THE CHÂTEAU MURDER

Molly Sutton Mysteries 5

NELL GODDIN

Beignet Books

ISBN: 978-1-949841-05-3

For my beloved mother, Cornelia S. Goddin. For a million reasons, I wish you were still here.

ꕥ I ꕥ

OCTOBER 2006

"Don't mess about with that." Marcel waved his hand with an effort at nonchalance but his tone had a slightly wary edge.

Aimed directly at his head, the barrel of the shotgun did not budge.

"Come on now," Marcel said, forcing a smile. "It's a Holland & Holland twelve-gauge, you know. Out of London. My grandfather gave it to me when I turned fifteen. Hard to believe I was ever that young."

The barrel advanced a few steps. And then, just like that, the trigger was squeezed and the gun went off, sending a spray of birdshot straight at baron Marcel de Fleuray. With that mysterious sense of premonition we sometimes have, in an infinitesimal fraction of a second, he felt the shot coming and turned to the side, trying to save his handsome face.

The blast would likely have stung but not been fatal, had not one single pellet happened to nick his carotid artery, which was exposed as he turned away.

Marcel slumped to the floor of the salon, which was hard stone but covered with two layers of sumptuous carpets. For a moment, speechless, he looked imploringly at the shooter, who lay the shotgun on an antique console table and meticulously wiped it clean of prints. By the time that was done, the baron had expired, and his murderer calmly went out through the open door and into the chilly darkness of a brisk October night.

❧

THE TWO-PERSON *GENDARMERIE* of Castillac was struggling to get its footing after a series of personnel changes. Gilles Maron was still acting chief, though unhappy in the job, partly because he strongly disliked the other officer. He found the snobby Paul-Henri to be insufferable, and organized their duties so as to spend as little time with him as possible. So on the morning of October 19th, Maron was making the rounds of the village alone, keeping his eye on the various businesses and chatting with residents, just as the former Chief Ben Dufort had taught him to do.

Maron was not naturally easygoing or sociable, but he wanted to do his job well, and every morning he walked the perimeter of the main village. By continuing in smaller circles, he eventually made it to the Place in the center of Castillac, greeting people as he went, and trying to see under the surface in case someone was in trouble but struggling to ask for help. Things had been quiet lately, and a yearning for a more urban posting kept swimming into his thoughts. He liked to imagine himself in a bulletproof vest, storming into a terrorist enclave on the outskirts of Paris, performing dangerous, important work—anything but monitoring this sleepy village where everyone knew everyone else's business and the main topic of conversation was what you planned to eat at your next meal.

Though no one could really call Castillac sleepy, not anymore. The villagers joked that it had turned into the French version of Cabot Cove, with another murder every time you turned around. Like all the best jokes, it came lined with a streak of truth and discomfort, and some didn't find it respectful—or prudent—to make light of such serious and unfortunate events.

It was a warm morning, with none of the chill of the past week. The terrace of the Café de la Place was filled with customers, most of whom Maron recognized. It was rather a loud group for mid-morning, he thought as he approached.

"Bonjour, Maron!" shouted Pascal, the young and very handsome server.

Maron walked quickly, understanding from his tone that Pascal was not simply greeting him. "What is it?"

"Have you heard? Babette just came by for a coffee with some news. You know Georgina Locatelli? She's the housekeeper out at Château Marainte."

Maron nodded though he had no idea who Pascal was talking about.

"Babette said Georgina told her that she found the baron dead in the salon! Shot to death!" Pascal could not contain his excitement at the news, but tried—and failed—to look appropriately sorrowful.

"Baron?" said Maron, lost.

"Yes, yes, the baron de Fleuray. I am not surprised if you've never met him. He didn't spend much time in Castillac, I don't think. And when he *was* here, he... well, I don't know what he did with himself, but he wasn't hanging around with the plebes here at the Café, I can tell you that!" Pascal laughed, tipping his head back and showing his straight white teeth.

"He hunted," piped up a young man leaning back in his chair. "The château has that huge forest behind it--the family owned all the land stretching north for many kilometers—where the baron had hunting parties. I know because I work at the *traiteur*, and sometimes he would order from us. Everything had to be packed in wicker baskets for them to eat out in the woods. Fussy about the menu."

Maron was nodding, his mind racing. With relief he thought: hunting accident! And then realized that was fairly unlikely to have occurred in his salon.

Possibly something had happened while he was cleaning his gun?

"Have you seen Georgina?" he asked.

"Oh no," laughed Pascal. "I'm sure she's making the rounds of the whole village with a story like that. It's not every day you stumble upon a dead aristocrat, after all."

"You think it's funny?"

"No! I mean, well, the thing is, Maron, the baron was known to be sort of a jerk. Not that anybody actually knew him. Barely ever came into the village because he didn't like to mix with the great unwashed, you know?"

Maron nodded. He was no great fan of the aristocracy himself, having come from a working class family in the north of France who talked reverently about the part their ancestors had played during the Revolution. "All right then, thank you for the information," he said stiffly, and took off for the station.

Not for the first time, he wished Ben Dufort was still the chief. He would know how to talk to the people out at the château. Maron jammed his hands into his pockets as he walked, brow furrowed, planning out the first steps in the new investigation.

"Bonjour, Paul-Henri," he said, entering the station.

Paul-Henri returned the greeting, his expression animated. "I just took a call from baroness Antoinette de Fleuray out at Château Marainte. Her husband has been shot to death."

"I know," said Maron, thankful that Paul-Henri hadn't surprised him with the news. "Let's get going."

"My parents might know them," said Paul-Henri as he put on

his coat. "I believe the baron spent most of his time in Paris, and you know my family has very many associations with the—"

"Let's get to the château, shall we?" said Maron.

"But the—"

"Paul-Henri, just stick to the matter at hand, if you will. A man has been shot here in Castillac. It has nothing whatsoever to do with who your mother knows in Paris."

Paul-Henri opened his mouth to answer, but changed his mind. It was difficult having a boss who understood so little about how the world worked, but he had learned that Maron did not listen when he tried to explain, so he pursed his lips while delivering a short lecture inside his head as they drove out to Château Marainte.

2

Molly Sutton, no longer a newly-minted expat but practically an old-timer in the village, was planting bulbs with Frances in the front yard of Molly's house, *La Baraque*. They made a mismatched pair, with Molly on the short side with freckles and unkempt red hair, and Frances slender and elegant, her red lipstick flawless. The two had been best friends forever.

"You have to dig deeper, Franny," Molly said, looking down at what Frances was doing.

"I keep hitting stones. Maybe this is a bad spot."

"Just pry them out, it'll be fine."

"I don't like gardening."

"So I gather."

"It's so...dirty."

Molly laughed. "But think how these daffodils will look in March! I'll bring you a big bouquet. They will smell better than the best perfume, I promise!"

"Well, I do like flowers," mumbled Frances, pressing her trowel under a stone and flipping it up out of the hole. "I'm just more of an instant gratification kind of person."

"Really?" teased Molly. They continued to dig in companionable silence for several minutes. Molly was thinking that she had been living in Castillac for over a year, and all in all, the move had turned out better than she'd ever dreamed. Her *gîte* business was... well, finances were perhaps a bit shaky as she headed into the off-season, but bills were mostly paid and she had some bookings over the next few months. She loved France unabashedly, and her adopted village of Castillac even more.

"So how are the wedding plans going?" Molly asked. Frances had come for a visit that winter, and ended up loving not only French village life but the bartender at their favorite bistro. She and Nico were talking about getting married, though no date had been set.

"Well..."

"I thought you were thrilled!"

"I was thrilled that he asked me—who doesn't like that part? But look, with my history, it's hard to get very excited about a wedding. I mean, I'm excited about Nico. I'm *ga-ga* about Nico. But the wedding part of it..."

"Two divorces is not that many."

"It's two more than Nico has."

"What difference does it make? Is he troubled about them?"

"Not that he admits. Or at least, not that I can tell, what with his English and my French. But really, how could he not be? I think I look kind of...flighty. On paper, anyway."

"You *are* flighty," laughed Molly, jamming a bulb for the white-flowered *Thalia* into a deep hole and filling it in with dirt. "But honestly? You and Nico are suited to each other in a way that you never were with your exes. I'd be happy to stick my nose in where it doesn't belong and tell him that, if you think it would help."

Frances sat on the grass, her legs crossed. "It's not really Nico, it's me that's the problem. I'm worried that...what if we get married, and then...you know, it's hard, sticking with the same person into eternity."

"You remind me of those cemetery plaques: 'Care in Perpetuity.'"

"See what I'm saying? Cemeteries aren't the best association with marriage, right? Something's wrong with me."

Molly's cell phone chirped, and she leaned back on her heels and struggled to get it out of her pocket. She had put on weight since moving to France and practically all her clothes had gotten a smidge too tight. "This guest isn't even coming for another couple of weeks, and already he's been totally high maintenance." She paused, looking harder at her phone. "Wait. It's from Lawrence. Murder at the château."

"Whaaat?"

"I know, right? I can't quite...another one? *Really?"*

"What else does he say?"

Molly checked her phone. "That's it. I swear he must be hacking into the gendarmerie system or something—he always knows everything practically the minute it happens."

"At the château! I've always wanted to get invited there for something. Do you know anything about the aristocrats?"

"Never met them. The...Fleurays, I think is the name."

"Well? I can't believe you're just calmly planting another bulb. A *murder*, Molls! Aren't you going to head out there and poke around?"

Molly shrugged. "I can't just show up at crime scenes and start asking questions. I don't know them or anything about them."

"So what's your angle gonna be, then?" asked Frances with a grin.

"Angle?"

"Oh, come on. You know you're going to get in on this one way or another. Too bad Ben's not around."

"Yeah," said Molly, allowing some wistfulness into her voice. Her romantic relationship with the former chief was a big question mark at the moment. Since he had been at the gendarmerie for many years, he still had an informal authority in the village and had been able to bring Molly into a few investigations on the side. But Ben had left Castillac for many months, off on a midlife crisis trip to Thailand. "I got a postcard from him yesterday with a picture of an elephant. Not much of a note."

"Well, that's no help," said Frances, standing up and brushing dirt off her knees. "But I have faith in you, my dear Miss Marple. If there's a dead body anywhere within fifty kilometers, you'll figure out how it got there...one way or another."

"Thanks for the confidence." Molly settled the last of the bulbs into a hole and scraped soil on top of it. "But enough about murder. Let's get back to Nico. Are you worried that once you're married, he'll turn out to be someone else, someone you don't know? That you've fallen for some kind of, I don't know, illusion?"

Frances pushed her straight black hair behind her ear and looked out across the road to the oak woods. "That's probably part of it." She took a deep breath and then spoke in a rush. "And also...what if it's *me* who's pushing an illusion? What if he finds out *I'm* not who he thinks I am?"

"Interesting," said Molly, pressing down on the newly-planted bulb and standing up. "So who is the real Frances, if you're not the wayward kook I've known since I was seven?"

"What if that's who I am to you, but to other people I'm someone totally different? What if I'm just a big giant *fake* and he figures it out right after the ink on the marriage license is dry?"

Molly stood with her hands on her hips, looking at her friend. "You've got mud on your chin," she said. "And I think you should just enjoy Nico and stop worrying. You're both clearly smitten, so why not appreciate that and stop trying to pick it apart?"

Frances bit the inside of her mouth and considered. "Eh, you're probably right. Got any pastries? All this backbreaking labor has me half-starved."

"Silly woman. Of *course* I have pastries."

The women walked arm in arm back to the house, Frances missing Nico even though she'd seen him only three hours earlier.

Molly wondered about her ex-husband, and whether this theory explained why that marriage had failed. Had she missed seeing who he really was until it was too late?

People are mysteries, that's all there is to it, she concluded as she opened the bag of almond croissants bought that morning at the beloved Pâtisserie Bujold, breathing in the buttery, almondy aroma and grinning in anticipation.

❧

LONG BEFORE THEY REACHED IT, the officers could see the imposing Château Marainte looming up before them, a red flag flying from a turret on the east end of the building. The 13th-century edifice stood on a hill surrounded by farmland, visible for many kilometers in nearly all directions. Maron turned into the drive, which wound up the hill through a wood and then straightened into an *allée* lined with two-hundred-year-old plane trees.

"To be clear, Paul-Henri, we are not here to interrogate anyone right now. We'll secure the crime scene for forensics and make whatever observations we can, and that's all. I do not want to hear you firing questions at the housekeeper or babbling on to the baroness about your mother's social connections. These situations take planning and strategy, and we can't do that on the fly."

Paul-Henri nodded, his jaw working. They pulled into a white-graveled parking area and got out. The château, a defensive building with slits for archers and two crenellated towers, was not in his favorite style. He much preferred the more delicate and artful architecture of later centuries such as the chateaux at Chambord or Challain. He rubbed a spot on one of the buttons of his uniform while waiting for Maron to decide what to do next.

Maron was looking at the vast building with his mouth open. The stone was dark and the place felt unfriendly to him. A wooden bridge crossed a dry moat, and he set off that way, wondering if the baroness was waiting for them inside, and what kind of person she would turn out to be.

The officers went through an immense gate and into a large courtyard planted with *parterres* outlined in boxwood, with an old well in the center, closed in on all four sides by the gray walls of the château, five stories high.

"Messieurs!"

They turned to see a middle-aged woman coming toward them, dressed in a long wool skirt and a velvet blazer.

"Bonjour, madame," said Maron politely. "I am wondering if you could direct me to the baroness?"

The woman smiled. Maron noticed that she wore no makeup, as though she had accepted the plainness of her face as fate, and did not fight against it. She looked pale and her cheekbones jutted sharply. "I am the baroness," she said, "though please, simply call me Antoinette."

Paul-Henri had been about to speak, but whatever it was, he choked it back.

"I must have spoken to one of you when I called. Marcel...my husband Marcel...has been shot." She held out a palm and bowed her head, taking a moment to collect herself. "It's quite horrible," she said, almost too quietly to hear.

"Can you show us where he is?" asked Maron, unsure how to behave, having had no experience around aristocrats and feeling pretty sure there were rules and protocols for what to say and how to say it, even if you were a *gendarme*.

"Follow me," she said. Antoinette crossed the courtyard and stopped before an ancient wooden door that was partly open. "This is his private salon," she said. "The place where he spent most of his time when he was here at Château Marainte. A man's place, you understand, where he kept his guns and cigars and that sort of thing."

Maron nodded, having never seen an aristocrat's man cave but figuring the concept was the same.

The baroness pushed on the door, and the three of them stepped into the dimly lit room. Old tapestries covered the stone walls, and a table lamp with a green shade pooled light on an antique desk. On the walls hung various hunting trophies: antelope and deer heads, a leopard skin, the impressive twirling horns of a kudu. An enormous fireplace held ashes and a few charred logs, but no fire was lit. Looking around, Maron noticed the shotgun on the console table, and when he moved farther into the room, he saw the baron lying in a pool of dark blood on a Turkish carpet.

Paul-Henri gasped and then tried to pretend he was coughing.

"All right, then," said Maron. "The coroner is on his way and forensics should be here any minute. Paul-Henri, go out to the gate so you can direct them in here when they arrive."

Paul-Henri glumly walked off.

"I'm very sorry for your loss," said Maron to the baroness, who inclined her head slightly and thanked him.

"I'm in rather a state of shock," she said. "We've been married, oh, close to thirty years. Raised two sons. I can't even begin to understand this. I'm struggling to grasp what has happened even though my eyes are looking right at it."

"Yes, madame. It sometimes takes the mind some time to catch up. Your sons? Are they on their way? Have you called a friend or anyone to give you some support during this difficult time?"

Antoinette waved off his concern and Maron worried he had been too familiar. "My sons live in Paris. I called them right after I spoke to you earlier. Not a phone call I relished making, I will tell you."

"I can imagine, madame. Is anyone else here at the château?"

"Georgina was here this morning. My housekeeper. She found Marcel, actually. I rather think it made her day."

Maron tilted his head inquiringly.

"Oh, I just mean that she likes a bit of drama. You know how people are." She looked over at her husband and Maron saw tears spring to her eyes.

"Anyone besides Georgina?"

"Hubert is around somewhere. He works for the château, doing whatever needs doing. Some carpentry and repairs, managing the hunting grounds, a gamekeeper of sorts."

Maron, who had grown up in a city, had no idea what that might entail. "What is Hubert's surname? And does he hunt as well?"

"Hubert Arnaud. And oh, of course, certainly he hunts. I don't know what kind of arrangement Marcel had with him about using our land for his own hunting, but he...are you thinking that the shotgun is the murder weapon?" she asked, her voice rising as she gestured at the Holland & Holland lying on the console table.

"Don't touch it!" barked Maron. "It will need to be dusted for fingerprints. There is some chance that another gun was used, and the coroner will have the final say. But I would guess, looking at your husband, that this gun was...the gun that killed him. Shotguns aren't the most efficient way to go about killing someone," he muttered, and then looked up to see that the baroness was staring at him aghast.

"I'm sorry, I just meant that most often a shotgun blast isn't fatal."

Antoinette nodded. "Made for killing birds," she said, a bit harshly. A border collie ran into the room and eyed Maron suspiciously.

"It's all right, Grizou," Antoinette said to the dog, reaching down to scratch behind his ears. The baroness's face relaxed for the first time since Maron had met her, and he had a fleeting glimpse of what she had looked like as a young woman.

The dog started to go around the table to inspect Marcel, but Antoinette held him back. "If it's all right, may I go? I don't mind if you have more questions but I would like to continue somewhere else, if we could?"

She's so polite, Maron was thinking. He had thought aristocrats were imperious and went around with their noses in the air, but here is Antoinette, not the least bit haughty and asking to be called by her first name, and doing her best to be helpful in what must be the most shattering time of her life. He was trying to put her in a category and failing.

"But of course," he answered, gesturing to the door.

"Grizou!" called Antoinette, and the dog shot through the door and into the sunny courtyard.

Florian Nagrand, the coroner, was just making his way into the courtyard, flanked by several forensics men who had made it from Bergerac in record time.

"Just sitting down to lunch," growled Nagrand to Maron, and the baroness burst into tears.

3

Alexandre Roulier stretched out on the hotel bed and put his hands behind his head, trying to think. He had just received a call confirming Marcel's death and he knew that his next moves were critically important. One false step and Antoinette might bar him from the château altogether, or worse, sic the gendarmes on him. He had to think through the details carefully, painstakingly.

The hotel was a solid two-star in an outer *arrondissement* of Paris. Hardly shabby—and the concierge was a pretty young woman, the breakfast better than average, the view from his window decent enough. But Roulier was not content with a two-star. He wanted to be at the Georges V, the Shangri-La, the Ritz. He wanted to have so much money that he never had to look at a price tag or comparison shop ever again. And once he had his riches, he had a few ideas about changing his last name to something with a bit more sparkle—*Roulier* referred to someone using a cart, a distinctly working-class name. But after losing a half hour daydreaming of more elegant possibilities, he sternly told himself to stick to the matter at hand and not get ahead of himself. Alexandre was nothing if not disciplined.

First thing was to take the train down to Castillac, just as he had numerous times with Marcel. He could comfort Antoinette in her time of grief. He could enjoy one last stay at Château Marainte, perhaps even get in a day of boar hunting.

And he could finally, with Marcel out of the picture, search for the box. Alexandre had never had a chance to search Marcel's Paris apartment, but he very much doubted it was there. For all his worldliness, Marcel had a sentimental streak, and Alexandre would bet his little finger that Marcel had hidden the box somewhere at Château Marainte, his boyhood home and that of his ancestors going back nearly four hundred years.

Alexandre liked to get up at dawn, finding that he did his best planning early in the morning. He enjoyed a long shower, spending a few moments regretting how small the stall was, and tiled in porcelain instead of marble. He was careful to dress in his most casual clothing, knowing that Antoinette would disapprove of his customary Parisian finery.

It was critically important to have her on his side, and as he packed a small bag he came up with a few ideas for winning her over. It was a delicate thing, as the baroness—though provincial and overly attached to her dogs—was quite perceptive and apt to be on her guard now that she was a widow.

He would need to figure out how to get Antoinette out of the way while he searched, and there might be others in the household who would need to be persuaded to look the other way. But this gave him little worry since he had yet to meet the housekeeper who was not open to a juicy bribe.

The one thing causing him anxiety was that he had no idea whether the existence of the box and its contents was widely known. Was Château Marainte going to be crawling with charlatans hoping to grab it? Or were the stories Marcel had told him over brandy late at night been actual confidences? Alexandre could think of no way of knowing except to show up at the château and assess the situation. Perhaps Antoinette did not even know about the box. Certainly that would make the operation easier, he thought, allowing himself to imagine finally holding the box in his hand with no one else around, no one to impinge on the rapture, the rapacious pleasure of holding that much money in the palm of his hand.

The box itself was elaborately decorated in jewels—or so Marcel had told him—but the emerald it contained was the real treasure.

All that remained was breakfast, and then to the train.

His fortune awaited.

❧

FLORIAN NAGRAND HAD BEEN the coroner in Castillac for twenty-six years, during which he had driven his white van to pick up around thirty bodies a year, give or take, the vast majority of whom had died of natural causes; taken countless photographs; smoked an infinite number of cigarettes; and consulted with a long list of gendarmes as they arrived in Castillac and then were posted elsewhere a few years later. At this point, a routine death by shotgun was nowhere near interesting enough to spark his curiosity, no matter that it was murder and not an accident, and had apparently taken place in a salon at Château Marainte.

"No chance the body was moved? He was definitely shot right here in the salon?" asked Maron, squatting down next to the body.

"Well, of course," answered Nagrand. "The bleeding from a wound like that would be instantaneous and copious. Yet there's no trail over the rugs or anything like that. I expect he dropped like a stone."

"Time of death?"

"Last night most likely. Or sometime yesterday at any rate."

Maron nodded. "Will you be able to be more precise?"

"It's possible," said Nagrand, who never liked being pinned

down about anything, even on what he would like to have for dinner.

The forensics team had already bagged the Holland & Holland and were looking around the room for anything else that might hide evidence—a glass, an ashtray with cigarette butts—but the room was noticeably tidy. "Did someone clean in here after the murder?" one of them asked Maron. "I don't think my house ever looks this immaculate."

"That's because you're a foul slob," said his workmate with a wide grin.

Maron got up and walked to the other end of the room, careful to watch where he put his feet. "If this is where the baron spent a lot of time, then yes, he appears to have been orderly in his habits. I will inquire about the housekeeper's activities. All right then, I'm going to leave you guys to it. Anything comes in from the lab, you know how to reach me. Paul-Henri, you stay here in case the guys need you." Maron patted his cell and went back outside to the courtyard.

Antoinette was kneeling beside one of the parterres, pulling some weeds, no longer crying.

"Excuse me once again," said Maron, trying and failing to find the right tone, something that expressed firmness of purpose, authority, and also a degree of personal warmth. "I apologize for the crudeness of Monsieur Nagrand. He...he makes light because death is so familiar to him, not because he's callous about your situation. I am sorry if he upset you."

"Oh no," said Antoinette, getting to her feet and brushing the dirt off her hands. "I didn't take offense. It's just...please understand, I'm still very much in a state of shock. This whole thing... when you're married to someone for a long time, as Marcel and I were, inevitably you consider...you think about things like, who will go first? What will life be like if I'm left all alone? But as you might imagine, Officer Maron, all the considering in the world makes no difference when the thing finally happens. So far, it's not a bit like I thought it would be."

"I understand," said Maron, though he did not. He looked around at the dark gray walls of the château. Instead of feeling protected there in the courtyard, he felt suffocated, even though he was standing in the sunshine and could feel a light breeze.

"Just a few questions, if you don't mind. Was anyone else here last night besides you and the housekeeper?"

Antoinette cocked her head. "Let me think. Georgina and her husband live in a cottage partway down the hill—you passed it when you drove in. I have no idea whether he was home last night or not. Hubert lives about four kilometers away, between the château and Castillac. Or do you mean right here, inside the gates of Château Marainte?" Antoinette paused and looked at Maron.

He looked into her hazel eyes. For a brief moment he had an urge to brush a stray strand of blonde hair out of her face.

"It was just me, as far as I know," she said, with a shrug. "We had dinner at about eight-thirty, then Marcel went to his salon. I went to our bedroom and got into bed with a book."

"And you heard no cars come up the drive, no one walking in the courtyard?"

"No. But the château walls are thick."

"Did you hear the shot?"

Antoinette shook her head. "I heard nothing. I read for a while, then went to sleep and slept like a baby until seven-thirty in the morning when Grizou woke me up with his wet nose in my ear."

Hearing his name, Grizou got up from a shady spot under a miniature peach tree and trotted to Antoinette's side.

"Did you and your husband usually breakfast together?"

"Oh, sometimes. Not if he was up early to hunt. But otherwise, yes, we would have coffee together in the lounge next to the kitchen. Marcel liked to watch the news on television first thing."

"And would the cook be here to take care of breakfast?"

"Oh heavens, Officer Maron, we don't have a cook! Yes, we have this immense pile—" she waved a hand at the château. "But in terms of cash flow, life here is not nearly as grand as one might think. I make the coffee in the morning, and cook all the meals for that matter."

"I see. How about trouble with burglars, anything like that?"

"Well, you should know as well as anyone," she said with a short laugh. "I'd certainly have reported that kind of thing to the gendarmerie. You know, I've always considered Castillac to be the safest place imaginable. I can't understand this recent rash of crime at all—it's almost as though an infection is spreading through the population—suddenly you hear of murder and abduction and all sorts of things that used to be common in big cities, but not here. Never here."

"Yes, madame." Maron paused to gather his confidence. "You'll understand that I must ask—how were things between the two of you, baroness?"

"Call me Antoinette, please," she said, putting her fingers lightly on Maron's arm. She tipped her face up to the sun, "Oh, *marriage*. Are you married, Officer Maron?"

Maron shook his head.

"Well, I suppose it's like anything else. It ebbs and flows. To be very honest, since that is obviously what is required, we did not have much interest in each other anymore. We knew each other as children, you see. Grew up together, raised a family, a lot of years went by. And so at a certain point it was as though all the feeling that could be wrung from sentiment had been gotten, you understand, and there was just not much of anything left.

"Which is not to say we were unhappy. We got along fine, Marcel and I. He did not try to order me about like some husbands do, and I was not a nagging wife as some become, at least I don't believe I was. For the last few years, he spent most of his time in Paris. First for his work as minister, and then because he enjoyed it. Had a good friend with a place in Berry, very good hunting apparently."

"You are not interested in hunting?"

Antoinette laughed. "Not in the least," she said. "At any rate, as you'd imagine I've been thinking all day about who in the world could have wanted to kill Marcel, and...for the life of me, I can think of no one. Where does that leave us?"

In a bad way, thought Maron, but kept the thought to himself.

4

It was Saturday morning, market day, and Molly was out of coffee. She dressed haphazardly, raked a comb through her tangle of red curls, fed Bobo, and zipped into the village on her scooter, planning to spend the first half hour at Pâtisserie Bujold getting her caffeine fix and feasting on the freshest and best pastry in the entire *département*. The air was chilly at eight in the morning. Leaves were turning color and summer gardens drooping, the sight of which always left Molly feeling melancholy. The problem with October was that the whiff of death was up in your face every time you went outside.

"Bonjour, Molly!" boomed Monsieur Nugent from behind the counter as he packed a box of pastries for an older woman at the front of the line.

"Bonjour, Edmond," said Molly with a wave. She walked over to the case and looked over the day's selection, always a wide variety on market day. As usual, the rows of delicacies were perfectly neat with not a crumb out of place. Cream puffs, Napoléons, *religieuses*, *palmiers*, éclairs, apricot tarts...impossible to decide.

"How are you?" asked Molly when it was her turn.

"Terrible," answered Monsieur Nugent with a smile. "My knee has been swelling up each night to the size of a succulent melon," he said, glancing at her chest. "I have to sit with ice on it for hours."

"What does the doctor say?" Molly said, ignoring his glance.

"Who has time for doctors? I have to be in the bakery at three in the morning, and so much work to accomplish. I cannot leave my customers unhappy, Molly!"

"We are grateful for your dedication, Edmond. I'll take four almond croissants, and what's that green thing in the second to last row to the right? Looks like white chocolate shavings on top?"

"Pistachio cream with white chocolate on an almond wafer. Gluten free. Something for everybody!"

Molly paid and moved to let the throng behind her have a turn, and since the tables were full, she walked back to the Place where the market stalls were set up, sipping coffee and nibbling a croissant along the way.

When she had first moved to France a little over a year before, market day had been both thrilling and intimidating. So many things she had never seen back in Boston: a fellow walking around with vials of vanilla beans attached to his clothing, selling them for four euros a pop; an old man sitting at a card table selling walnuts he had gathered in his yard; more varieties of cheese than seemed humanly possible. But Molly was not satisfied just being an observer—she wanted to be in the thick of it, laughing and talking to everyone. Which she had managed, in time, but those first few months had been a bit like jumping off the high dive and belly-flopping over and over, since her language skills had been pretty dismal.

But that was then. As with many pursuits, a willingness to make mistakes leads to fast progress, and a year later, Molly would still not have said she was fluent, though she really was. She understood jokes most of the time, and could almost always find a way to say what she meant and understand what someone was saying to her.

"Molly!" called her friend Manette, who presided over a vast array of vegetables, both imported and locally grown.

"Bonjour, Manette," said Molly. "I was hoping you'd be here."

"When have I ever not been? Oh, that one time when my brother-in-law took my place because I had the flu. I think he sold three potatoes and that was it for the day."

Molly laughed. "Those radishes look very good. Give me a bundle of those and two handfuls of beets, if you please."

"So let's get right down to it," said Manette, leaning in close to Molly as she loaded beets on a scale. "You heard about the baron?"

"Oh, I heard all right."

"Any ideas?"

"Ideas? The poor man's been dead for fifteen minutes and I know absolutely nothing about the case! Nor will I, now that Ben's left town."

"Eh, you'll find a way. Well, look who it is," said Manette, still whispering.

Molly raised her eyebrows.

"Antoinette!" Manette boomed out.

Molly whirled around to see a slender woman dressed in a quietly smart wool suit, wearing an expensive pair of leather boots.

Manette came around from behind the counter to hold the baroness firmly by the arms and kiss her cheeks. "Antoinette, I was so, so sorry to hear about the baron. What can I do? Would you like me to deliver some things to the château? Surely you don't need to be here at the market, not with everything you're going through."

"It's helpful to me, actually," said Antoinette in a low voice. "I'm so...it's just such a shock, you understand. So a bit of normalcy...it's a good thing to be out and about, and just carry on with things."

Molly stood with her eyes wide and her ears open, hoping Manette would introduce her, but after talking a minute more, the baroness bought an eggplant and four potatoes, waved goodbye, and moved back into the throng in the center of the Place.

"Manette!" hissed Molly.

"I know, I know. But after what's happened, I felt I had to respect her privacy. She's a baroness, after all, and doesn't really mingle with villagers. It just didn't seem like the right moment to make an introduction. I hope you understand."

"Well, not really," Molly answered, scowling. "Besides," she added under her breath, "I thought all the aristocrats got the guillotine."

Manette grinned. "You're going to the gala this year? Perhaps you'll meet her there."

"Oh, the thing at L'Institut Degas?"

"Of course. It's, let's see, I think it's next Friday. They'd best get to work on their advertising, I've barely seen any notices about it."

Molly kissed Manette goodbye and tried to think about what to make for dinner. Sausages and sauerkraut? With a dry cider?

"La Bombe!" called out a familiar voice.

"Good morning, Lapin," said Molly, stopping to let the big man dodge through the crowd to catch up to her. They kissed cheeks and exchanged how-are-yous. Market day took three times as long now that Molly had so many friends in the village.

"Are you rushing back to do changeover?"

"Alas, not this week. No guests coming. I'm expecting someone next week though, and he's super fussy so at least I'll have a whole week to get the cottage just so."

"I know you've heard about the poor baron."

Molly sighed. "Look, I've very much enjoyed being involved in past investigations, but I'm afraid that's all over now. I don't know the family and apparently won't be getting to know the family, so let's just move on and talk about something else."

"You're adorable when you get snippy."

"I'm not being snippy!"

"Have you finished your marketing? Walk with me to my shop, I have something juicy to tell you."

Molly looked at her friend and narrowed her eyes. "Yes?"

"Come on, walk this way." He took her arm and pulled her along in the direction of his antique shop on rue Baudelaire. "I won't torture you by dragging it out. The rumor is that the late baron, Marcel de Fleuray, owned *La Sfortuna*, the famous emerald. It was kept in a jeweled box—also extremely valuable—hidden somewhere at Château Marainte."

Molly rubbed her chin. "How do you know this?"

"Well, it's true that the Fleurays have never hired me to appraise anything at their estate. But still, people in my business talk. I have at least two associates who claim to have seen the box, if not the emerald itself."

"And how widespread is this rumor?"

"Oh, everyone in the village knows about it."

"You do realize you've just given pretty much everyone a rock-solid motive for killing him?"

"I knew you'd know valuable information when you heard it," said Lapin with satisfaction.

"*La Sfortuna*...is that Italian? I've never heard of it."

"Do you keep up with jewelry news, *ma chérie?*"

"Well, not exactly."

"You stick to the sleuthing, Molls, and let me cover the antique side of things. We make a great team, if I do say so myself."

Molly nodded glumly and said her goodbyes before reaching the shop. She had left her scooter parked beside Pâtisserie Bujold and she gratefully entered the store and bought a loaf of sourdough and an almond croissant to have for breakfast the next day.

Because really, a village murder, and at the château no less? And here she was, shut out entirely. It was hard to bear. As she sped home, she told herself not to be so selfish, that plainly it was the baron and the baroness who had the worse end of the stick by far. But sometimes, all the self-criticism in the world doesn't budge you an inch, and she walked into La Baraque, tossed the bakery bag on the counter, dropped to the floor and let Bobo lick her face until she couldn't help smiling just a little.

❧

NICO AND FRANCES had skipped the market that Saturday, preferring to spend all morning in bed and then linger over coffee and the newspaper. But by lunchtime Frances was starting to get a little antsy.

"How about a bike ride?" she said with enthusiasm.

"We don't have bikes. Plus—don't take this the wrong way, *petite chou*—but is athletics really your sort of thing?"

Frances rolled up the paper and bopped him on the head. "Well, we can't just laze around for the entire day. Isn't there some secret magical place somewhere that you've forgotten to show me?"

"Like what, a tourist attraction?"

"Nah, you know, a witch's cottage or something. A house where a whole family died of typhoid."

"You have a grisly imagination."

"All the best people do."

Nico laughed and stepped into a pair of blue jeans, then pulled a T-shirt over his head. "There are plenty of chateaux around if you'd like to do some sight-seeing."

"What about the one right outside the village?"

"Château Marainte?"

"I think that's it. Is it open to the public?"

"No, I don't think so." Nico went into the bathroom and

loudly brushed his teeth. Then he came back into the room, scooped Frances into his arms, and said, "Marry me."

"Aren't you supposed to be at Chez Papa by now?" said Frances, giggling.

"Ten minutes ago," answered Nico, kissing her on the neck.

"Alphonse is going to blame me for your lateness."

"Let him try." He put his hands on her thin shoulders and ran his palms all the way down her arms. "You are a bony thing. If you won't marry me, then let me cook a big lunch for you."

"Nico! You've got to get to work!"

"Who knew you were such a slave to convention?"

"I like paychecks. Learned that one early."

"I thought your family was mega-rich?"

"Oh, they are. But we, uh, well...I figured out pretty early that it would be best if I made my own money and didn't depend on them. I got my first job—wait a minute, nice try, I'm not falling for your delay tactics! Get your silly butt over to Chez Papa on the double!" She reached under his T-shirt and tickled him.

"Okay, I'm going, I'm going. But one more try. Frances," he said, his voice serious, putting his hands on either side of her face. "Elope with me. Right after I'm done with this shift. We'll go to Bergerac, get married, and take a month of honeymoon. Alphonse will be fine with it, you know he will. And you don't have any contracts at the moment, right? Nothing is in the way!"

Frances looked at Nico with love, successfully hiding the panic his words had stirred up. "Just go to work, monkey," she whispered. "We can talk about all that later."

He looked momentarily crestfallen, but pulled himself together, kissed her unhurriedly, and left the apartment.

5

Sundays were quiet in Castillac, especially now that summer was long over. Families spent the day together, some going to church and some worshipping at the altar of a well-stocked lunch table. The roads were empty as Acting Chief Maron trudged through the village, wandering the streets and thinking over the details of the murder, at a loss for how to proceed.

It had been difficult to take over when Ben Dufort resigned as Chief, but at least Dufort had stayed in town and been available for consultation. Now he was on the other side of the world cavorting with elephants, and Maron was stuck with another murder that so far was offering up nothing but dead ends. Nagrand had called the day before to tell him he approximated the time of the baron's death to be eleven o'clock the night of the 18th. He might easily have survived, but a single ball of shot had caught his carotid artery, and he had bled to death in a matter of minutes.

Not the worst way to go, said Nagrand, but Maron had no interest in pursuing that line of conversation with the coroner, whom he viewed as a necessary vulture but not a friend. Not that Maron had many friends at all in Castillac, or prospects either.

In theory, death did not especially bother him as long as it wasn't his, and having a murder to solve should have brought some welcome excitement from the usual round of parking tickets and petty theft that was Castillac's normal fare. But to Maron's surprise, it was decidedly *not* welcome. Ironically, the pressure of the being the top guy—even if only provisionally—in such a small village was far more difficult for him than the very real dangers of urban counterterrorism would be. It felt as though all eyes in the village were trained on him and him alone as everyone waited for results.

All right then, he thought, trying to bring some order into his straying, jumpy mind. Let's be methodical about this. We have the murder weapon, the expensive, antique Holland & Holland twelve-gauge shotgun, belonging to the victim. No prints. No one known to be at the château except the baroness, who appears to have no motive for killing her husband—though of course more interviews are necessary—and the housekeeper. Got to see what the opinion of the village is on that one, at least if the couple mingled enough with the village for anyone to have an opinion. Maybe I should go see Madame Tessier, the font of all knowledge...

He let himself into the station and went to his desk to read Nagrand's report once more. Time of death, eleven o'clock. Penetration of the carotid artery. Otherwise fit and in good health for his age. Some arthritis in his left thumb. An ingrown toenail. Not overweight; defined musculature.

He heard a rustling at the door and Maron looked up to see Paul-Henri come in, his uniform immaculate.

"Bonjour, Paul-Henri."

"Bonjour, Chief. Any word from Nagrand?"

"Yes, I just emailed you his report. I'll reserve comment until you tell me your thoughts."

Maron leaned back in his chair, stretching his arms up over his head, and waited for Paul-Henri to read what Nagrand had written.

"Okay. Well," Paul-Henri began, looking up from his computer after a few minutes, "obviously there's not much here. But in my opinion, what we're dealing with is some kind of attempted robbery or burglary."

"Explain."

"Well, you've heard about the emerald, of course. That, to me, is the most obvious motive. I mean, you don't keep something of that massive value at your house, with no security to speak of, and expect that you're never going to run into trouble."

Maron had not heard of any emerald but did not want to say so. "So in your opinion, someone went to the château on Friday night looking for this emerald, and ended up shooting the baron?"

"He probably had to, didn't he, if he had just forced the baron to hand over the goods? Getting rid of the witness, you see."

"I see," said Maron sarcastically. "And your evidence for this dramatic tale?"

"A murder *is* dramatic, Chief, it's not me trying to make it so. And a murder at that gloomy château—even more so."

"Oh, you don't approve of Château Marainte? Not your style?"

Paul-Henri wanted very much to explain the features he believed to be the most aesthetically pleasing in château architecture, but had no confidence Maron would appreciate a word of it, so he steered the conversation back to the case.

"Certainly the jewel would have been hidden somewhere, not sitting out where anyone could snatch it. So I believe the baron was alive long enough to show the thief where it was—at gunpoint, no doubt."

"No doubt," said Maron, sneering.

"And so," continued Paul-Henri, ignoring Maron's glares, "on the assumption that the murder did not take place until the emerald had been secured by the thief, and thereby that the thief has the emerald in his or her possession—because otherwise why kill the baron?—we should monitor all avenues of jewelry sales, auctions, and that sort of thing. Though I suspect the thief is too clever to try to sell it on the open market. It's probably a private sale, and if our luck is very bad, it's already changed hands, the money untraceable."

A long quiet moment in the station while Maron digested this explanation and Paul-Henri straightened his posture, looking very pleased with himself.

"So you're saying a professional jewel thief killed the baron?"

"I am," said Paul-Henri, puffing out his chest.

"And this professional jewel thief just happened to find a loaded gun at hand at just the moment he needed it?"

Paul-Henri started to speak but stopped. He looked up at the ceiling as though a movie of the murder scene was playing on it. "He could have brought his own weapon, of course, perhaps a dagger? But decided to go with the shotgun since obviously it's better to kill someone with his own gun if it can be managed."

"Is it now," mumbled Maron, rolling his eyes. "Did you by any chance think about going to film school instead of the police academy? Perhaps you were writing screenplays? Your imagination is certainly...vivid. Daggers and jewel thieves, huh? How much does a ticket to the matinée cost?"

"Very funny," said Paul-Henri. He turned back to his computer and pretended to be looking over the report again. "Shame the baron had such bad luck. According to Nagrand, the guy was in very good shape for his age."

"Fifty-seven," said Maron. "Not exactly an old man. Spent a lot of his time hunting, so I suppose that means a lot of walking. Do you hunt?"

"Me? Oh no. I grew up in the suburbs and liked going to museums and cafés in Paris. Forests aren't anyplace I'd choose to be."

Maron had little interest in nature either, but the shared

opinion did not make him look at Paul-Henri with any less contempt.

"All right, one thing we can agree on: someone else was at the château the other night. So let's get out there, chat up everyone we can think of, and find out who it was, shall we?"

❧

MOLLY FELT a little lonely that Sunday. It seemed as though the entire village was snuggled up on that chilly morning with their families and lovers, and she had no one, not even any guests. Which—forget loneliness for a minute—was the much bigger problem, she thought, looking over the numbers for her gîte business for the last month. Her bank account wasn't empty, not all the way, but dwindling by the day. After a booming summer when she'd been fully booked most of the time, with a delightful cash flow, the booking calendar for November looked bleak.

She had used much of the summer money for improvements around La Baraque. That would pay off, eventually...but how to keep food on the table in the meantime?

"Come on, Bobo!" she said, getting up from her desk and heading to the kitchen to top off her coffee. She had learned from sore experience that sitting around the house checking her email every thirty seconds did not actually produce more bookings, and it was better to get out of the house, away from the temptation.

She put on some sturdy boots which made Bobo leap about the room because she knew that meant a long walk, and then off they went, down the meadow behind the house, past the empty *pigeonnier*, and into the woods. Of course, she wondered about the baron's murder, but those thoughts fizzled quickly since she had no knowledge at all of any of the details, and could not even picture where it had taken place since she had never even been up the driveway to Château Marainte.

Probably his wife did it, she figured, or a disgruntled relative. Fighting over an inheritance or something.

But such ruminations were not very entertaining since they were based on nothing at all, and soon Molly was not seeing the woods and the bright day but instead worrying over her financial situation and what to do about it. She had spiffed up her website and taken out a few ads. She had joined a site that represented many hundreds of gîte businesses, but so far had only produced one booking. What could she do to make visiting Castillac in the off-season more appealing?

And then she stopped, spilling coffee on her jeans. "Yes!" she said to Bobo, "That's what I'll do: I'll have a series of dinners, with different themes, and put notices up in Bergerac and Périgueux. It won't be like running a restaurant because I'll only be making one menu—everyone eats the same thing. An event where tourists and villagers get to mingle for an evening. What do you think—will it be enough to keep the wolves from the door until spring?" She bent down and rubbed Bobo on her speckled chest, where she loved being petted the most. And then Molly apologized for cutting the walk short and turned and ran back to La Baraque, full of enthusiasm for the new idea, and the murder most happily forgotten.

6

The next day Molly rushed around getting things organized for her first dinner. She wasn't thinking haute cuisine or anything too fancy, but she did need to get a decent tablecloth and some new napkins. She sighed as her bank account shrank still further, but pressed on in the hope that the plan would be lucrative enough to cover expenses at the very least. And it gave her something to do besides sit at the computer willing new bookings to show up in her inbox.

By the time cocktail hour rolled around, she was ready to see some friends, and rode her scooter to Chez Papa, a bistro where she could almost always find someone she knew to talk to. Mondays were usually convivial after everyone had been holed up all weekend, and this Monday was no exception—sitting at the bar were Frances, Lapin, and Caroline Dubois, with Nico behind the bar.

"Salut, tout le monde!" Molly sang out, and all three spun around on their stools and greeted her. "I haven't spoken to a human in two days. Tell me some good news! Entertain me!"

Caroline, who worked in the office at the village school, shook her head. "There is no good news. Have you read the paper today?

More strikes coming. I don't know how our children are going to get an education if schools are on strike all the time."

"You don't have to be in a classroom to learn," said Nico, making Molly a kir without having to ask.

Caroline shrugged a shrug that said *Your statement is so inane I'm not even going to reply.*

"They don't do a lot of striking in the States," said Molly. "But maybe things would be better if they did."

"Oh please, let's not talk about politics tonight!" said Lapin. "We've got a stolen emerald to discuss, which is infinitely more fascinating."

Molly told herself not to take the bait. Her finances had to be job number one at the moment, not chasing around after jewels and a murder. She walked to the end of the bar where Frances was sitting. "How's tricks?" she asked her friend.

Frances shrugged. "I can't really say right now," she said quietly. "Let's text Lawrence and tell him to get his butt over here. Now that he has a boyfriend, we never even see him anymore and that kind of behavior is just not allowed."

"Agreed!" Molly pulled out her phone and tapped a message.

"So Molly," boomed Lapin from the other end of the bar, "what would *you* do if the baron's emerald fell into your hands—completely legally of course—and you suddenly had nine million euros?"

"Pay off my Visa bill?"

"That is too mundane, my dear. Of *course* all bills would be paid. But what I am asking is, what is your heart's desire, as far as money can make that possible?"

Everyone looked at Molly, curious about her answer.

"Well," she said slowly, "I'm drooling at the idea of no outstanding bills. I mean, that alone..."

"*Chérie*, you're going to have to do better than that. Come on, tell us your heart's desire."

Molly smiled. "All right, but don't blame me if I get sentimental. Here I am, living in Castillac in the southwest of France. I have a wonderful house even if it still needs a hundred repairs. I have you sorry lot to hang out with. I'd say I have my heart's desire already."

"Oh my heavens above, you sound like you're running for office," said Frances.

Lapin came over and put his beefy arm over Molly's shoulder and gave her a side-hug. "I love you too, *La Bombe*," he said, kissing her on the forehead.

They were startled by a sudden cool gust of air and turned to see Lawrence sweeping into the room, dressed in his usual beautifully tailored suit, hair freshly cut, skin still holding on to the golden glow of summer.

He walked down the row, kissing cheeks and exchanging greetings as he went.

"And where is the boyfriend?" asked Frances. "I'm beginning to think he's made up. We hear he exists, but we never actually see this person."

Lawrence laughed. "Do you really think I would dare bring him here, to this shark tank? He's far too sensitive for that. And I rather like having him all to myself," he said impishly.

"What's his middle name?" Molly asked.

"Terrance," shot back Lawrence. "I'm way too quick for you, Missy," he said, ruffling her hair, which was even more out of control than ever. "Would it kill you to find a comb? You are familiar with such implements and their uses?"

"Ha ha."

"Have you discussed the murder yet? I don't want to miss out on the latest."

"We haven't really talked about it because no one knows anything," said Molly. "Nico, bring a plate of *frites*, will you?"

"Anyone else?" Nico asked.

Frances raised her hand, Nico grinned at her and disappeared into the kitchen.

"Well, who are our suspects?" asked Lawrence, leaning with one elbow against the bar.

"It's not a game, you know," said Caroline Dubois. She finished her beer, and tossed some money on the bar. "You can't just treat people's lives like they're contestants on a game show."

"We can't?" said Lapin.

"*Bonsoir*, everyone. Time for me to go walk my dog." Caroline hopped off her stool and made for the door.

The others were silent as she went out.

"I suppose we seem terribly rude," said Lawrence after the door had banged shut.

"It's not as though we knew the baron," said Lapin. "And Caroline didn't either. She just likes being huffy."

"Well, she *was* close to that case last summer," Molly added.

"So tell me more about this emerald," said Frances. "Is it huge? About as big as a basketball?"

"Ah, the emerald! A tantalizing subject!" said Lawrence.

"He probably gave it to Esmé," said Lapin with regret.

"Who's Esmé?" said the other three, all together.

"You haven't heard of Esmé Ridding? The actress?"

"Oh, of course I've heard of her," said Frances. "What does she have to do with the baron?"

"Only his mistress," answered Lapin, grinning ear to ear with pleasure that for once, he was the person everyone was paying attention to.

❧

THE THEME for Molly's first dinner was "Classic Périgord." Not exactly cutting edge, but she figured that could come later, once she'd built up some repeat business. And it made for an easier menu for the first time as she ironed out the process. She spent a contented hour surfing her favorite French recipe sites online and forcing herself not to check her email.

So let's see, she thought. Duck breast is the obvious choice, so maybe I'll avoid that. How about starting with a *salade Périgourdine*—a lot of tourists have probably never eaten duck gizzards and it will be hilarious telling them what they've just eaten and proclaimed delicious. Always good to put in a few opportunities for a laugh. And then, hmm, oh this looks amazing! *Filet de Bœuf Grillé Sauce Périgueux*. Beef tenderloin with a sauce of Madeira and truffles. I know I was thinking it wouldn't be fancy, but that looks too good to pass up. And dessert...something that fits with the season...yes, this *pompe aux pommes du Périgord* fits the bill perfectly. A layered apple puff, I'll probably need to make two or even three, if I get as many customers as I hope.

And there went the morning, in a daydream of a house packed with paying, hungry guests, the smells of roasting meat and pastry, hearty local wine, a few laughs, and a gently fattening bank account. Sometime the week after the gala seemed like a good time to schedule it. Once the menu and shopping list were written out in detail, Molly broke up the tasks by day. First she needed to make flyers about the dinner and post them all over Castillac, and some in Bergerac and Périgueux as well. No sense doing any shopping until she had some idea of how many would be coming.

And they *will* come, right? she thought, having the first pang of insecurity as she printed off a stack of notices.

But she brushed that off, quickly ran a comb through her hair and said goodbye to Bobo. She jumped on the scooter with the flyers stuffed in a knapsack, and headed into the village with a short list of things she felt she could safely buy ahead of time, such as pre-made puff pastry for the *pompe aux pommes*. At that time of day Edmond Nugent was safely behind the counter at Pâtisserie Bujold. If he ever found out that she was buying premade puff pastry he might never speak to her again. And in principle, she agreed with him. Homemade *was* always better. But she was still a novice when it came to making that labor-intensive dough, there was so much else to do...and she would absolutely search for a brand that used real butter. Smart cheating is how she thought of it.

Molly made good progress in Castillac, tacking up flyers everywhere she could think of and chatting with acquaintances and strangers as she went. Late in the day, when she was almost done, a woman stopped her as she was putting a flyer up on the bulletin board of the organic market.

"Excuse me very much for troubling you," said the woman, whom Molly recognized as none other than the Baroness de Fleuray. Her accent was posh. She looked to be in her mid-fifties, dressed casually but expensively, her hair pulled into a low chignon. Her nose was too large for her face and her eyes too close together, which Molly noticed and then quickly chastised herself for being shallow and judgmental. She made an effort to stay poised and not shriek with excitement at meeting her.

"Bonjour, madame," said Molly with a big American smile. "How can I help you?"

"I know this is terribly forward of me," the woman said. "I am Antoinette de Fleuray, from Château Marainte."

"I am very pleased to meet you."

"I have asked some people I trust, and they have told me you are the person to see when something terrible has happened."

Molly laughed, then stopped abruptly, realizing it sounded very rude. "I don't know about that," she said, "but I have heard about your husband, and I'm very sorry."

"Yes," said Antoinette, casting her eyes down.

A long moment of silence. Molly's thoughts and plans about the dinner were quickly pushed to the side as she dared to hope that she would be getting in on the baron's case after all.

"He was shot right in his salon," Antoinette murmured. "And there are...as you can imagine, when a great deal of money is involved...at any rate, I apologize for having this conversation here on the street. I would prefer to go into details somewhere more private, if you are willing?"

Molly nodded. A million questions had already jumped into her head, but again she held herself back.

"Would you come to the château for a more complete conversation? Would it be possible perhaps on the Monday morning, after the gala?"

"Of course. I would be more than happy to help, if I can."

The baroness smiled, though Molly noted it was hardly a smile of happiness, and went into the organic market to do her shopping. Molly forgot about the pre-made puff pastry, the flyers, the dinner, and everything else, and began, with very few facts to work with, to think seriously about the murder of Baron Marcel de Fleuray.

7

"My darling, it is absolutely magnificent to see you! I'm only regretful that it is under such harrowing circumstances," said Alexandre Roulier, settling himself on the sofa in the lounge at Château Marainte.

Antoinette's face remained composed, not giving away any hint of the contempt she felt for this supposed business associate of her husband's who tried so hard to speak the way he imagined aristocrats speak, but which conversation of course came out utterly wrong and false. Where did Marcel find these people, she thought, pouring Alexandre another cup of coffee.

"Thank heavens I find myself at loose ends for the moment, so I shall be able to stay for a short while to help in any way I can. I expect there is much to do and it is far too much to manage all on your own. Will the boys be arriving soon?"

Antoinette grimaced as Alexandre poured half of the small porcelain pitcher of cream into his coffee and bit off the end of a croissant. "Yes, they will be here tomorrow. The funeral is on Saturday. No need to stay after that," she added.

"And who will be the *notaire* administering the estate? Shall I make some calls to see who can be trusted?"

"Really, there's no need to bother about any of that, Alexandre. My sons and I, we are grieving but not incapacitated. In any event, there is nothing complicated about the probate. Marcel, quite lovingly I must say, told all of us what was in his will a few years ago. There will be no surprises."

"As long as no new will is found," said Alexandre, slurping his coffee.

"You must watch a lot of television dramas," said Antoinette drily. "I'm going to go do my morning chores. You are settled in your room? Anything you need?"

"No, my dear Baroness, not a thing. Would you like some help? Admittedly I am not a country boy, but perhaps my enthusiasm for helping you would compensate?"

"Oh no, I am happy to do them myself. The more I carry on with regular duties, the better."

"Understood," said Alexandre with a solemn expression. Antoinette wasn't sure, but he appeared to be on the verge of tears. Crocodile tears, no doubt. She went out into the courtyard and stood for a moment with her face up to the sun, long enough to feel its warmth, and then continued to the barn to tend to her menagerie of a donkey, three goats, and a small flock of fancy chickens.

Alexandre leaned back on the sofa and smiled broadly while drinking his coffee and contemplating the various places he might search for the jeweled box. Thus far Antoinette had made no mention of it, which he knew meant nothing if he were going to appraise her silence objectively, but which he hoped meant that she did not know of its existence. He understood Marcel to be a man of secrets, and it would not be surprising if he had not told his wife that he owned *La Sfortuna*. Of course Marcel had told *him* about it, and Alexandre held that fact close to his heart as proof of the baron's high esteem and trust.

He got up and peered through the small slit of a window to see if he could see Antoinette or anyone else wandering about, but the courtyard was empty. Château Marainte was vast with many outbuildings, but there was no tumult, no hubbub of staff or family members going about their business. It was quiet and sedate, with not even a leaf moving on the small European weeping birch trees that punctuated the parterres.

Alexandre glugged down the last of his coffee, jammed the rest of the croissant into his mouth, and went down the long, dark corridor toward the baron's salon. Surely that would be the first place to make a preliminary search? And best to get a jump on it before those insolent sons arrived.

The salon was in another wing of the building, and to get there without cutting across the courtyard took much longer. Alexandre walked slowly, imagining himself as Baron Alexandre, then improving that to Marquis Alexandre, rich beyond all reckoning, with a pack of sycophants at his heels attending to his every comfort and anticipating his every whim. He knew where the salon was, having visited the château several times over the last few years for Marcel's famous hunting parties. He would miss those terribly. It had not been easy getting so close to Marcel that he was allowed to mingle with various government ministers and titans of industry. Once, the president of France had been due to attend, though he had backed out at the last minute because of some sort of emergency in the Middle East.

At any rate, thanks to cutting Marcel in on some extremely profitable business deals, and taking on more than his share of the risk (not to mention the application of a tedious amount of flattery), Alexandre had broken into a stratum of French society that was normally closed to people like him. And he did not for one second intend for Marcel's death to shut him out again.

He had forgotten that one could only gain entrance to the salon from the courtyard, not from inside the château, so after checking again to see if anyone was outside, he let himself out and made straight for the door as quickly as he could without running, hoping the gendarmes hadn't locked it up.

And they had not. The door eased open without a creak, and Alexandre was back in the room where he had smoked many cigars and enjoyed the smutty jokes of the baron's friends, drunk the finest cognac, and suffered through endless discussion of shotguns and boar in which Alexandre had no interest at all. These weekends in the Dordogne with Marcel were wonderful for the food, drink, and most of all, contacts—but the hunting itself bored him to tears.

He walked around the console table to the main part of the room, flinching when he saw the large bloodstain on the rug. But there was no time for contemplation. He ran his eyes over the bookshelves, the gun rack, the antique desk. Marcel must have hidden it someplace ingenious, he thought, but why not give the obvious a chance, just in case? Quickly he opened all the drawers of the desk and rifled through the sparse contents. Nothing but papers and a small stuffed bear no more than two inches tall. He took a set of books out of each row of the shelves and looked behind them before putting the books back. He rapped on the mahogany-paneled wall, listening for hollow sounds, thinking that there might be a secret compartment in there somewhere. He peeked behind the tapestries. He peered through the glass in the gun rack, looked under the cushions of the sofa, checked the pockets of a hunting coat that hung on a coatrack by the door.

Nothing.

It would ruin the fun if he found it right off, Alexandre thought. I've got time. There's no massive rush. Just got to think like Marcel and try to imagine where he would keep his most treasured object. Remember all the nights when he drank too much and talked about how much trouble it had been to buy, and how powerful he felt when he was alone and holding it in his palm.

Alexandre was a man of many interests. Apart from business, in which he had been spectacularly successful mostly owing to a lack of conscience, he had an incongruous interest in spiritual matters. He believed that if he wished for something hard enough, completely enough, that he could physically draw the item toward him. And so, leaving his friend's salon for the moment, he went off in search of Antoinette, happily trusting in the belief that the jewel was somehow inching itself in his direction and would soon be revealed to him.

❧

IT WAS LATE in the evening, and Chez Papa was empty except for Lapin, who had drunk more than usual and to Nico's annoyance seemed in no hurry to go home.

"Just tell me one thing," said Lapin, slurring his words a bit. "Why would you keep something like that a secret, and never show it off to anyone?"

"Keep what a secret?" asked Nico.

"*La Sfortuna*, of course! Aren't you paying attention?"

"To your drunken ramblings? Not so much, old man," said Nico. "I don't know anything about *La Sfortuna*, including whether it even exists. The whole thing sounds to me like a fairy tale."

"Oh no," said Lapin, steadying himself on his elbows. "*Au contraire*. I know it's real. I've seen photographs, anyway. The story I heard—privately, you know, at a meeting of antiques dealers years ago in Paris, many knowledgeable people in attendance I can tell you—the story I heard was that *La Sfortuna* was once the featured jewel in a necklace owned by none other than Lucrezia Borgia."

"Oh I see, the emerald is not only huge and worth a fortune but historically significant? You antiques people are all the same, always trying to make something out of nothing. The thing is probably a chunk of worthless green glass Fleuray kept in his pocket to impress people."

"No," said Lapin. He emptied his glass and banged it on the

table. "No, that's...*La Sfortuna* is *real*, Nico. And it's worth millions, for certain, even in a bad market. These days, with stocks flying so high? Probably couldn't even put a price on it. Those crazy American traders have *so* much money and they're absolutely dying to spend it something like *La Sfortuna*. Something real, a treasure from history that no one else has."

"Lucrezia Borgia," said Nico, shaking his head.

"Yes, *Borgia*. You know Fleuray's brother-in-law was Italian, after all. Aristocrat, industrialist, more money than God apparently. Now, you wouldn't know them because they didn't live around Castillac, but the baron's sister Doriane was very beautiful, and she married Gianni...can't quite remember the name... Conti, I think it was? They used to visit the Fleurays sometimes, but lived in... Milan, I believe, or at least somewhere in northern Italy. I don't remember the details. Anyway, I heard that he gave *La Sfortuna* to his wife for a wedding present. Just imagine! And then of course, you might remember this part—the couple died in a plane crash, in the Alps coming back from skiing—you remember that, don't you my boy? It was all over the tabloids for a short while—doubtless it was at that point that the baron got his mitts on his sister's jewel and didn't let go."

"So you say, Lapin, so you say." Nico reached under the bar for a fresh rag and began polishing up the bar for something to do. "About ready for bed, old friend? As you can see, the rest of the village is all tucked in."

"I don't like October. Every afternoon it gets dark a little sooner. Depressing."

"So hop down to Morocco for a few weeks and bake in the sun."

Lapin laughed. "Not when *La Sfortuna* is about to come out of hiding! I've been waiting to have a glimpse of that stone since the minute I first heard about it over thirty years ago."

Nico just shook his head. "It's no good believing in fairy tales, Lapin, I'm telling you."

❧ 8 ❧

"It's not that I think it's a bad idea, Molls. It's just that it sounds like so much work."

"Eh, not to me. The organizing is the worst part. But the cooking, and actually throwing the party—that part will be fun. I'm going to ask Nico if he'll bartend and help in the kitchen a little. Maybe Constance will agree to serve, though she might be flipping plates upside down in guests' laps."

Frances grinned at the prospect. "Sometimes an upside-down plate makes for the most memorable dinner."

Molly nodded, staring down at her list and trying to sort out what needed to be done when.

"So are you going to the gala tonight?"

"Gala?"

"Molly! It's like the biggest social occasion of the whole year. You went last year, you told me all about it."

Molly looked blank, still thinking about her list.

"The fundraiser for L'Institut Degas. Come on, snap out of it, kiddo!"

"Right. The gala. Listen, I haven't even told you my big news. Did I tell you I met the Baroness de Fleuray yesterday?"

"No, you did not. Spill."

"I don't really have anything to tell. At least nothing very juicy. But...she wants to meet with me. Said she'd heard I was the person to talk to when there's trouble."

Frances hooted. "That's my girl! Lord almighty, a baroness is going to hire you! Have you figured out what you'll charge?"

"Honestly, I hadn't even thought about getting paid."

"Are you not in some financial hot water?"

"I wouldn't call it hot water exactly."

Frances looked exasperated. "Look, you need money. We're headed into the cold months and unless I've got it wrong, your calendar is not crowded with bookings. Right?"

Molly nodded reluctantly.

"Well, so when a freaking baroness knocks on your door and asks for your help, don't be all timid about it. And don't agree to do anything without talking about your fee first. I don't know anything about aristocrats, but believe me, I know plenty of rich people. They'll fleece you if you don't demand your share. And lose respect for you as they're doing it, too."

"So you're saying...I'm a private investigator now? A legit one?"

"If you've got clients approaching you out of the blue, I'd say yeah, that's what you are. And if that client lives in a humongous château and is rolling in do-re-mi, make that invoice a hefty one!"

Molly laughed. "Okay, okay. I'm a little uncomfortable asking for money but I see your point. So...you and Nico are going to the gala? What time does it start?"

"Eight. You can't weasel out of going just because you're sort of single for the moment. Who knows, you might meet someone."

"Ha. I'm not looking to meet someone. Romance is really just not my thing."

"Uh huh. If I only had a euro for every—"

"Oh shut up, Frances," said Molly.

"And you're on a murder case. Murderers always go to big parties."

"What are you even talking about?"

"Pretty much everyone in the village will be there, right? So if the baron's killer is local, he's not going to risk staying home when the whole village is at the same party. It would attract attention, and he might miss out on important gossip. So my brilliant deductive powers say that *ipso facto* the murderer will be at that gala. And so should you."

"Oh *ipso facto* alakazam!"

"No need to get salty," said Frances, pretending to be offended.

Molly loved her old friend deeply, but sometimes even old friends can grate on your last nerve. She announced she was going to mop the floor, and Frances scurried off, leaving Molly to contemplate whether she could muster the enthusiasm to go to the gala this year. It had been so much fun with Ben last October, and going by herself just wouldn't be the same. It made her feel lonely just thinking about it.

But Frances was probably right. It might not be a night of romantic pleasure this time, but there was sleuthing to do, and staying home really wasn't an option.

❧

MARON STOOD up from his desk, still looking at his computer screen. He was expecting Georgina Locatelli to arrive at the station any minute, the first of several interviews of the employees at Château Marainte.

"I would be more than happy to conduct this interview, if you have more important things to attend to," said Paul-Henri, anxious to get in on the action.

"Actually, that call just now was from Madame Vargas. I'm

afraid her husband has gone wandering again. Check the usual places, will you?"

"If he always goes to the same places, why can't Madame Vargas just fetch him?"

"Well, that's the thing. Sometimes he shakes things up and doesn't go to the cemetery, and it takes some detective work to figure out where else he might be. Hop to, Paul-Henri, wouldn't want him out in the road on a blind curve. ..."

Paul-Henri sighed, and Maron turned away to hide his amusement. It was not so long ago that Ben Dufort was giving him the Vargas assignment, and he remembered very well how onerous it felt.

Just as Paul-Henri was leaving, a dark-haired whirlwind came through the door. She was short and slender, around forty years old, dressed in a black skirt and low heels. Waving her arms, she quickly moved next to Maron, glaring at him, and he took a step back.

"All right then, here I am," she said defiantly. "But don't get it into your head that I'm going to sit down and blurt out all the family's business because that is not how I operate."

"Good morning, Madame Locatelli."

"Just make it Georgina. I'm a housekeeper, not the Queen of England."

"Yes, madame," said Maron. "Please have a seat, and thank you very much for coming in."

Georgina narrowed her eyes at him.

"Please begin by talking to me about last Friday night. Start early, before dinner. Do you cook for the Fleurays?"

"*Al diavolo!* We did not...we did not see eye to eye on food, officer."

Maron rubbed a palm over his face. "What do you mean?"

"I am *Italian*, if you have not noticed, Mr. Police Investigator. The Fleurays are *French*. Do I need to spell it out?"

"I'm sorry, are you saying you simply like different kinds of food?"

Georgina did not alter the intensity of her stare as she slowly shook her head without answering. Maron felt sweat break out under his collar despite the room being rather cool.

"So who cooked dinner? Was there dinner? Did the Fleurays eat together?"

"That night they did, yes. I had been working on the third floor readying some guest bedrooms, so I was there later than usual. The baroness cooked. When I was done mopping the floors I went home."

"And where is that?"

"A cottage partway down the hill, on the drive up to the château. My Angelo and I live there."

"Angelo is your husband?"

"What kind of woman are you implying I am?"

"I am implying nothing, madame, simply asking—"

"Very impertinent. Insinuating. Let me tell you, I may be only a housekeeper, but that does not give you license to—"

"Excuse me, madame, I have really only a very few questions left to ask. I am not in any way trying to insult you or—"

"So you say, Mr. Police Officer. Are you the head detective? Who else works in this office?"

"I'm going to ask the questions, Georgina. All right. Who were the guest rooms for, if you know?"

"I don't."

"So you finished up work and went home. You heard nothing else that night?"

"Why would you ask the question that way? Is that what you want me to say? 'Oh yes, Mr. Important Detective, I went home and went to bed and never heard a thing.' Is that what you're after? You've already wrapped this case up, over and done?"

Maron inhaled slowly. "Can you tell me what happened after you finished cleaning?"

"I walked down the hill to my cottage and made spaghetti carbonara for my Angelo. We drank a Barolo I'd saved up for and went to bed around ten."

"And did you hear or see anything else that night, or notice anything at all?"

"Apart from the sports car that came screaming down the drive at around midnight, no Monsieur, I did not."

Georgina folded her arms and continued to glare at Officer Maron, though now she allowed herself the tiniest hint of a smile.

9

She was ready but not enthusiastic. It was nearly nine o'clock, and the gala was in full swing already, but Molly dawdled, wiping off her eyeliner and putting it on again, tying a scarf and retying it three more times, spraying her hair with something meant to dampen the frizz. Uninspired, she was wearing the same black dress she had worn to last year's gala, only this year it was tighter, and not in a good way.

It wasn't that she was embarrassed to be without a date, or felt incomplete without a partner, or anything like that. Just that a big party like this was so much more festive when the zing of romance was in the air.

Though *really*—wasn't she getting too old for such thoughts? She was going to be forty next year, after all. Time to let go of the picket fence and babies dreams, Molly.

Ugh, way to cheer yourself right up, she thought, glumly giving Bobo one last scratch behind the ears before heading outside and climbing onto her dented scooter. As she cut through the village on the way to L'Insitut Degas, she remembered last year's gala, when she hadn't been in France more than a few months. All of it —leaving Massachusetts, the first big village social occasion, the early efforts at detective work—it seemed a million years ago now. She missed Ben, but the pang bubbled up and faded away quickly, and she told herself to quit moping and get ready for a good time. Her friends would be there, she had a new case to work on, the dinner plan for more income...all in all, life was good. Or good enough for now.

The streets of Castillac were empty. There weren't many streetlights and she passed pockets of shadow and darkness on her way. Chez Papa was closed, as were the other bars and restaurants, the Presse, everything. When Molly stopped for one of the few stoplights in Castillac, she shivered while looking around at the shuttered windows. Not even a cat slunk along an alley.

Just outside the village, the central building at L'Institut Degas was modern, with big rounded windows, a series of large skylights, and a strange external covering that made it look like a jellyfish. Molly could see that the place was packed, and groups stood out on the lawn chatting.

The first person she recognized after parking the scooter was Rex Ford, a teacher at L'Institut whom she had met briefly during the Amy Bennett case. He was lanky and serious, and greeted her with the same sour demeanor she remembered.

"Everyone inside is talking about how you're investigating the baron's murder," he said, lighting a cigarette and somehow making his disapproval clear.

Well, that didn't take long.

Molly tried to smooth her hair back under control after taking off her helmet.

"You do know this village is packed to the brim with the biggest gossips on earth," he said.

"Yes...but, generally speaking, the gossip tends to be pretty lighted-hearted, wouldn't you say?"

"No."

"Just, you know, mostly affectionately interested in what other people are doing?"

"Are you kidding? No, Molly, I'm afraid you're looking at this with more optimism and good spirits than are called for. People here like to drag others down, is how it is. They feed on bad news, and they'll chew you up and spit you out if you're not careful."

Molly sighed inwardly but nodded. "Well, it's nice to see you again, Rex. I'm going to head in and get to the bar!"

"Cheers," he answered gloomily, and Molly could not wait to put some distance between herself and the embittered teacher. Her mood was precarious enough as it was.

"Molly!" shouted Lawrence, who was just inside the door selling tickets.

"Oh, I am glad to see you!" she said, falling into his arms for a hug.

"I was worried you wouldn't show."

"I didn't feel like coming. But here I am. Have I missed anything?"

"Actually...not a thing. You're not the only late arrival. But the baroness is here—she got here about fifteen minutes ago and caused quite a stir. Apparently, she usually sends a yearly check to the Institut but never actually attends the gala."

"Oo, I'm going to rush off to find her—"

"Not before you buy your ticket, Missy."

Molly fumbled in her tiny evening bag for cash, then looked in the crowd for Antoinette while Lawrence made change.

"And um, who else is here, Lawrence? Has your infamous boyfriend with the middle name of Terrance made an appearance?"

"He's here. Just...be gentle, will you?"

"You wound me, you really do. What do you think I'm going to do, push him up against a wall, shine a light in his face, and interrogate him?"

"Well...yes."

They both laughed. Then Molly caught a glimpse of the baroness, kissed his cheek, and disappeared into the crowd.

❧

THE ROOM only had a few streamers for decoration, apart from some bowls of flowers on the tables along the walls of the room. A DJ was set up in one corner and was blasting pop, a gang of villagers danced in the center of the room, and a few people sat at the tables eating plates of duck breast and frites. After the quick glimpse of the baroness, Molly could not find her, so she stood on the edge of the dance floor feeling awkward, looking for anyone she knew.

Then someone grabbed her hand, spun her under his arm, and pressed her close. "Lapin!" she said, pushing him away.

"La Bombe! I have been patiently waiting for your arrival all night. When oh when is La Bombe ever going to arrive? I have said this to myself ten thousand times."

"Pfft, you've said that to the last six women to come in."

"Never!"

Neither of them was familiar with the song but they valiantly danced until the end of the song, Lapin showing more enthusiasm than Molly.

"You should eat something," he told her. "It's duck, like they serve every year. Why change something when it works, that's what I always say."

"Not a bad idea. First I think I'll get a kir—"

"Allow me," said Lapin, bowing low with a grand gesture of the arm, and then working his bulky self through the crowd.

I wish Ben were here, Molly couldn't help thinking.

"Molls!" shouted a familiar voice. Molly turned around to see Frances and Nico, their arms entwined around each other, both beaming.

It was impossible not to smile back. "Having fun?" asked Molly.

"You should see the moves Nico's got on the dance floor,"

shrieked Frances. "He's been practicing at home, as a secret surprise. Learning from YouTube videos!"

"Well?" said Molly to Nico. "Show me what you got!"

Nico led Frances out to the center of the dance floor just as an electronic song started up that sounded like something composed by a computer. Nico stood absolutely still, then began moving various parts of his body along with the bass beat, isolating each part so that he magically seemed to become a robot right before their eyes, his limbs segmented and autonomous.

"I...." started Molly, impressed but disturbed.

"Isn't he *amazing?*" said Frances dreamily, and then she went to Nico and he wrapped his arms around her and they slow-danced like a couple of ninth-graders in their first infatuation.

Molly sighed. She kept scanning the crowd but not seeing anyone she knew. Where were Manette, Rémy, Constance and Thomas? Usually Molly was gregarious to a fault, but that night she felt out of step and reluctant to go up to people whose faces were familiar, but whom she hadn't actually met.

And where was Lapin with that kir? She decided to go fetch one herself, and squeezed through the crowd to the bar where the always gloriously handsome Pascal was on duty.

"The usual, Madame Sutton?" he asked charmingly.

"Of course," said Molly. "I hear the baroness is here tonight?"

"She is! Right over there, no, to the left—"

Molly stood on tip toe and nodded. "Oh yay! I want to have a word with her."

"I'm sure you do," said Pascal. "Any progress yet?"

"I haven't even begun! Slow down!"

"I have supreme confidence in you, Molly," he said, and the real charm of Pascal was that he was not only beautiful but honest, so when he gave you a compliment, you could trust that it wasn't just a pile of empty words.

"Thank you. And thanks for the kir, too."

Pascal flashed a smile and began to chat with the old man who was next in line. The room was packed and Molly slowly made her way toward the baroness, who was talking to a small group of people just on the edge of the dance floor.

"Bonsoir, Baroness," Molly said, catching her eye.

"Oh please, Molly—call me Antoinette. When people use the title it makes me feel like we're still in the Middle Ages!"

The others in the group tittered.

Molly saw that Antoinette was wearing a glamorous gown that fit her slender frame closely and gave her movements a sinuous grace. It was an odd color, in between yellow and green, that was flattering to her complexion, and the gazillions of tiny beads sewn into the fabric made her glow with reflected light. Yet her face, Molly thought, her face...it's a shame she's so plain. But what is this weird assumption I keep making—that if you're rich you're automatically supposed to be physically attractive? She shook her head as though to change the direction of her thoughts.

"I *love* your dress," Molly said, leaning close to the Antoinette's ear because the music had gotten louder.

"Thank you." Antoinette sipped her drink and looked out at the dancers.

The song ended, and Frances saw Molly and started to come over with Nico.

"Allow me to present my best friends in Castillac," Molly began as Frances approached. "This is Frances Milton, a childhood friend who has also chosen to live in Castillac full time. And this is—where did Nico go?"

Frances turned around and looked momentarily crestfallen. "I—no idea. He was right here a second ago. Oh well, you know how men are, he probably felt starved and ran off for another plate of food."

Molly and Antoinette laughed politely. The three women all craned their necks looking for Nico, but he was nowhere to be seen.

10

"Oh my God, oh my God, oh my God—*look!*" said a young woman in a mini-dress. So Molly looked.

Pausing in the wide doorway was a heart-stoppingly gorgeous woman, her chin lifted slightly as she surveyed the crowd. Her glossy blonde hair spilled over her shoulder in artful waves, her darkened eyebrows framed her exotic eyes, and her full lips were a sensuous red. But more than beauty, this woman had *it*: the kind of charisma that stopped a room dead. The music kept pounding but no one moved. All the faces in the crowd had turned to the doorway, mesmerized by the tall woman dressed simply in a silk shirt and dark, fitted trousers.

"That's...who *is* that?" Molly asked.

"Esmé *Ridding*," said the woman, looking at Molly as though she were mentally challenged. "Are you kidding me? The face of Chanel? Plus all those movies? Oh my *God*." And she scurried off to get closer to the stunning celebrity who was taking her time in the doorway, an expert at knowing how to make an entrance with optimal impact.

"There you are," said Lapin, appearing at Molly's elbow carrying a kir and a glass of local red for himself. "I've been looking all over for you. The gala is so crowded this year, more people than ever. You saw who just came in?"

Molly tossed back the rest of her drink and took the new one from Lapin. "Thanks, pal," she said. "So what in the world is Esmé Ridding doing in Castillac?"

"The baron's mistress, what else?"

"Wait, *what?* I thought you were joking the other day."

"I never joke about gossip," said Lapin with a grin. "Oh yes, the affair's been going on for months. In all the tabloids. Don't you look at the papers?"

"I tend to go with *Le Monde*."

"Ah," he said rolling his eyes. "If you want to keep up on what's really going on, you've got to read all the trashy papers that are willing to break the laws about spying on people. Sure, they publish some made-up stuff to boost circulation, but there are some nuggets of gold in there every so often."

"But here's the thing, Lapin. I actually feel sorry for celebrities. Once you hit a certain level of fame, you can't even go to the *épicerie* for a candy bar without being photographed and the world mocking you for it. And God forbid something embarrassing happens."

"Remember when the princess of Liechtenstein tripped going up the steps to the palace and her dress flew up and we saw she was wearing Little Kitty undergarments? I live for moments like those," he said dreamily.

Molly shook her head, smiling. "You are a complicated man, Lapin."

"Indeed. Esmé *is* stunning, you must admit. Makes me think she was part of the baron's hoard, you know? He possessed *La Sfortuna*, and wanted another prodigious jewel for his collection."

"Do you really think anyone is like that? Or are you talking sort of metaphorically?"

"Oh yes, people *are* like that. Literally. Men especially. I see it all the time in the antiques world. People get a fixation on something—a type of furniture, or jewelry, or maybe a particular artist's work—and they don't just want to own a piece or three and get the pleasure of having some nice things in their house. No, they want all of it. And they want to keep other people away from it, too. That's part of their motivation."

"And control? Like if they own every last piece, it belongs to them completely. No one else has any say at all."

Lapin nodded and sipped his wine. "A lot of messed up people in this world, La Bombe."

"So did one of his women kill the baron?" asked Molly, almost to herself. A famous mistress suggested at least the possibility that his wife could have done it. Or Esmé herself. Maybe the actress wanted the emerald, and the baron refused to give it to her. Maybe she wanted him to leave Antoinette and marry her.

A world of possibilities, really—and Molly couldn't wait to get started.

✥ 11 ✥

The morning after the gala, promptly at ten o'clock, Molly rode her scooter up the winding drive to Château Marainte to meet with the baroness. She passed the empty gatehouse and the cottage where Georgina and Angelo lived, the scooter struggling a bit on the steep incline. Once at the top of the hill, the drive flattened out and she went through the *allée* of plane trees, trying not to run off the road from looking at the incredible view, the green patchwork of farmland and villages of the Dordogne.

When she reached the parking area outside the walls of the château, Molly stopped and looked up. It was a forbidding sort of place, clearly built for defense and not for beauty, the stones not the warm and inviting golden limestone typical of the area but a dark gray granite. She wondered what it was like to live in such a dreary place in the twenty-first century—would it make you defensive and wary to live in a building built for war? Would it make a person colder or harder of temperament than someone who lived in a cozy, cheerful place with lots of light? And how on earth did they heat the place in winter?

Molly walked the scooter across the bridge over the dry moat.

She had a vague memory of alligators in moats and shivered even as she guessed those memories came more from cartoons than historical fact. The courtyard was more welcoming than the outside of the château had been. The yellowing leaves of birches fluttered in the breeze, the gravel was neatly raked, the parterres still showed plenty of life since they had not yet had a hard frost. Asters bloomed in profusion, and Molly noticed some flowers she wasn't familiar with, some sort of autumn bulb, possibly?

"Madame Sutton," said a voice, and Molly turned quickly to see the baroness walking toward her with a border collie at her side.

"Please, call me Molly! Your home...well, I can't even find the words! It's magnificent. Of course, for an American, it's just so outside my experience to imagine living in history like this. Has it been in your family forever?"

"Not mine, but my husband's, yes. The Fleurays have been at Château Marainte since sometime in the seventeenth century. Right around the time your country was being settled by the English."

"Incredible. I suppose we have families in the U.S. that go back that far, who know their history, but for the most part we are much more fractured. I couldn't even name my great-grandparents, which now that I think of it, seems downright horrible of me."

Antoinette laughed. "Well, as with anything, there are pluses and minuses. Ancestry can be a sort of unhealthy fetish that distracts one from the present." She squatted down to pet the dog, running her hand down the border collie's back and then ruffling her ears.

Molly suddenly remembered the dramatic entrance of Esmé Ridding the night before, and wondered how to bring it up without seeming unforgivably rude.

"Well," said Antoinette, "come inside, and let me explain what I would like you to do. Would you like coffee, or a cup of tea?"

"Coffee would be lovely."

They walked across the courtyard and through a door that opened into a small dining room, and from there into the kitchen. In the center of one wall was an enormous fireplace, almost tall enough for Molly to stand up in and more than two meters wide. A pair of massive andirons held some charred logs and a black pot —a classic witch's model—hung from an iron hook.

"Wow," said Molly.

Antoinette smiled. "If you'd ever like to roast a whole boar, we can handle that here."

"I see that you could! I've never tried roast boar. I bet it's amazing. Do you eat a lot of game? Did your husband do a lot of hunting?"

Antoinette looked momentarily taken aback and Molly reminded herself to proceed with more sensitivity and not pepper the baroness with so many questions.

"He was an avid hunter, yes. He lived for it, in fact."

Molly bit her lip to keep from talking, hoping Antoinette would elaborate, but she was giving her attention to the espresso machine and said nothing further for the moment.

"Thanks," Molly said when Antoinette gave her the small cup and saucer.

"You're quite welcome. Let's go in the lounge where we'll be more comfortable. Come on, Grizou, you may join us." They went into the lounge, a small room with a television and two sofas that had seen better days, and several Turkish throw rugs. Molly was surprised to see that the room was comfortable and pleasant, and did not feel a bit like part of a fortress despite having only one small window and being made completely of gray stone. The dog followed Antoinette and curled up at her feet. "Molly, I know you have been in Castillac barely a year, so perhaps there are bits and pieces of local gossip and history you have not yet heard. I will need to fill you in if you are to undertake the task I have in mind. By any chance have you heard of *La Sfortuna*?"

"The emerald?"

"Indeed. So you have heard of it?"

"Just barely. All I know is...that it's big. And valuable?"

"Yes to both, though I cannot put an exact price on it. It belonged to my husband and was, for sentimental reasons, one of his most treasured possessions. So treasured, in fact—ironically enough—that he absolutely refused to keep it in a safe place. His friends and I begged him to put it in a safe deposit box but he would have none of it. He liked, much of the time, to wander about with the stone in his pocket where he could caress it anytime he liked."

"I get that. I mean, what's the point of having something beautiful if it's going to be locked up where you can't even see it?"

"You and Marcel would have gotten along famously."

Molly listened for bitterness or jealousy in that remark, but heard none.

"The problem is, with Marcel gone, we have no idea where the emerald is. It was not in his pockets when he died, so either he had hidden it away somewhere—which he did from time to time —or it has been stolen. What I would like to do," continued Antoinette, "if you are amenable, is hire you to use your prodigious detective skills to figure out where it is hidden, if it is. I've looked everywhere I can think of and can't find it anywhere. As you might imagine, it's worth far too much money to remain lost."

"Understood," said Molly, trying not altogether successfully to hide her disappointment at the job Antoinette was giving her. Then she decided the hell with it, she would speak her mind. "I... I'll admit, Antoinette, I thought you were going to ask me to investigate your husband's murder. It *was* murder, right? Not an accident? If you don't mind my asking?"

Antoinette bowed her head. "Not an accident, no." She looked up and Molly could see her eyes were reddish and damp. "Let me be clearer. I'm asking you to find the emerald not *instead of* Marcel's killer, but because it's a necessary first step in that process. The jewel is the key," she said in a low voice. "I believe the chance is fairly good that he was killed by someone who wanted it, and that finding it might bring that person into the open, force his hand so to speak. And not only that—do you know any Italian? *La Sfortuna*...it means *misfortune*. Not exactly subtle, whoever gave it that name. Maybe it sounds silly to you, but the emerald...it truly does seem to be cursed, and believe me, I'm not a superstitious person, I don't go in for that sort of thing normally. Let me explain a bit of the history.

"The jewel came to this family through Marcel's brother-in-law, Gianni Conti. You've heard of him? Fabulously wealthy, a captain of industry in Milan, an aristocratic family going back many centuries. I do not know precisely how he got the emerald, but back in the fifteenth century, it belonged to none other than Lucrezia Borgia, and surely you have heard of her."

Molly nodded, racking her brain for details. "A lot of poisonings?"

"Oh yes, although many of the reports are unverified. Her enemies were legion, and it is difficult to sort out their attacks from the truth. But in any case, it is clear that Lucrezia was a powerful woman and she did not always use the gentlest means to achieve her goals, shall we say. The emerald was the central jewel in a famous necklace of hers—it shows up in at least one portrait that I know of, currently hanging in the Uffizi."

"That's some story," murmured Molly.

"There's more," said Antoinette with an ironic smile. "Fast forward to the 1990s. Marcel was devoted to his sister, Doriane. She was ten years younger than he, and he believed she could do no wrong."

Ah, thought Molly, now there's a note of bitterness.

"So Doriane marries Gianni Conti, they live a life of great luxury—although to give her credit, she was actually something of an intellectual, always had her head in a book. But Gianni wanted to show her off and was always dragging her to Gstaad or Cannes, to the latest jet-set party. In any case, to give you the short version of this long story—Gianni and Doriane were killed in an airplane crash in the Alps, almost twenty years ago now. That is when Marcel came to own *La Sfortuna*, as an inheritance from his sister. Excuse me if this sounds, oh I don't know—it does sound absurd, there's no getting around it—Marcel seemed to treasure that stone as though it were the embodiment of Doriane's soul. As though by keeping it in his pants pocket he was holding her there as well, keeping her close to him. It seemed to give him a great deal of comfort, though he would tell anyone that her death had broken his heart.

"So you see—again I'm going to sound superstitious, so perhaps I am. But I believe the emerald is nothing but trouble, and I absolutely want it out of this house. If indeed it is still here. Two accidental deaths and a murder, in only one generation. If that is not a curse, then I don't want to imagine what is."

Molly looked solemn. "I'm not usually superstitious either, but I can see why you feel that way." She drank the last of her now-cold espresso, forgotten in the excitement of the tale Antoinette had told. "Well, I'd be happy to help you if I can. I'm not sure my talents fit exactly with the problem—I'm better at thinking about people than objects. I suppose for a start, what I need to do is get a good sense of your husband, so that I can make some guesses about what he might have been thinking when he decided on a hiding place. Can you tell me about him, what he liked and disliked, what kind of man he was?"

Antoinette's face fell slightly, and then she drew herself back up, her posture straight though her eyes were full of sorrow. "I understand what you are asking. But I'm afraid this morning...I am not feeling up to it. It's a conversation that will be...you understand? Quite painful to have."

"Yes," said Molly, reaching out and putting her hand over the baroness's. "Whenever you're ready, of course. I'm sure there's so much to do just now, and surely if the emerald really is cursed, it doesn't do its evil instantly. There's time."

"Thank you, Molly," said Antoinette. "You'll come back soon? No need to arrange anything in advance. I'm almost always here at the château, most often down at the barn taking care of various animals, sometimes working in the garden in the courtyard or the *potager* outside the walls. Give me a few days, then return?"

"You can count on me," said Molly, rising from the tattered sofa and feeling a bit relieved to be leaving. "We'll find that stone somehow!"

Though as she climbed on her scooter and headed down the hill, she thought about the vastness of the château and how easy it would be, if someone desired, to hide something that small so that no one would ever be able to find it, not in a million years.

12

Maron had sent Paul-Henri off on an errand in Bergerac and was eating a baguette with ham and butter at his desk when Hubert Arnaud came into the station. Maron shoved the last of the sandwich into his mouth and drank down some water before thanking him for coming in.

"Please understand, monsieur, you are not a suspect in the murder of Marcel de Fleuray. I only want as much information as you can give me about the operations at the château, the baron and baroness, their friends...anything you can think of that might help point us in the right direction."

Hubert nodded his head vigorously. "I want to help. I was gutted by the news. My family has worked for the Fleurays for generations, and never has anything so ugly taken place at Château Marainte. And of course I knew the baron quite well. He spent a lot of time in the forests, you know—in big hunting parties, but also by himself or just the two of us. Nothing he loved more than shooting, being outside in any weather. Nature, that's what the baron cared about. You know, he was called Little Bear when he was a kid, because anytime his parents or the nanny wanted to find him, he would be rambling around in the forest, or huddled in a cave somewhere."

"Yet my understanding is that recently he spent most of his time in Paris."

"Well, yes. He had business to attend to. It's not like most of the aristocratic families can just bob along without a care in the world, can they? They have to make a living like anybody else. It's not 1770, Officer Maron."

"No, of course not," said Maron. "All right, the baron was a nature lover. What else can you tell me about him?"

"He was a very good shot. Could nail a pheasant on the rise at a good distance, just like that, ninety-nine times out of a hundred. Used to impress his city guests, I can tell you."

"And his relation to you—was he a fair person to work for? Treated you well?"

"Yes. Like I say, my family has worked for the Fleurays for something like two hundred years. We consider it an honor. And if you are asking about details like salary and things like that, he paid me regularly and about the same as anyone else in my job gets, as far as I know."

Maron nodded. "And what exactly is your job?"

Hubert sat up straight and expanded his chest. "You could call me a gamekeeper, I suppose. I manage the hunting lands," he said. "There's more to that than you might think. It's not like you can just open a crate of baby pheasants and that's the end of it. There's an art to it. I keep an eye out for poachers—that goes back and forth, some years it's a big problem, and others not as much. And the rest of it, well, the baron, as you say, was out of town quite a bit. Sometimes the baroness needs help with something at the château, and I take care of that for her."

"What kind of help?

"Oh, a tree fell over in the driveway once, and I brought my chainsaw and cut it up for her. I fix things around the château, handyman sorts of jobs—replacing a broken windowpane, a rusted hinge, little jobs like that."

"And the baroness, how do you get along with her?"

"Quite well. She's pretty self-sufficient and doesn't call me often. I think she likes seeing what she can do on her own, before asking me to step in. I found her trying to rewire a lamp once and she only gave it to me when I insisted."

"And how does she treat the other people who work at the château?"

"There's only me and Georgina." Hubert leaned forward and lowered his voice although there was no one else in the station. "Confidentially, the Fleurays don't have the best cash flow. But apart from that," he said, sitting up again, "they aren't really the type to want to be waited on hand and foot. Neither of them are like that, and Percival and Luc aren't either. Not spoiled, like you might think."

"Those are the sons?"

"Yes, officer."

"I'd like to return to them in a moment. Tell me about Georgina."

Hubert started to grin but stopped himself. "She's a right firecracker, that one," he said, but went silent and looked around the station as though only then realizing where he was. "It's just you and the new guy now? I heard Dufort is off riding elephants somewhere. Is he never coming back?"

"Not to the gendarmerie. Back to Castillac, I have no idea. Now—Georgina. What do you mean, firecracker? She has a temper?"

"Oh, yes!" said Hubert with relish. "And she and Antoinette, they don't get along so well. Some women are like oil and water, you know?"

"You're saying temperamentally they don't get along?"

"Yeah, that's what I mean. The baroness is on the quiet side. Doesn't show how she feels about things right off. You know—

reserved, like a baroness should act. But Georgina, holy mother of Jesus, she'll start up screeching at the drop of a hat. If you're within a hundred meters, you're gonna know her feelings about everything, you know what I'm talking about?"

Maron remembered his interview with the housekeeper and understood Hubert's point very well.

"And this difference in temperament, you think that is the cause of their not getting along? Any other reason?"

"Well," said Hubert, delighted to have an opportunity to show his intimate knowledge of the goings-on at Château Marainte, since his friends in the village had tired of the subject long ago. "Yeah, there's reasons. See, Georgina's not from a family that has served the Fleurays for generations, like mine. She was the baron's sister's maid. Doriane de Fleuray," he added reverentially.

"Who is Doriane de Fleuray?"

"The baron's sister, like I said," Hubert said, annoyed that anyone could be so out of the loop about Castillac's aristocracy. "She grew up at the château with the baron, his little sister. Famous for her beauty. And not at all in a show-off way, either. Beautiful and kind-hearted, that was Doriane de Fleuray.

"I knew her quite well, you see. We were all gutted when she... when she died," he added.

Maron cocked his head and studied Hubert. This loyalty and even reverence was strange and distasteful to him, but he managed not to show it.

"How did Doriane die?"

Hubert bowed his head. "I'm astonished you don't know. The story was in all the papers. I kept many clippings, if you would be interested to see them. Do you not remember the tragic plane crash in 1986, when she and her husband were going back to Milan after a ski trip at Chamonix? Of course they were both instantly killed. A terrible, terrible tragedy."

Maron had never been even slightly interested in the activities of celebrities or the very rich, so no, he had no memory of the crash. "So Doriane lived in Milan? Then how did her maid end up at Château Marainte?"

"Because the baron hired her. All I know is, after Madame Conti's death, Georgina showed up. And she and the baroness sometimes went at it hammer and tongs, I'll tell you."

Maron considered. The two men sat for a few quiet moments, each lost in his own thoughts about the world inside the château. "One more question," said Maron finally. "On Friday night, the night of the murder—do you know anything about a sports car being at the château?"

"Sports car? What kind? I never saw anything like that, but I wasn't there after about four in the afternoon. I'd been working on a tractor and gotten covered with grease, so I went home to get cleaned up. The night the baron was shot, I was home watching television."

"You married?"

"No."

"Live alone? Anybody to corroborate what you just told me?"

"What are you getting at? Why in the world would I—you think *I* had something to do with it? Excuse me, Officer Maron, for telling you your business. But if you want to catch the baron's murderer, you are really barking up the wrong tree." Hubert stuck out his chest, clearly affronted.

"All right, then," said Maron. "Thank you, Monsieur Arnaud, you've been quite helpful. Please don't take offense, my questions are standard protocol and I will be asking anyone else connected with the château the very same things. Also—I understand that you might feel reluctant to speak freely since you're obviously a very loyal employee. Just remember that anything you tell me could lead to the baron's murderer."

Yes, sir," said Hubert solemnly.

"Anything you think of, even a little detail—just give me a call," said Maron, handing him a card with his cell number.

❧

WEDNESDAY AFTERNOON, and Chez Papa was empty except for Frances perched on her stool at the end of the bar, and Nico putting glasses away behind it.

"Where is everyone?" moaned Frances melodramatically. "It's not like it's pouring rain or anything."

"What's Molly up to?"

"I don't know. She's been impossible lately. Either staring into space thinking about the baron, or running around like a chicken with her head cut off getting ready for this dinner tonight. Are you still going to help her out? I think she's got maybe eight or ten people signed up."

"Yeah, I told her I'd make *apéros*, but that's it. She sounded confident she could manage the kitchen end of things if I took care of the drinks for her."

"Seems like a lot of work to me, with high expenses."

Nico shrugged. "She can't whip off jingles for big money like you," he said, leaning in for a kiss.

"Okay, maybe I'm wrong. I just think there's got to be an easier way to improve cash flow than going to all that trouble for one meal."

"Frances, *chérie?*"

"Yeeeessss?"

"You've lived in France how long?"

"Nine months, give or take."

"And do you still not understand that in France, there is nothing more important than a meal? Nothing!"

Frances laughed. "How about Italy? Isn't it pretty much the same there?"

Nico's smile faded. "I haven't lived there since I was a boy, so it's hard to say. Sure, Italians enjoy food immensely, no doubt about that. But my point is that you don't...not to insult you, *petit chou*, but you don't really cook. Sometimes I think you live on air. For the French, everything else comes second to food and drink. The meal is the focus of everything, the axis the world spins on!"

"Okay, okay, I get it. You know, you could spin out a plate of frites while you're standing there blabbering on."

"How about a proper meal for once? Your favorite frites, with a nice green salad and a hangar steak. Since no one's here, I'll join you."

"What if Alphonse comes in?"

"You think Alphonse is going to be upset about my eating a nice meal with my beloved? No, no, he would be delighted. I already told the chef to go home."

Frances grinned. "Can I come help? Maybe you could teach me a few culinary tricks of the trade."

Nico turned away so Frances could not see his expression of dismay. He had tried showing Frances how to make a few things in the small kitchen in their apartment, but it had not gone well. At all.

He gave her a lettuce and told her to separate the leaves and wash them in the sink, and went to get the steak which was marinating in the cold box. When he came back, the lettuce was still sitting on the counter and Frances was tapping her fingertips on the counter, lost in thought.

"Hello?"

"Oh—sorry. I had a tune running through my head and was just...what was I supposed to be doing?"

"Never mind," said Nico, picking up the lettuce. "But listen," he said, taking her by the shoulder and turning her toward him. "Just marry me," he said, leaning his forehead against hers.

"You want to wash my lettuce every single day?" she said lightly.

"Don't joke, Frances. For once, don't joke."

"It's just...we don't have to make a decision this instant, Nico. I love you, you know that. I'm just...."

"I know, twice burned. But you agree that what we have isn't like those other times."

"It isn't. No doubt about that."

"Then what?"

Frances looked away, uncomfortable.

"Is it my job?" asked Nico. "Would you rather I did something more respectable?"

Frances hooted. "Respectable? Are you kidding me? First of all, if you've been hired to do something, and you show up every day and do it well, that's respectable right there. And second, where in heck did you get the idea that respectability is what I'm after?"

Nico looked away but did not take his hands from her shoulders. "I'm just trying to understand why you don't say yes," he murmured.

"All right, I'm just going to say it then. But I don't want you to take this the wrong way. It's not personal, not about you in particular. But the thing I wonder—especially after my two divorces—is this: can we ever *really* know other people? I mean, who am I, really? You don't know."

"Frances!"

"Well, you don't, not really. You know my skin is pale and I can make up jolly tunes for jingles. You know I'm ticklish under my chin, have a desperate love of frites, and don't get along with my parents. You know some facts, I'll grant you that. But I hate to tell you—sometimes in here it is nothing but chaos and I do my damnedest not to let that show," she said, tapping on her temple.

Nico smiled a slow smile. "You think I don't know that? You'd be wrong," he said, kissing her on the neck, just under her ear, where he knew she liked to be kissed.

13

When things are going wrong, it is tempting to think that the bad stuff has been gotten through and things will turn right again any minute. At least, that's what the usually optimistic Molly was thinking that Friday, the day of her first dinner. She had woken up to hear Bobo throwing up, and then realizing the dog was in her bed and puking on her pillow. Then, drinking her first cup of coffee and checking her email, she got her first gîte cancellation. It was the fussy guest, the one who kept emailing with more and more demands. Apparently she had failed to respond quickly enough to his last petulant email and he had canceled on her.

Just in time to get a refund of his deposit. Of course.

Undeterred, Molly spent an hour doing prep work in the kitchen before running out for last-minute ingredients. Just as she was heading out of the driveway onto rue des Chênes, Constance came flying in on her bicycle.

"Molls!" She jumped off her bike and left it to clatter, embracing Molly and kissing her on each cheek. "I've missed you! Now that I'm taking that online course I just haven't been out and about like usual. So tell me, what's this plan of yours?"

Molly went over her evening of Classic Périgord cuisine, and how she hoped it would be the first in a string of lucrative dinners. "So for cleaning? Just do the public spaces—kitchen, living room, foyer. Don't bother with the cottage or any of the bedrooms for now. I'd love to stay and chat but I've got to get to the store—"

"Go, go, go! I'll have everything gleaming by the time you get home!"

Molly smiled and waved and sped down the road, thinking that it would be half a miracle if Constance actually performed her job with any competence. Usually Molly had to follow along behind, putting away dirty dust cloths Constance had left on tables, and mopping up puddles of water. So, not the most efficient cleaner in the world, but Constance had other qualities, and Molly felt a great deal of affection for her.

Sure enough, when Molly returned, Constance was gone and a bucket of dirty water stood in the foyer. A dust mop leaned against the kitchen counter. It was always this way—as though Constance had been suddenly removed from La Baraque by aliens, vaporized where she stood. But Molly knew that most likely her boyfriend Thomas had called, and Constance had quickly taken off without quite meaning to, swept away by love or fury.

The afternoon flew by with too few hours to get everything done. Bobo smelled the beef and stuck close. Molly scavenged enough flowers from the fading front border to fill a few vases, the rooms looked neat enough, the salad was made, steak seasoned, dessert baking in the oven. For a moment, she stopped to breathe in the comforting smell of baking apples and sugar, and crossed her fingers that the menu would be a success.

Dinner was at eight, with guests to arrive at seven for an apéro. Nico was due at 6:45 to help set up.

6:45...7:00. No Nico, and no guests.

Molly felt a rising panic. She texted Nico to ask where he was.

If this were her own party, she could call a few guests and make sure they were coming, but in this situation, with all the guests strangers, there was nothing to do but wait it out. Four of them had prepaid—surely they wouldn't bail without calling? She stood in the living room staring out at the road, then decided that looked sort of pathetic so she went into a small room off the living room where she could watch the road hidden behind some curtains.

7:15.

She texted Nico again. The thought of all the money she had spent on food was making her queasy. Oh, why did people sign up if they weren't going to come?

Almost instantly—and with great relief—she got a text from Nico. He was home throwing up.

Well, all right, I'll just have to manage without him, she thought. *Débrouiller*, as my French friends would say.

Then a car appeared, driving slowly. It stopped at the driveway and Molly could see an older man looking at the sign for La Baraque. Then he turned in and parked close to the house.

"Bonsoir, Monsieur!" said Molly, too loudly.

The man had gotten out of the car but shrank back. "Bonsoir, madame," he said softly. "You Americans, you never learn that you do not have to shout. I am right here, after all."

"Excuse me," said Molly, realizing that he had a point. "I'm Molly Sutton. I'm very pleased you could come."

"Hans Gosse," said the man, with a nod. "I am curious about your cooking. It is brave of you to take on the classic food of the region when you are not a native. Did you not consider serving something you might know better like, I don't know, meat loaf?"

Molly heard the contempt in his voice but ignored it. "I do love a good meat loaf," she said. "In any case, I won't claim to be a four-star chef, but I don't think you'll starve."

Hans shrugged. "And please, enlighten me on why tourists and locals would have any interest in eating together?"

Molly stared at him. "We'll see," she said finally. "Come inside, don't mind Bobo—" And thankfully, two more cars pulled in at that moment, and Molly crossed her fingers that Hans's mood would improve once he had had something to eat and drink.

❧

But his mood did not improve. Molly began serving drinks and she could hear Hans continuing his litany of complaints to the others. How am I going to keep this guy from poisoning the whole thing, she wondered, making herself a kir after all the guests were served.

Bobo was entertaining two younger women from Amsterdam who were biking through the Dordogne. A single woman, middle-aged, sat at the dining table with her kir in front of her, looking at the somewhat bedraggled bouquet with her lips pursed. Molly was not getting a friendly vibe from her, but she was sitting alone and someone had to talk to her, so she slid into the seat next to her and smiled.

"Madame Baker? So glad you could join me tonight."

"Is that so? You've been talking to all the other guests and ignoring me. I arrived in Bergerac yesterday and saw your flyer on the bulletin board of a pastry shop. I'm feeling a bit homesick for Dorset and thought the dinner sounded like a good way to socialize. But I'm sorry to say that thus far, the whole thing has been quite a disappointment."

"But Madame Baker, you just got here! I'm sorry that my bartender has been delayed and I'm trying to juggle about three jobs at once. I hope that once everyone is seated at the table and I've served the first course, things will look up."

Glancing over at the group talking to Hans, Molly saw nothing but furrowed brows and dark looks. The dinner was on the brink of completely flopping, and she jumped up to get some hors d'oeuvres out of the kitchen.

"Who would like an herbed palmier?" she cried, pulling a tray from the oven and cringing at the tense tone of her voice.

The young Dutch women came over and took some, nodding and smiling as they ate. "Very good, Miss Sutton!" one said, reaching for another.

Please infect the others with your positive attitude, Molly thought.

"I do believe I see a hair in my drink," said Madame Baker.

"Are you going to give us an update on the murder case?" asked Léonie, an elderly woman with an encouraging smile. The rest of the guests stopped what they were doing and waited for an answer.

"An update? What murder case?" said Molly nervously.

"The baron's, of course. Unless there has been another?" said Léonie hopefully. Several of the others nodded.

"Do you—oh, no. No. This dinner...it's just an occasion for a good meal. Meet some new people. It's not...it's not a...whatever you were thinking. It has absolutely nothing to do with murder."

Madame Baker stood up and asked, "Who was killed?"

One of the Dutch women, speaking in perfect English, said, "You haven't heard? The baron who lived in the huge castle just outside of Castillac. Shot dead in his own house!"

"Did he have a butler?" asked the other Dutch woman wryly.

"It's almost certainly the wife. It's the spouse something like a million percent of the time," said Léonie with a twinkle in her eye. She had not had a chance to speak English in some time and was enjoying herself immensely.

Molly sighed and went behind the kitchen counter. The guests were animated now, happily discussing the case that she was not quite on. It was disconcerting to realize that so many people—even tourists just passing through Castillac—had somehow heard of her reputation as a detective, and assumed she had been hired. Flattering, in a way, she admitted. But she was not going to disrespect Antoinette by using the baron's murder as some kind of cheap gimmick to make her dinners a success. The queasy feeling came back again.

In a mad whirlwind of cooking and serving and catering to the whims of Madame Baker, Molly somehow made it to the end of the dinner. Dinner for eight is no snap to pull off without help, and none of the guests volunteered to do a single thing, but instead chatted away about the murder and criticized Molly's food as though the meal were part of a Top Chef contest.

Hans Gosse had been passionate in his certainty that she had used premade puff pastry for the *pompe aux pommes*, and she had quickly come clean and tried to use that fact as a way to discuss the bigger picture of how making food had changed in France over the last twenty years with the development of such conveniences. But no one was interested. They only wanted to talk about the murder weapon, have a vote on whether the beef was under- or overcooked, and then on to immigration and whether foreigners should be allowed to move to other countries at all.

"Everything would be better if people would simply stay put," said Hans Gosse, "and eat the food they were given as children. It would make everything so much simpler!"

"That's crazy," laughed one of the Dutch women. "We adore traveling! And especially eating new food in different countries. Dutch cheese is of course the best in the world," she said grinning, "but you can get tired of the best if you have it every day."

And actually, Molly thought at the end of the evening, as she stood waving to the last of the guests as they drove off—it seemed as though their favorite part of the evening had been evaluating and criticizing each dish. She sat down on the stone floor of the foyer, exhausted, and Bobo flopped into her lap and licked her face.

"I'm not sure I ever want to go through that again," she said, rubbing the dog's speckled chest. "I'll just have to come up with something else. I can't give up now, right girl? If I had to go back to Boston at this point, I really don't know what I would do."

14

Antoinette had never been happier to see her sons, Luc and Percival. They had finished their studies a year earlier, doing better in the final semesters than when they first left home, having matured and not been as tempted by Paris night life. Luc had gotten a job as a reporter for a newspaper, which suited him perfectly, not being a man who liked being confined to an office; Percival had joined the management of a company whose purpose was still a bit murky to Antoinette. They created some sort of particular software that she did not come close to understanding, but as long as Percival was happy, she did not question it.

"I'm only sorry that you came home for such an awful reason," she said to them after dinner, when what was left of the Fleuray family sat together on the sofa to watch a little television before bed.

"What time is the funeral tomorrow?" asked Luc.

"Ten. I thought it best to get it out of the way early. Your father and I talked about this; he expressly said he did not want any fuss. So it's going to be only the three of us, plus a very few others at the graveside. Nothing afterward."

Percival shrugged. He had no friends in Castillac since he had left for boarding school when he was very young. He had not been close to his father. All he wanted was for the whole thing to be done with so he could get back to Paris.

"Of course, that wretch Alexandre Roulier will be attending. I haven't been able to get rid of him matter how rude I've been. It's just extraordinary. However, I plainly told him he should leave after the funeral so certainly he'll be gone sometime tomorrow."

"You're too polite," said Percival, using the clicker to flick through the stations. "Are you ever going to get a satellite dish? A few clouds and the reception is utterly shot."

"Give me that thing," said Luc, jostling him, and they play-wrestled for the clicker as though they were fourteen.

"You do realize," Antoinette said slowly, "that Percival will hold the title of Baron from now on. I hadn't even thought of it until now."

"No one bothers about any of that anymore," said Luc, giving up on the clicker and straightening his clothes. "Well, except... does that mean he gets more money than I do? Because screw that." He gave his brother a sharp jab to the ribs.

Antoinette looked puzzled. "Oh, don't you remember when your father sat us all down and went over his will? He wanted to be sure there was no inequality, no surprises." She smiled at her younger son. "I know you and your father struggled to get along. He was very hard on you. But he would never have punished you in his will," she said, ruffling his longish hair.

Luc looked skeptical. "I have no memory of that meeting. Which is not to say it didn't happen, it's just—you know me, sitting around listening to Father drone on was never my favorite thing. The question I have is—what about the emerald?"

Percival and Antoinette stared at him. They all knew about *La Sfortuna*, and were familiar with the sight of Marcel jiggling it in his pants pocket with a faraway look in his eye. But after the death of Doriane, no one in the family had ever spoken of it, not wanting to do anything to remind Marcel of his sister's death—never mind that he never forgot for a second, and obviously enough the emerald was not a source of pain as he often carried it around with him. Not talking about it was just one of those unconscious decisions that happen in a family, and after no one questions it, it becomes habit.

"I don't know where the emerald is," said Antoinette quietly. She smoothed her hair behind her ears and tried to sit up straight, but she looked tired and thinner than usual.

"Father was ridiculous, carrying that thing around," said Luc, shaking his head. "Perhaps we should rename it 'Marcel's Folly.' Did you check his trouser pockets? That's the only place I ever knew him to put it."

"I...as you might imagine, Luc, when your father was discovered, the emerald was not the first thing on my mind."

"So maybe a gendarme pinched it. Or the coroner. Or maybe he gave it to Es—"

Antoinette did not speak for a moment. Then she wet her dry lips and clasped her hands together. "Esmé Ridding. You can say the name, my dear, it doesn't trouble me unduly."

Percival had moved into an armchair beside the sofa. He and Luc exchanged a glance.

"Perhaps it's odd to discuss such things with you, but you're grown now, and your father is dead, so why not? I will tell you honestly: your father's liaison with Esmé Ridding was not high on the list of things that caused me pain. I have other things to worry about, you understand? Look at what's happening to elephants in Africa, for instance. Magnificent beast, the elephant, and they're killed by poachers at an alarming rate. That is something that keeps me up at night. Not your father and Esmé Ridding."

"Mother...."

Antoinette shrugged. "I didn't say I felt nothing. It was humiliating to be compared to her, yes. She's not really of this world, is she? Not of my world, anyway. My world is the barn, my dog, my sons...and of course, having lived here for over three decades, Château Marainte. So you see, in *my* world...."

"I understand," said Luc. "I find her a bit scary to be honest. Always performing, you know?"

"Do you want us to look for the emerald?" asked Percival.

"Heavens no, you don't have time for that. Let's just get through tomorrow, and afterward, we'll go out for a very nice dinner. I know you both have to get back to Paris. I'll be in touch about anything related to your inheritances once your father's affairs are settled."

Luc finally found a show he could stand to watch, and he leaned back on the sofa and put his head on his mother's shoulder.

"My boy," she murmured, closing her eyes and reaching her hand out for Grizou to sniff before he turned around three times and lay down on her foot.

❧

TRYING to be as unobtrusive as possible, Alexandre had gone out for dinner in Castillac after telling Antoinette that he didn't want her to go to any trouble for him. *La Métairie* had no Michelin stars, but he found it interesting enough, and after eating three courses at a corner table and putting away a fine bottle of Médoc, he called a taxi and returned to his room. Knowing Antoinette was annoyed with him, he figured staying out of sight was the best idea for the moment, which, in a place the size of Château Marainte, was perfectly easy to do. The family's bedrooms were in the central part of the building, but Alexandre had been put in a large suite in the west wing. He had a small sitting room with a sofa covered in blue and white toile, the walls decorated with portraits of Fleurays long dead, a white-tiled bathroom with an enormous cast iron tub, and a canopy bed trimmed in antique lace.

It lacked the room service of the Georges V, but other than that, Alexandre had no complaints. The water pressure was stellar and the west wing was very private. As long as he kept an eye out for Georgina, he had all four floors to himself. It was silent in the house apart from the occasional banging of radiators. He had no reason to think that Marcel would have hidden *La Sfortuna* in the west wing rather than the east or the north, but why not start where he was and expand the search as necessary?

All the while, in the background of his thoughts, he was bidding the emerald to come to him, to reveal itself. And he absolutely believed this would have an effect.

Instead of Roulier, how about Alexandre Valois-Saint-Rémy? he mused. So much more elegant. I might spend the first three million euros on an apartment in Paris. With staff, of course....

He made quick work of his own rooms, tapping on the walls and opening drawers, checking the undersides of chairs, the bed, the small desk. Early in the morning, when he knew Antoinette was at the barn and her lazy sons still asleep, he went through the other rooms on his floor. They were sparely furnished, usually only with a bed, small table, and an empty armoire. The stone floors were cold even through his shoes. He opened every drawer, lifted mattresses, shook out curtains. After several hours, there was still no sign of Georgina or any of the family—he could wander from room to room, going down to the third floor and then the second, pretending that he was the baron, grandly moving down the staircase with his nose in the air, lord of his domain.

On his final night at the château, the night before his friend's funeral, he lay under an eider down quilt covered in maroon silk, hands behind his head, feeling a surge of anger. It was not going to be easy to stay on afterward—Antoinette had not been subtle about wanting him gone. But the château was so vast that he had barely scratched the surface of all the places to search. He was irritated with Marcel for not making this easier for him, but at the same time, he realized he was not giving Marcel enough credit. Of course the baron hadn't simply shoved the stone under a mattress in some random room! The box was going to be hidden somewhere meaningful, somewhere clever. Alexandre needed to think harder and smarter. He had to get inside his friend's head, understand what Marcel had been feeling and thinking, and then he would be led to *La Sfortuna*.

Of course, other people's feelings were not exactly Alexandre's strong suit. As he lay in bed, he remembered his friend, but felt not so much as a wisp of regret about his death. He recalled a dinner they had eaten together in Paris about a month earlier. Alexandre had ordered the veal with a Marsala sauce and been quite satisfied with it. The wild boar had been excellent as well. As for what Marcel had talked about, he had no memory whatsoever. He had only pretended to pay attention at the time.

Sighing, he rolled over on his side, visions of the jewel gleaming in his hand pushing out all other thoughts. Suddenly, sickeningly, he wondered if Marcel had given the jewel to Esmé Ridding. As far as Alexandre knew, Marcel had not been one to get overly sentimental about his mistresses; he enjoyed them, he treated them well, but they did not gain influence over him concerning anything that mattered. But perhaps Esmé was different. She was not just any good-looking woman, after all—she was France's most treasured beauty, an international star. Marcel might have given it to her on a whim. Admittedly, it would be a gesture with real impact.

What had Esmé Ridding wanted with Marcel anyway? All he ever talked about was hunting boar and forest management.

That's it! he thought, sitting up and pumping one fist in the air. He'd been an idiot to think *La Sfortuna* would be lying around the château. The hiding place would of course have something to do with what Marcel loved more than anything—hunting. The small lodge out in the forest, that's the place to look.

Alexandre swung his legs out of bed and sat for a moment, visualizing the moment when his hand grasped the box, the fantasy so real that his hand reached out into the air and closed over the imaginary box. Then he bathed, dressed carefully in a dark suit, and descended the wide, red-carpeted staircase, intending to comfort the grieving widow for as long as she would allow, and hoping that the service would be short.

15

Molly was up and drinking coffee, slumped on the sofa with Bobo at her side, feeling morose at the failure of her dinner. The guests had gobbled up all the food—that hadn't been the problem. It was that the assembled personalities hadn't gelled into good spirits, but instead endless complaining and expressions of disappointment. They told Molly her table setting wasn't very elegant, that the *pompe aux pommes* was too dry, that they expected some inside information about the baroness and the murder. By the end of the evening, Molly's face had hurt from fake-smiling and she had never been more glad to fall into bed, leaving the kitchen a disaster.

When she heard a knock at the door the next morning, she had a stab of anxiety that one of last night's guest had shown up looking for a refund.

"Constance!" she said, opening the door with relief.

"Molly!" said Constance mournfully, and collapsed into her friend's arms.

"Uh oh," said Molly, hugging her. "What's going on?"

Constance sobbed into Molly's neck until her shirt was quite damp. *"Men!"*

"Ah," said Molly. "Come in, would you like coffee? Tell me what Thomas has done now."

"Yes to coffee. You got any croissants?"

"Sorry, all out."

"What?"

"I know. I'm...not having a great morning either. I'm afraid I only had two and I ate them both."

"But I'm starving."

"Let's see. I could make you some eggs? I made a couple of incredible *pompe aux pommes* last night, but the guests ate every crumb of both of them."

"How did the thing go?"

"Eh, I'll get to that later. So, scrambled eggs?"

"How about chocolate pudding?"

Molly laughed. "A woman after my own heart. Chocolate pudding it is. Come sit at the counter so we can talk while I cook."

"Okay," said Constance, settling on the stool and spinning from side to side. "So, you know things with Thomas have been going super well. I mean, for months and months, barely any fighting at all. Anything comes up, we talk about it, problem solved."

"All good," said Molly, tapping on a pudding recipe on her tablet. "Very good, in fact."

"Yeah," said Constance, her eyes welling up. "I thought we were on the brink of getting married, even starting a family...."

Molly looked up quickly. Constance, a mother? Well, sure. Why not? But Molly felt a pain in between her ribs, like a sharp blade had jabbed her. Every time she thought she might be letting go of the desire to have children of her own, she got reminded that the desire might hide out of sight but never really went away.

She sipped her coffee and with some effort turned her thoughts to Constance instead of herself. "So has something happened? I'll just jump in to say—I know at your age getting married seems really important, but I'll be your know-it-all big sister and tell you that I don't think that's actually true. Nothing wrong with just letting relationships deepen over time, without the pressure of something official."

"Oh, I don't really give a rat's ass about getting married," said Constance. "But—okay, you're probably going to think I'm making a big deal out of nothing. Yesterday I got back from doing some marketing—buying his favorite prunes stuffed with foie gras and everything—and when I came into the apartment, he's acting all hinky."

"Hinky?"

"Guilty. Like he jumped up out of an armchair like it had suddenly caught fire, and it looked like he was trying to hide what he'd been doing."

Molly scraped the melted chocolate into the egg mixture and whisked everything together, waiting for Constance to continue.

"So later on, after he'd gone to work? I went over to the chair and looked around. And I found a magazine—one of those trashy tabloids, which if *I'd* been reading he'd have teased me like crazy—and the pages were folded back to show this photograph..." She bent her head and wiped a tear away.

"It was that Esmé Ridding. He bought the stupid magazine because it had a feature on stupid Esmé Ridding, and then sat around our apartment drooling over her. Can you even believe it?"

Molly poured the pudding into small cups which she had put in a roasting pan halfway full of water. She did a poor job of scraping out the bowl so she could give it to Constance to lick. Then she leaned her elbows on the counter and looked hard at her friend. "You're telling me you're furious with Thomas because he looked at a picture of a movie star in a magazine?"

Constance wailed, "It's not that he was only looking at the picture! He obviously *wants* her, Molly! And not me!"

"Oh, dear," said Molly, not giving in to the desire to roll her eyes. "I know this is going to sound rude, and I don't mean it that way at all. But so what if he wants Esmé Ridding? *Everyone* wants Esmé Ridding. Hell, I'm sure if I ever had a chance with her, I'd want Esmé Ridding too, and I don't even swing that way!"

"But Molly. It's just...how can I even compete?"

"You're not competing, dear heart. She's a movie star. Thomas is not trying to decide between the two of you. The fact that he finds her interesting and attractive—that's just fantasy. You never, ever, ever for one second have any interest in any man but Thomas? Absolutely never?"

Constance smiled a complicit little smile. "Not telling."

"Thought so."

"But he really hurt my feelings. It's not even the magazine so much as the way he tried to hide it from me. If he had only talked to me about it, I think I wouldn't have freaked out so much."

"Being open with people...it's hard. Especially sometimes with people we love."

"Were you able to do it with Donnie?"

Molly snorted at the mention of her ex. "I don't even know at this point. I hardly ever think of that part of my life anymore, now that I'm here in Castillac with a whole new life. And by the way, I'm probably the worst person to come to for relationship advice, given my string of failures in the romance department."

"Not your fault."

"That's what they all say," Molly shrugged.

"It's just...I thought I knew Thomas, and now he's thrown me this curveball of his secret lust for Esmé Ridding, and the worst part—once I get past the insane jealousy—is that now I feel skittery around him, like I don't even know who he is anymore."

"It's just some pictures in a magazine, Constance. Not important, really, is it? And no doubt he tried hiding it because he was embarrassed."

"I haven't forgotten Simone Guyanet." Nine months earlier, Constance and Thomas had broken up when he started seeing

Constance's old classmate Simone, but before long he had begged Constance to forgive him. And she had.

"Of course not. Stuff like that shouldn't be forgotten. But it shouldn't be the first thing you think about whenever you hit a bump in the road either."

"What would I do without you, Molls?" asked Constance, grinning. "How long until the pudding is ready? I'll eat it straight out of the oven."

"You don't think it would be better cold?"

"You trying to tell me there's something wrong with warm pudding? How in the world could that be?"

"You make a solid point," said Molly, looking at the timer on the stove. "Another half hour. Listen, while we wait—would you tell me everything you know about the baron and baroness?"

"I knew you'd get on the case!" Constance leapt off the stool and did some hip-hop dance moves, making strange noises that sounded like the call of a tropical bird. "But wow, chalk me up for a big fail on this one. I never met 'em. Never really heard anything about 'em either. Two sons, I think? But they went to boarding school and didn't really grow up here. I've seen the baroness around the village every once in a while at the market and such, but never exchanged so much as a bonjour with her. And sad to say, I don't think anyone I know has, either. But I'll keep my eyes and ears out, Molls!"

Molly sighed. It was going to be very difficult to figure out anything about *La Sfortuna*, never mind the murder, if no one had any idea who the Fleurays were. So far, the family—beyond the public face—was almost a complete mystery.

16

SEVEN MONTHS EARLIER

Paris in April. Marcel de Fleuray had met Esmé Ridding in December, at an *apéro* held by his sort-of friend, the minister of public works. She was, unsurprisingly, the center of attention, and nearly every man in the room was vying for her notice. She was dressed in a white silk sheath that made her look impossibly narrow, almost boyish. Her blonde hair spilled down over one eye, curling just past her shoulders, and she looked like a Gallic reincarnation of a young Lauren Bacall, sultry and sophisticated. Esmé sat on the back stairs of the apartment that led up from the kitchen. Men crowded around, some staring, some desperately trying to be witty.

Marcel, however, stayed in the other room talking about grouse-hunting to a Scot who was in Paris for a week with his wife. Eventually the Scot and his wife took off, leaving Marcel alone, and still he did not go into the kitchen where Esmé was surrounded by courtiers, but stood by the window looking out at the spectacular view of the city—the Seine winding its way through, the Eiffel tower spendidly lit up, the beautiful Haussmann apartment buildings across the street.

Eventually, as he had guessed she would, Esmé emerged from the kitchen to see who else was there. She looked at him curiously. And in that moment, with total confidence, he knew he had her.

So they had been involved from December to April, a bit over three months, and for once in his life, Marcel was off balance, uncertain of what to do. He had had mistresses for most of his adult life—secret liaisons with unsuitable women before he was married, then secret affairs during his marriage, as well as not-so-secret flings. It was part of living life to its fullest, he and his friends told each other. And he considered himself lucky to be married to someone who did not carry on or punish him for it, but went on with her life and the things she cared about no matter what anyone else did or did not do.

But so. Three months, and now Esmé had flung a vase at him, demanding he leave his wife and marry her. To Marcel, this was incomprehensible; it was as unexpected and nonsensical as though she had suddenly been unable to communicate except in Swahili.

But Esmé was unrelenting.

Her apartment was in a stunning block of the 6th, just off boulevard Saint-Michel. Marcel gave his name to the concierge, who scowled at him as she always did, and waited while she called up to Esmé's apartment. As he rode the ancient elevator with its elaborate ironwork up to the penthouse, he was thinking not of Esmé but of the particular shade of green the leaves were in the Dordogne in April, and he was swept by a wave of homesickness for Château Marainte and its forests.

"My dear," he said, stepping inside and taking her hands. She pulled back slightly but he leaned in and kissed her cheeks, then kissed her on the mouth, at first gently, then more insistently.

"Marcel," said Esmé, pulling away, her voice cracking.

"You are making everything more complicated than it needs to be," he said, looking into her dark brown eyes. She was wearing no makeup and dressed in blue jeans with a simple cashmere sweater, and looked incredible.

"I hate fighting with you, *Petit Ours*," she murmured, withdrawing her body but beckoning with her tone of voice.

Marcel nodded. He put his hands on her shoulders and squeezed them, and she felt tension drain away. Then he moved his hands down her arms, touching firmly, and with a quick move had one arm around the top of her shoulder pulling her to him, and the other around her waist. He pinned her up against him and kissed her again, kissed her like he meant it, like she was everything to him and nothing else in the entire world mattered.

"Marcel," she said softly, leading him to the sofa with a faint smile. She did not sound contented, or satisfied, but rather doomed.

17

Outside the château, on the other side of the moat, stood a small chapel built in the seventeenth century. It had an unusual turreted roof that went in a spiral, which students of architecture believed might have been copied from the twisted spires of the Loire known as *baugeoise*. The building itself was made of limestone, with three unremarkable stained glass windows along each of its long sides, an arched doorway, and a hideously salacious gargoyle on the northeast corner of the roof. The Fleuray family had never been known for its piety, and while the chapel had not been allowed to fall into ruin, neither was it given much attention or upkeep beyond the bare minimum.

Inside were vaults containing the bodies of Marcel's parents, grandparents on his father's side, several uncles, great-grandparents, and even great-great-grandparents. Marcel had, in fact, discussed his funeral arrangements with his wife, and he had been quite firm about not wanting to be "stuck in a box of stone" but instead wished to be buried outside, in the earth. He had chosen the spot, under a magnolia tree beside the chapel. From there, high on the hill, the view was serene—rolling hills and farmland, with the cluster of red-tiled roofs that constituted Castillac not far away. The sun was out and warm, billowing clouds floated overhead, and it was altogether a beautiful day for a funeral.

Antoinette was dressed in a black wool suit, tailored and well cut. Her hair was pulled into the usual loose chignon at the back of her neck. She wore no jewelry and very little makeup.

"Maman," said Luc, kissing her on both cheeks when she appeared up in the lounge. "You look tired."

"I'm burying my husband today. You expect me to look invigorated?"

"Sorry, I didn't mean anything by it, just wishing you were getting better rest. Who's doing the service?"

"The priest from the village church is coming up. He should be here any minute. Where's Percival?"

"Did you or Father ever actually attend a service in that church?"

"Are you set on being an annoyance this morning? Make yourself useful and go find your brother."

Luc put his hand on his mother's shoulder for a second and then went into the kitchen and then to the courtyard. He kept waiting for a wave of emotion to crash over him—sorrow, regret, grief, *something*—but it did not come, which was not entirely a surprise, since he had barely known his father. When he had turned eight, and was old enough to hunt but showed no interest in it, his father consequently had no interest in him. Luc had been sent away to school and not spent any time at home except on vacations, and often he had gone to visit classmates instead and skipped coming to Château Marainte entirely.

In his adult life, he was happy in Paris. Luc was good-looking, charming, from a good family, and had plenty of girlfriends. His job as a reporter got him out on the streets where he liked to be. His life was in the city, not here in sleepy Castillac. He was sorry for his mother, but could locate no other feeling about the events of the day at all. The funeral was just one more official ceremony to get through.

"You taking the train back?" said Percival, trotting down the stairs while straightening his tie.

"Yeah, the one after dinner. I figured Maman might want us to stay that long at least."

"You still seeing Chloé?"

"Ha! Can't wait to get your filthy mitts on her?"

"That's right, little brother. I know how to make a girl like her happy."

"In your dreams, in your dreams."

Percival was more money-minded than his brother. He had gotten a degree in business and found work at several firms where he was valued for his astute analysis, though he was known for having expensive tastes he did not yet have the money to support. He was taller than his brother, and broader across the shoulders. He gave Luc a shove and Luc grabbed his arms, and they grappled for a moment before Antoinette appeared in the doorway.

"Boys! The priest is here. Stop your monkeying about and come outside so we can get started."

The three of them filed out through the enormous wooden door of the central building and into the sunny courtyard. Hubert was there, holding his hat in his hand, and Georgina stood beside him, dressed in a tight black dress. Alexandre Roulier was there as well, standing apart from the others. Antoinette thought his suit in bad taste but of course only smiled faintly and thanked him for coming.

"You going clubbing after?" Luc whispered to Georgina as the group made its way to the chapel.

"Bad boy!" hissed Georgina, but she threw him a quick smile. She was older than the young Fleuray men, but not so old that there hadn't been flirting during some of their trips home from school over the years.

Antoinette's face showed deep lines in the harsh sunshine.

Tendrils of her washed-out blonde hair escaped her chignon and blew around her head, and she walked haltingly, as though she might have a pebble in her shoe.

Hubert and the funeral director had arranged things competently. The paperwork was in order and the grave was neatly dug exactly where Marcel had asked for it. A gust of wind blew everyone's hair in their faces and a cloud drifted over the sun.

"First, I would like to give a blessing to the three of you," the priest said, walking closer to the family.

"That will not be necessary," said Antoinette, shrinking back. "Boys, the casket is inside the chapel. All three of us will carry it, and Hubert, perhaps you will help?"

"Of course, madame," he said, seeming to come awake.

Alexandre was out of place, but he was a not a man to bother about that. He stood next to Georgina, throwing admiring glances her way until she reached over and pinched his arm and told him to knock it off.

The priest waited under the tree while they went inside the musty chapel. Marcel had been quite slender, and the casket was not too heavy.

"Maman, you really needn't—" said Luc, trying to wave her off.

"Yes, I want to, I must," she said, gasping with effort as the edge of the casket dug into her shoulder. It was too heavy for her and she started to buckle, but the others saw what was happening and lifted it up. Hubert was behind her and managed to keep the casket high enough that it rested on her shoulder but did not put much weight on it.

"Ready? Back up and then turn for the door," said Percival, the usual leader when people needed to be managed.

Back outside, with Marcel on their shoulders, everyone was immersed in Marcel de Fleuray's final moments above ground. Everyone except Alexandre and the priest felt a little breathless, knowing the moment wouldn't be forgotten.

The journey to the gravesite was short and managed without

difficulty. They placed the casket on the ground next to the grave and the priest began intoning prayers. The others stared at the casket, their hands folded.

As the priest kept going, talking on and on about God and faith and rebirth, and then Heaven, one by one the Fleurays began to look out at the view, following the progress of a hawk swooping into the sky, then a blue car meandering down a country road far in the distance. Hubert was the only one thinking about Marcel. His eyes were moist as he remembered the joy they had felt together tromping through the forest in the early mornings.

For her part, Georgina was thinking about how her job was probably hanging by a thread now that the baron was being planted. He'd been the one to bring her to this dark château, and the baroness couldn't stand her, so she figured she'd get tossed out any second, maybe even before she had a chance to change out of her black dress.

Which she *had* been clubbing in, on a quick trip to Bordeaux four years earlier, not that she would admit that to Luc. The dress had seemed like the perfect thing to wear to the funeral—it was black, anyway—but who would've guessed the day would turn so hot? Georgina was sweltering. She was fleetingly sad for the baron. He had been good to her, and she admired him for his devotion to his beautiful sister.

They heard the loud sound of an engine, and the priest raised his voice. Then the sound was impossible to ignore, and everyone turned to see a late-model sports car flying up the drive and turning with a spray of white gravel into the parking area.

A tall, very thin woman climbed out, dressed in something filmy and black, almost as though she were wearing a storm cloud. Her head swathed in a scarf, sunglasses on.

"It's Esmé Ridding," said Luc, amazed.

THE ACTRESS MOVED across the parking lot with quick grace, her limbs sinuous, as all the mourners watched. Antoinette was expressionless and pale. Luc's eyes were wide but he quickly put on a knowing smirk. Hubert was confused. The priest continued to read from his prayer book.

Esmé stood next to Percival for a moment, with her head bowed, as though she had merely slipped unobtrusively into a pew at the back of the church instead of crashed a funeral with only five attendees. Luc wanted to reach out and touch the ethereal fabric of her dress, but restrained himself.

When the priest said, "We commit his body to the earth, for we are dust and unto dust we shall return," Esmé let out a little moan. Antoinette jerked her head up and stared. Percival moved his weight from one foot to the other, trying to decide whether to take Esmé's arm and lead her away, or let her be.

"Oh, Marcel!" Esmé cried out, her voice breaking. She stepped away from Percival and toward the casket, and then fell to her knees and threw her arms over the mahogany box, pounding the top with both manicured fists.

The priest stopped reading.

"What in hell do you think you're doing?" cried Georgina. "Get up offa there!"

Antoinette said nothing. She seemed to shrink a bit, as though her suit suddenly became almost too big for her. Alexandre looked on with open amusement.

"Marcel!" cried Esmé, lifting her head and showing them her stunning face, with mascara running theatrically onto her dewy cheeks.

"Come on, now," said Hubert, as though only just realizing what was going on. He moved quickly to her and pulled her up to standing.

"You don't belong here, don't you realize that?" shouted Georgina. "This is a family event, you hussy! Get lost!" To Georgina, the appearance of this woman was an insult to the

Fleuray family, and she still felt a great deal of loyalty to Doriane, who had been so good to her.

"Hush now," Hubert muttered. He took Esmé by the arm and walked her back to her car. She stumbled in her strappy heels but Hubert did not let her fall, talking to her along the way like an animal that needed reassuring. He got her in the sports-car and leaned over and spoke in her ear, but by then the priest had continued the service and no one could hear what he was saying.

"Is she bawling because he didn't give her the emerald, or because he did? That's what I'd like to know," muttered Luc to Percival.

"Shut up," said his brother, and then it was time for them to lower their father's casket into the grave, and then for Hubert to start shoveling the dirt on top. When the first shovelful thumped on the casket, Antoinette began to cry, and then Georgina cried too, partly because she was afraid of having no job.

Luc and Percival watched the dirt fall on top of the father they barely knew, and then it was as though a page was turned and they reentered their individual lives, the funeral over. Percival considered whether his travel arrangements could be improved, and Luc thought simultaneously about a story he was researching about a fashion house, and a suit he had to pick up from the tailor's.

Antoinette felt alone in her grief, and noticed that it was Marcel whom she might have gone to for comfort, Marcel who might have enjoyed the spectacle of his mistress prostrating herself on his coffin. She understood that others would expect the appearance of Esmé Ridding to be painful for her, but it was not. At least not in the ways that anyone thought it was.

❧

WHILE THE FLEURAYS were standing under the tree next to the chapel, a teenager named Malcolm Barstow ran silently across the drawbridge and into the courtyard. He had been waiting since dawn, keeping a lookout from a bank of bushes at the top of the drive, guessing that the funeral of the baron would take place that day, and he might have his chance.

Malcolm was clever, and thus far had never been caught or even close to it, as he carried out his various criminal activities when he was supposed to be in school. He had worn a pair of rope-soled espadrilles, which weren't great for speed but were quiet, so that as he streaked across the drawbridge, no one at the gravesite turned in his direction even though he would have been in plain view if they had.

La Sfortuna. What thief in the entire département didn't dream of it?

Malcolm slowed down once inside the courtyard, uncertain whether the château was empty. It could be teeming with servants for all he knew, never having visited a château on a social basis. But he was young and friendly-looking, and always ready with an easy excuse that he was a delivery boy for the local épicerie, even though the idea of a regular job gave him the willies.

He saw by the pattern in the gravel which was the most-used door, and avoided that one. Quickly he went past the central part of the building to the north wing and tried a door, but it was locked. Malcolm got a tingle then, as he often did when on a job and hit an obstruction. It made the whole operation that much better, since overcoming obstructions was at least half the point of the enterprise. He went quickly to the next door, which opened with a creak, and he found himself in the baron's salon.

Malcolm closed the door behind him and stood for a moment, assessing the room. Gun rack. Antique desk, console, bookshelves. No television. Could really be a room from a hundred years ago, he thought, looking for anything electronic and finding nothing. Of course *La Sfortuna* was the goal, but he understood that the chance of finding it was as likely as being struck by lightning. He could always make the trip worthwhile by picking up a few laptops and tablets to resell.

He squatted down and looked on the underside of the desk and the console table, having found that people taped interesting things there more often than you'd guess. The leather sofa went down so close to the floor that he couldn't see under it, but he swept his hand underneath as far as he could reach. Nothing.

The boy hopped back to his feet and looked around at the various stuffed heads on the wall. The deer...was there something a bit funny about the mouth? Maybe something in the cavity? He went on tiptoe but it was too high up. A wooden folding chair leaned against the paneled wall, and he set it up and carefully climbed up, barely able to reach into the deer's mouth. His fingers moved about, feeling the animal's teeth, but the light must have been playing tricks because he could feel no box, no jewel.

One of the reasons Malcolm had never been caught was that he had neat habits, and he folded the chair back up and put it exactly where he had found it before moving on to the bookshelves. Philosophy, economics, poetry...then he spied a thin book titled Sportsmen's Essays, and took it down. The book was so short that the second he opened it, the two envelopes that were inside fell to the floor. He bent to pick them up, grinning as he always did when he found something that had been hidden.

18

On Monday morning, after his walk through the village, Maron sat at his desk glaring at the coroner's report. Marcel de Fleuray, dead from loss of blood after receiving a shotgun blast to the face. No drugs, .017% alcohol level, no chance of suicide or other compounding factors to the cause of death. He had been in good shape, with a strong heart, healthy liver, and impressive muscle tone for a man in his late fifties.

That was more or less it. Florian Nagrand padded the report with a lot of data from the autopsy, but Maron suspected he had done it only for show, painstakingly measuring this and that, when they both knew it was all beside the point. The man had been killed with his own shotgun—an extremely nice one at that—and been unlucky enough that a pellet hit him at the only spot that could have made the shot fatal.

Perhaps, thought Maron...perhaps the shooting hadn't been meant to be fatal? Maron stewed over that idea for awhile. But if it had been an accident, why wouldn't it have been reported? And who accidentally discharges a shotgun in someone's face, at close range, inside the house? No one innocent, that was plain enough.

Of the people who were at the château that night, he could eliminate no one. Nor had he uncovered any particular motive that pointed to any of them. For all he knew, an entirely different person—a stranger, a business associate, a random psycho—could have entered the château, snatched up the baron's gun and blasted him, and then continued on his way. And so, as usual, where he was on the case was...nowhere. He had interviewed the wife, the gamekeeper, and the housekeeper, and was no closer to any leads than when he started.

Except for one small detail. Georgina had claimed that a sports-car drove away from the château late the night of the murder. No one in the family owned such a car. Maron had not forgotten about this little tidbit but had not told Paul-Henri, instead guarding it like a dog with a treasured bit of gristle, unwilling at first to investigate it further because it represented the only hope he had, and he feared having it come to nothing. He had skipped the gala this year without Dufort there to urge him to go, and so had not seen Esmé Ridding make her entrance. But in his morning stroll around the village, several people related the story to him, as well as some admiring talk about the white sports-car she drove.

It was time to move on the lead. He made some calls to a gendarme in Paris whom he had been friendly with at the police academy, and was able, after several more calls, to procure a phone number for Esmé Ridding.

He did not expect that she would agree to come to the station in Castillac for a chat. He thought for sure she would say work commitments made that impossible, the filming schedule with her current movie was grueling, on and on with a million excuses—and he was already looking forward to the prospect of traveling to Paris to interview her. But to his surprise, she agreed immediately. The next morning, Maron was to collect her at the Castillac train station, and she told him she would be more than happy to answer any questions he might have for her, and hoped very much that she would be useful to the investigation.

Esmé Ridding, he thought, leaning back in his chair and putting his hands behind his head. Could she have killed the baron? Maybe she wanted him to leave his wife, and he refused. Maybe she begged him to give her *La Sfortuna*, and he refused.

Though why any man would refuse Esmé Ridding anything, Maron could not understand.

❧

MOLLY SLEPT LATE on Monday morning. The cottage and *pigeonnier* were empty, and she had no guests to take care of, and nothing in particular on her calendar for the day...not that she even looked at a calendar anymore, except to keep track of bookings. Which for the next few months were few and far between. It took Bobo's increasing insistence on breakfast to get Molly up and in the kitchen making coffee. The day was chilly and La Baraque was about five degrees colder than was comfortable, even wearing a thick sweater and her very American sweatpants.

After feeding Bobo some table scraps, she rested her elbows on the counter and sighed. With a pang of anxiety, she remembered that the baroness was expecting her to come to the château and search for that emerald. Molly glugged down some coffee and took a quick shower, trying to simply put one foot in front of the other and not let worry about money ruin the day. Frances was right, she did need to bring up the subject of payment, but the idea made her *so* uncomfortable. Maybe she needed some official-looking cards, with Molly Sutton, Private Investigator and her cell number.

Oh, that was ridiculous. She'd just gotten lucky a few times on some easy cases. It wasn't like she had any actual credentials and would be able to get real jobs. Antoinette probably thought Molly was just being helpful, for the fun of it.

Which actually, she was happy to do. More than happy. If her bank account were healthier she wouldn't have dreamed of asking for a fee. Well, she would feel the situation out as she went along. If she got to know the baroness better, she might be able to tell whether payment made any sense or not. She had used the word *hire*, after all. In any event, Molly had to find the emerald before she could expect any kind of reward. So she gave Bobo a good scratch behind the ears, checked the mirror to make sure she was presentable, and took off for Château Marainte.

It was chilly riding the scooter, especially on either side of town where there was no traffic and she could go fast. The wind made her ears cold and she wished she'd put on a hat. Once again, she admired the chateau's driveway as it curved around the side of the hill, lines of plane trees on either side, and parked in the parking lot, hoping Antoinette would offer her a second cup of coffee and maybe even a little something to nibble on.

As she walked over the drawbridge, Molly glanced up at the towers on the château side, looking at the archer's slits and imagining what it must have been like to wait inside, bow drawn, waiting for enemies to broach the top of the hill. Despite the clear October day, the blue sky, the quiet...again the place felt threatening in some way, and she was confused about whether she was simply feeling how it must have been to live there centuries ago, or noticing something in the present—a tension, a jittery vibe underneath the calm. The place was so forbidding with its gray stone rising so high, and crenellations along the top where more archers had hidden. And probably soldiers ready to dump boiling oil on anyone who made it into the courtyard, she thought with a shudder. The courtyard was empty and most of the leaves on the white-barked birches had dropped.

Molly walked to the door she had entered on her previous visit and gave it a sound rap. "Bonjour, madame!" she called, hoping it wasn't rude to call the baroness *madame*. She wondered if she should have called first, but realized she did not have Antoinette's number.

She heard barking from inside, and then the door opened and Antoinette smiled and gestured for Molly to come in as Grizou leapt and spun around. "Bonjour, Molly," she said, and Molly noticed again that her accent was posh but could not put her finger on exactly why it sounded that way. Maybe it was not her voice but her manner as a whole, which was most definitely aristocratic, even stately, though Molly did not detect even a hint of snobbishness. The baroness's clothing, as always, was lovely and expensive-looking.

"Do you mind walking with me while I do my morning chores? I'm afraid I had trouble sleeping last night and then overslept in the morning. The goats are probably thinking I've abandoned them."

"Sure!" said Molly. "I know yesterday must have been very difficult for you," she added, watching Antoinette carefully.

"Funerals are...well, both horrible and wonderful, in a way. The feelings are so concentrated, so pure. Do you know what I mean?"

Molly nodded. No question that the funerals of both her parents were imprinted on her mind like nothing else. She remembered which flowers covered the caskets, who else was there, the way the canopy over the grave was frayed on one corner. Her relationship with her parents had been loving, if not especially close, and the grief over their deaths wasn't finished fifteen years later.

"Grief never really ends," she said, and instantly wished she could take it back.

"I know," Antoinette said simply. "I miss my mother every single day, and she died when I was only fourteen."

"I'm so sorry."

Antoinette waved her off. "It's the natural order of things, yes? When one loves, one opens oneself to pain and grief. It's simply the way of this world."

Molly reached down to pet Grizou, who had been staring at her intently.

"Although—I tell you this in confidence, of course—I found it a bit troubling that my boys did not appear to feel the death of their father as I would have expected."

"Maybe it just hasn't sunk in?"

"Perhaps not. The violence of it...it puts a different spin on the situation. Maybe that is it."

"Yes," said Molly. "Has Maron—have the gendarmes made any progress on the case?"

Again Antoinette waved a hand in the air. "Eh, not that they've told me. I have every confidence they'll catch him before too long. If he managed to steal the emerald, it will be sooner rather than later. It would take an extremely knowledgeable and connected thief to sell *La Sfortuna* without being caught. And don't you imagine that he was at least smart enough to force Marcel to hand it over before shooting him?"

"That would have been the clever thing," agreed Molly. "And you're right to try to put yourself in the killer's shoes and think like he thinks. That's more or less the secret to figuring out what happened. In my limited experience," she added.

They had left the courtyard by way of a narrow passageway which led outside the château walls. The top of the hill was large enough that behind the château, there was room for a stable and cavernous barn, along with a small pasture. When the two women came into sight, three goats began bleating and trotted over to the electric fence.

"Oh now, have some patience," Antoinette said to them affectionately. "Please forgive my lateness. I'll get your hay out this minute. They're such funny animals," she said to Molly. "Very developed sense of the absurd."

Molly reached out to pet one of the goats on the head and it reached up and nipped her hand.

"Ouch!" said Molly, "I'm not your breakfast!"

Grizou growled at the goat, who suddenly leapt backward all at once as though it had been given a shock. Molly was pretty sure it was laughing at her.

Antoinette brought out the hay and the three goats ran over and stuck their faces into it and began munching away.

"So, if I'm understanding you, there's a real possibility the jewel has been stolen, so I might be looking for something that's not here?"

Antoinette stood by a pump, filling a rubber bucket with water. "That's correct," she said. "The thing is, we just don't know either way. So for all the reasons I told you when you last visited, I would like for you to search, if you're willing. I'll pay you, of course. I was thinking...ten percent of the sale price? I plan to sell it immediately. Horrid thing."

"Oh, I—well, thank you! That's very generous. And yes, I am willing." Molly took a minute to regain her bearings. Ten percent! That would be enough to make all kinds of problems disappear. She turned to Antoinette, feeling suddenly very motivated. "Can you talk to me some more about Marcel, so I can get a better idea of his personality?"

"Well, let's see. He was a simple man, in a lot of respects. He loved to hunt, as I've said. Was happiest out in the forest with Hubert, probably. Much happier doing that than doing any kind of business, or politics, which he was involved with for many years."

"In what way?"

"He was minister of the interior. Sorry, I thought you knew that. But you did not live in France then, so of course it's unlikely that you would know. He took the post as a favor to the president. They were hunting friends, you see. But the work didn't suit him." Antoinette laughed. "Well, not to put too fine a point on it —no work suited him, if it required anything other than walking through the woods with a gun under his arm."

"I see. And...family life?"

"It's different these days. Fathers are expected to be involved in ways they were not when Luc and Percival were small. As for Marcel, he was proud of his sons, he was glad of them, but he didn't spend much time with them. He wanted *them* to come to *him*, you see, and was unwilling to do things the other way around."

Molly nodded. "You're saying...they didn't hunt?"

"Just not interested. And Marcel felt that as a rebuke, even though I don't believe it was."

"And...excuse me for the indelicate question...please understand, I am only trying to get the full picture. What about your relationship with Marcel? What was that like?"

Again Antoinette surprised Molly by laughing. "Has the story hit the village yet, how his mistress crashed his funeral and threw herself on his coffin? As delicious as that bit of gossip must be, it only tells the surface of the story."

No doubt. Molly felt a tingle of anticipation as she waited for the baroness to continue.

She was all ears.

19

That was pretty much the best funeral ever, thought Alexandre with satisfaction. The vision of Esmé Ridding draped over Marcel's casket, her flowing black dress fluttering in the breeze—every detail was like a photograph in his mind. He liked that dress. He kept thinking about it, how silky and ethereal the fabric was, how soft her skin must be underneath—anything to keep his mind off the terrible trudge he was engaged in, as he went deeper and deeper into the forest around the base of Château Marainte, looking for the lodge where he had stayed once with Marcel several years earlier, at a November hunting party for wild boar.

Alexandre had been smart enough to pack up and leave the château immediately after the funeral. The sons didn't give him the time of day, so self-important about their lives in Paris; little did they realize Alexandre was making ten times what they were. Probably more, he thought smugly. And his network of associates, well, there was little they weren't capable of, given enough inducement.

He had taken a taxi to the bottom of the hill and gotten out when he thought he recognized a road leading into the dark woods. It was unpaved but wide and nicely kept, and for a while the walk was almost pleasant. Then the road petered out and became a path, but Alexandre got distracted by thoughts of *La Sfortuna* and Esmé's smooth skin, and failed to pay attention to which way he was turning. Soon enough, the path was narrow and occasionally crossed with logs and underbrush so as to barely qualify as a path at all. He should have bribed that gamekeeper to take him to the lodge! But the guy might have told Antoinette... not worth the risk.

Alexandre had grown up in a concrete apartment complex that had an asphalt playground with a broken swing set and a small dusty field to play soccer on. The only trees he knew were those lining the streets in nicer neighborhoods than his. He liked cities, hard surfaces, neatly made hotel beds, technology. He had never been in a forest alone before, and he was deeply uneasy. Most of the trees had lost their leaves and the bare branches looked skeletal and forlorn. He turned up his collar and kept trudging, figuring something would be at the end of the path, for why else would it exist?

He supposed the lodge was so secluded it wouldn't be locked. He would arrive, open the door, and go inside. Perhaps, after such an arduous morning, he would light a fire and have a glass of whiskey. Doubtless Marcel kept the place stocked with something to eat, and he might sit down at the table by the window. He remembered sitting there with the baron as he tediously recounted a hunt from several years earlier in which the boar had wheeled on the hunters and ended up goring a friend of his. He might want to fortify himself before settling down to the search.

Or maybe, since it was way out in the middle of nowhere, after all, maybe the box containing the emerald would simply be sitting on the table, waiting for him.

"So you're going to stage a reality show in Castillac, right here at La Baraque, is that what you're saying?" Frances cackled as she made herself another kir, having invited herself over for dinner.

"Well, sort of. My new idea, since the dinner last week went so horribly, is to have a series of cooking contests. We could have three or four contestants, and people would pay to come watch some kind of cook-off. They make their best dish, or we have them figure out how to make a meal with only four random ingredients, stuff like that. Maybe we could have the audience do the judging?"

"No, that would never work. Too much tasting, too much food would have to be made, it would take forever. Have a panel of judges, people in the village who know something about food. Nico, for instance."

"Just as a random example," Molly teased.

"He is a very good cook. He's tried to teach me a few things but he got so frustrated his ears turned all red."

"Remember that time you called me to find out what a scallion was?"

"Oh come on, I knew what they were, I just thought they were called green onions! How was I supposed to know things have multiple names?"

"Too bad you never spent any time in the kitchen with your mom, growing up."

Frances hooted. "As you remember, my mom never spent any time in the kitchen, period. Thank God we had a cook, but even then for a while there we were all forced to eat macrobiotic. I nearly died."

"I remember that one cook who made the best cherry pies. You don't know how lucky you had it, Franny. A cook? I can't even."

"Yeah. Well, I know it's annoying as hell to hear coming from someone who grew up in the velvety soft lap of luxury, but money doesn't actually solve anyone's problems, unless those problems are specifically and only bills that need paying."

"That would be an excellent start," said Molly. "Anyway, not sure whether my idea would be much of a money-maker. It's not like I could charge people much just for coming to watch."

"How about you make the event free, and charge for snacks?"

"Wait a minute. You're brilliant!"

"Why yes, kind of you to notice. But why are you even bothering with all this anyway? It'll be a huge amount of work. And you've got ten percent of a bazillion dollars just waiting for you out at the château!"

"Yeah," said Molly, with no enthusiasm. "I got all excited when Antoinette mentioned it. But then I thought about the château. It's like ten houses' worth of rooms, Franny, I mean the place is *immense*. There's not a snowball's chance in hell I'm gonna find that little gem."

"From what I hear, it's not so little. But whatever you say, you're the detective. If you think you can't figure it out..."

"So now you're breaking out the reverse psychology on me?"

Frances nodded and grinned.

Molly dropped a couple of anchovies in a mortar and ground them up to a paste. "So, change of subject: how've things with Nico been lately? He still got marriage on the brain?"

Frances sipped her kir and chewed on the inside of her mouth.

"Frances?"

"I'm thinking. It's just...a little...on the one hand, he's all 'Let's get hitched, you are my everything,' and I don't deny it, that sounds pretty good even if it also inspires panic. But then the next minute, he's Mr. Mysterious. I try to have the kind of conversation you and I just had, where we're talking a little about what it was like growing up in our families—and he gets all stony silent."

"We don't like stony silent."

"No we do not."

"Do you think it's something painful and he doesn't want to go there?"

Frances shrugged. "How would I *know?* And also, his timeline begins roughly at age eighteen. I know he studied in the U.S. for a few years, and thank God because if his English wasn't so good we'd never have gotten together. Obviously he came back to France at some point, and has been in Castillac for at least seven years or so, working at Chez Papa the whole time. But even that—why go to all the trouble to do foreign study and get a degree in philosophy, and then choose to be a bartender? And you know I have nothing at all against being a bartender. What I want to know is, what happened to lead him there? I want him to...tell me the story of his life, you know?"

"And he won't talk about it?"

"Gives me a whole song and dance about living in the present moment. And I'll tell you Molly, trying to have an argument with a philosopher is like wrestling with bubble gum."

Molly thought that over while she took lettuce out of the refrigerator, along with a container of feta and another of olives. "I'm feeling a little Greek tonight, hope that's okay with you?"

"*Si.*"

"Are you trying out Spanish?"

"I thought you could say *si* in French!"

"Well, you can. But it's only for answering negative questions. So if I said, 'You don't like accordion music, do you?' you could answer *si*. I see I'm losing you."

"French grammar—forget about it. I just like it when Nico murmurs French things into my ear and I can't understand what he's saying. Maybe it's better that way," she said with a guffaw. "You're almost out of *cassis*," she added, shaking the bottle. "So wait a minute, hold on, you haven't told me the details about your meeting with the baroness. So where are you supposed to start your search for an emerald hidden in a gigantic château? Did she give you any ideas?"

"I guess if she had any good ideas, she'd look herself. I assume she's already done so. And yeah, like I was saying, it's a daunting job. I've got a few ideas cooking along though."

"Of course you do. Got any of those cheese crisps you had last time?"

"Have you eaten anything today?"

"Maybe?"

"Okay, salad's done. How about we eat it, and if we're still hungry after, I can make something else. Not exactly the French way of doing things but it's what I feel like tonight. You game?"

"You're cooking, of course I'm game." Molly brought the bowl over to the dining table and then fetched forks, plates, and napkins while Frances tossed the salad. A few leaves flew out and landed on the floor where Bobo pounced, but declined to eat them.

"Actually, Antoinette seems like a really decent sort of person," said Molly. "She's very down to earth. I spent a little while talking to her while she fed her goats this morning."

"That does not sound all that interesting."

"But this is. The baron's funeral was yesterday. He was buried under a tree outside the château walls, just the immediate family present plus the couple of people who worked for him. And guess who showed up?"

"Santa?"

"Esmé Ridding!"

"No!"

Molly nodded. "And not only that, according to Antoinette she threw herself on the actual casket and sobbed! Right there in front of the family!"

Frances got up and ran around the table shrieking, then dropped into her chair. "Sorry, that's just too juicy for words! Holy bananas, Molls! I wonder if any paparazzi caught it?"

Molly shrugged. It was always interesting, telling Frances a story—her reactions were always unexpected, even when Molly was expecting the unexpected.

"Well? Was she absolutely furious?"

"Antoinette? No, actually. She seemed...almost amused by the whole thing. Not quite—it's not like she was laughing or anything. But not at all angry. Or even disapproving, really."

"Curious."

"Indeed."

"When I heard the baron had Esmé Ridding for a mistress, I figured the baroness must've plugged him. I think *I* would have."

"I know what you mean," said Molly, thinking of Constance and Thomas. Esmé caused all kinds of trouble she wasn't even aware of. "She said the romantic, sexual part of her relationship with Marcel had been over for years, and she was just glad when a mistress made him happy because he was more pleasant to be around."

"Okay, first of all? Your husband seeing somebody on the side, out of sight, that's one thing. It's a whole other thing for the somebody to show up at the funeral and make a big fuss. And second, yeah, okay, mistresses. All very French and sophisticated. But with Esmé Ridding of all people? Wouldn't that make anyone feel puny, even if you didn't ever want to see your husband naked again for the rest of your life?"

Molly stabbed a cherry tomato and ate it. "I know. I've got no answers. One big question is why was Esmé with Marcel anyway? I mean, I know he was a catch in certain respects. But Esmé could literally have any man on the planet. Why choose a middle-aged one who by all accounts wasn't happy unless he was out shooting at something?"

"He must have had another side to him."

"Apparently."

Frances and Molly spent a long time eating the salad, drinking wine, and thinking the whole thing over, but neither one came up with so much as a sliver of an insight. Once she was full, Frances went home to her apartment, where Nico waited impatiently for her return.

20

Maron was nervous. He'd never met an actual movie star before, and Esmé Ridding was not just any movie star but the most famous, most beloved in all of France. Her perfect face was everywhere, so that people she met often took odd liberties with her, as though they had known each other for a long time. He vacuumed the police car thoroughly and wiped out any specks of dust, and drove to the station fifteen minutes before the train was to arrive, paced the empty platform and glancing up at the electronic board every twenty seconds to see if there was any change in arrival time.

The train station in Castillac was tiny. Since it took two train changes to get to a station with the super-fast TGV, people didn't use it much anymore. That morning no one else waited, either to get on the next train or pick up a passenger. The young woman at the ticket counter was reading a novel. Once there had been a bustling café, but that was closed now, so if you were hungry there was nothing but a vending machine in the hallway by the bathrooms.

He heard the whistling, grinding sound of the train before he saw it. The grimy engine finally came poking around the curve and with much squealing and shrieking of brakes—even though it had been moving quite slowly—the train stopped. A conductor hopped off and lowered the steps.

Maron waited.

The conductor looked at his watch.

"Is anyone getting off?" Maron asked.

"She's coming," said the conductor with a grin. He shook his head as if to say he could hardly believe Esmé Ridding was actually going to walk down these steps, these same steps that he went up and down a hundred times a day.

"Officer Maron," called Esmé, standing at the top of the stairs and waving to him. Maron startled, realizing that he had been expecting her to arrive in some kind of costume from one of her movies—long gloves and stiletto heels, a tight sequined dress—when of course she wasn't on a set, and was dressed like any sophisticated woman, casual yet expensive-looking in wool slacks and cashmere, with Italian ballet flats.

"Thank you for coming in," said Maron, wincing at himself for sounding obsequious.

"Delighted," said Esmé, with a crooked smile and roll of her eyes, and Maron laughed and was instantly put at ease.

"Do you have any bags?"

"Just the one," she said, gesturing to a porter who was holding a small overnight bag. Maron took it from him though he resented doing it, feeling that the general rule should be that people carry their own bloody bags unless they were old or infirm. He glared at Esmé out of the corner of his eye as they went out to the station parking lot, bristling at the feeling of inferiority her mere presence bestowed on everyone else.

"I hope you're going to tell me about all the progress you've made in Marcel's case," Esmé said as she buckled her seat belt.

"I'm afraid I won't be making any sort of report today. It's in process. I'm looking forward to our interview."

Esmé sighed. "If it's a matter of funds, I can certainly hire investigators or whatever you need. Obviously Castillac is...low on manpower?" She cut him a look, checking to see if her dart struck home.

But Maron did not respond. After the initial agitated moment —when there in front of him stood Esmé Ridding the movie star, two feet away and smiling at him—had passed, he slid a door down between them, *bang!* and determined that whatever he thought or felt during the interview, she was not going to know about it. He had a talent for keeping his face impassive and still.

He parked outside the station and they went inside. Maron had of course sent Paul-Henri off on a wild goose chase up in Thiviers that would take him all day, so he and Esmé had the place to themselves as long as Castillac remained crime-free for the duration.

"Now then," said Maron, when he was seated at his desk and she was in a chair next to it, her long legs elegantly crossed to the side. "First, please tell me the character of your relationship with Marcel de Fleuray."

"The character of it? What an interesting turn of phrase, Officer Maron," she said, looking up at him innocently. "We were lovers," she said, lifting her chin with some defiance. "I don't mean simply that we were having an affair, and yes, this time the tabloids are correct, we *were* having an affair. What I mean is that it wasn't just a dalliance. We loved each other. Very deeply. Without restraint." She reached to wipe a tear from the corner of one eye, carefully so as not to smear her eyeliner and mascara. "It is a nice feeling to be able to say that, to open up to you," she added. "Though I must ask—is this interview confidential? Would it be lawful for you to run out and call up *World Wide News* and tell them what I've said? I ask not because I'm going to lie, but you must understand, this battle with the tabloids, it's never-ending for me."

"What you tell me is in confidence, though it might be brought up if there is a trial."

"Oh." Esmé looked up at the ceiling and blinked back tears. "I am sorry. You'd think I'd have cried out all the tears ever in existence by now," she said ruefully, again wiping carefully under her eyes, this time with a lace-edged handkerchief she retrieved from her bag.

"How long had you been romantically involved?"

"December 23rd of last year. I met him at a party, a terribly boring party—long story but I attended as a favor to someone. Only it turned out that I was the lucky one, because the instant I met Marcel, I knew there was going to be something very special between us."

"You felt you could see the future?"

"Disparage if you must, Officer Maron. I stand by my intuition. I remember coming out of the kitchen and seeing him standing by the window. He was very handsome, you know—did you have the good luck to meet him, by chance?"

Maron shook his head.

"Well, very, very handsome. Craggy, weathered, intensely masculine. And more than that—he...he *saw* me."

"I would imagine that was not a new sensation for you, Mademoiselle Ridding."

"Ha! Actually, yes it was—the way Marcel looked at me was entirely different. It was as though he could see right down into my soul, that he missed nothing about me, took *all* of me in...this is what he told me with his eyes. He did not say a word. He did not have to."

Maron tapped his fingertips on his desk, feeling impatient.

"I'm not making this personal as I do not know you, Officer Maron. But the thing about Frenchmen," she said, uncrossing her legs and turning in the chair, "is that they think they know all about women—am I right? You do know what I am talking about?"

Maron shrugged, but yes, he did know.

"And they will talk on and on, telling you how much they

understand women, how they appreciate them, blah blah blah... but Marcel? He understood women all right. Splendidly. *Superbly.* But he didn't have to say a word.

"Marcel would have made a magnificent detective," she said, leaning forward, "because he would have been able to figure out who the killer was without even asking any questions." She leaned back in her chair and watched Maron.

His face showed no expression. "He sounds like a talented man," he said, a bit lamely.

"Oh yes—that too," agreed Esmé, giggling as a blush washed over her cheeks. Maron wondered if she could do that on purpose.

"All right. So you started seeing him last December. Nearly a year, then. How was it going? Were you happy?"

"Blissfully."

"It did not bother you to be in a relationship with a married man?"

"No."

"You were not jealous of the baroness, of Château Marainte, his family? You did not want Marcel all to yourself?"

"Not at all. I have a full and busy life, as you might realize, Officer Maron. I travel all over the world and spend much of the year on location. The last thing I would want is to settle someplace like Castillac, which is the back of beyond if I may say so without any insult intended."

Maron was surprised to feel a surge of defensiveness about his village even though he himself thought of it as a backwater.

He continued the interview for another hour, doggedly trying to ferret out whether any tension had existed between the actress and Marcel, but not succeeding in getting any such admission out of her. To hear Esmé tell it, Marcel was a natural diplomat who loved his family and her, and managed to navigate the potentially perilous waters of a serious affair by being kind and understanding both to her and his wife. Talented indeed, Maron was thinking to himself, not sure what to believe.

"And...one last question for now. Did Marcel ever show you the emerald, *La Sfortuna*?"

Esmé let out a laugh that Maron recognized from movies, throaty and sensual. "Of course he did! He was absolutely gaga over that thing. It reminded him of his sister. Which—do you see? He was, *above all*, devoted to the women in his life, and remained heartbroken over the loss of Doriane. That, to me, is an exceptional man. A man who feels deeply, and who doesn't put you on a shelf and forget about you, even after death."

Maron wanted to grin at Esmé's theatrical delivery of that last bit. He reminded himself that she could have been acting all the way through the interview, spouting prepared lines every step of the way.

But if she was lying, he had to admit—she was very, very good at it.

❧

WHILE MARON INTERVIEWED ESMÉ, Molly was back at Château Marainte to continue searching for *La Sfortuna*. When she arrived, Georgina answered the door and told her that Antoinette had gone to a livestock auction that day, south of Bergerac, and would not be home until late in the day.

"Thanks for the message," said Molly. "Do you mind if I ask—did you ever see the famous emerald? Was the baron in the habit of showing it off to people?"

Georgina stood very still. She did not like the idea of this American barging in and asking a lot of questions that were none of her business. "I would not say 'showing it off,' madame. I did see *La Sfortuna*. It was an item with history, you know, an Italian jewel that once belonged to the Borgias."

"Incredible! Was it amazing to see? Did you get to hold it?"

Georgina controlled herself with effort. "You've got to understand, the emerald belonged to Doriane Conti, and I was her maid. She showed it to me, of course, but she was not at all a show-off and I think she might've been a little embarrassed to own it. I was devoted to Doriane, madame. *La Sfortuna* is not something to drool over, but something precious that belonged to a person we loved."

"Yes, of course, I do understand that. I'm sorry if I sounded rude. You know that the baroness has hired me to find it? Apparently it cannot be located, and you realize that something of that value—sentimentally as well as financial—has got to be found and kept somewhere safe," she added. Antoinette had given her a thorough description of the jeweled box that contained it, although she had warned that it was possible Marcel had hidden it separately from the box.

"The baron carried it in his trouser pocket," said Georgina. "It was a way to keep the memory of Doriane with him."

Molly cocked her head. "Did you ever know him to stash it somewhere, just temporarily?"

"Madame, I have no idea."

"Well, thanks for your help. If you do remember anything that you think might help me in my search, please let me know?"

"Of course."

"Thanks again. I'll be roaming around the château, just tell me if I'm getting in your way."

Georgina nodded, thinking it was extremely unlikely that she would stop the American from anything she was doing, no matter how disruptive it was. After all, the baroness had hired her, and now that the baron was gone, she was in charge of everything.

Georgina went to do the breakfast dishes and Molly stood in the lounge and looked around. Obviously, Marcel had not hidden the jewel just anywhere, the way you might hide an envelope of cash or some papers you'd rather no one saw. Besides, if she were to search under every cushion and behind every painting, it would take months and months given the vastness of the château. She had to think of a different approach, something more selective, more discriminating. In the back of her mind—she couldn't help it—she was fantasizing about paying every last bill off and then having so much money to spare she could go on a trip. Even a luxurious trip, to Venice or the Canary Islands. She could afford to find someone to restore the barn finally, and perhaps even a part-time gardener. There was no end to the things she could think of to spend money on, same as anyone.

The day before she had not really searched in earnest, but walked around the château trying to get a feel for the place and seeing if anything led her to one place over another. Like Alexandre, Molly quickly concluded that since hunting was what the baron had loved above everything, it was reasonable that the hiding place would have some connection with that. She figured there must be a place in the château where he kept his guns and other equipment, and deciding to leave Georgina alone, she set off to find it herself.

On the first floor, the ceilings were quite high in some rooms and low in others. Some floors were stone and some had glossy parquet. The incredible thing for Molly was simply how many rooms there were—she kept walking and discovering more and more, some barely furnished and others jammed with furniture, the walls covered with paintings in elaborate gilt frames. Eventually she came to a dead end, and went outside to the courtyard. There were other rooms on the first floor in a different wing, and she knocked and then entered the first door she came to, heavy and wooden, probably many hundreds of years old.

Ah, she thought, once her eyes adjusted to the dimness. The room exuded a clubby masculinity with its stuffed heads, leather furniture, and deep green walls. She crossed the room with her eye on the gun rack, opened it, but saw nothing but a couple of guns and a box of shells in the bottom. Turning on a green-shaded lamp on the desk, she stood still, breathing deeply, focusing on Marcel de Fleuray, trying to imagine his state of mind.

Had he guessed someone was trying to kill him? Did he see it coming?

It seemed that a man in his position might have any number of enemies—political from his time as minister of the interior, romantic from his years of affairs, even neighbors who might be jealous of his title and position in the community. The bigger you are, the more people hate you, right? Molly thought, walking away from the desk and seeing the bloodstain on the rug for the first time.

Molly squatted down and put her finger on the dried blood. She imagined the solidly built man lying slumped, the life draining out of him. Did the murderer stand there watching, taking pleasure in the sight? Or did he—or she—grab the emerald from the baron's pocket and make a run for it?

Or perhaps both?

She stood up and went over to a shelf crammed full of books, some of which looked well used. On one shelf was a row of photographs in silver frames. A beautiful woman leaning against a pillar, reading a paperback, her brow furrowed. Perhaps that is Doriane? wondered Molly. The next was a picture of Marcel holding a gun in the crook of one arm, and his other around the shoulders of a smiling man also holding a gun. A dead boar lay at their feet. The next was a faded photograph of a boy who—wait a minute. Molly picked up the frame and looked at the photo more closely. The boy had longish dark hair pushed back from his face and no shirt on. He was about ten years old, standing on a rock with water behind him.

The boy looked a hundred percent like a young Nico. Molly peered at his face. The same aquiline nose, the same dark eyes, angular cheekbones, full lips. The same *aura*.

It *was* Nico.

What in hell was Nico doing in Marcel de Fleuray's salon?

21

That night Molly set off for Chez Papa, hoping to catch Nico alone but dreading the prospect. It was a typical October night as she drove in on her scooter—a few couples out taking a walk in the cool evening, a kid riding a skateboard, otherwise empty streets—but for once, Molly didn't pay attention to the village, instead lost in her own thoughts until she parked outside the bistro. The scraggly tree was lit up with a string of lights but it looked half-hearted instead of festive, with one light blinking and two others dark. She saw the place was crowded and wasn't sure whether to be disappointed or relieved.

"Nico," she said, nodding when they made eye contact.

"The usual?" he said, smiling and picking up the bottle of cassis.

"Not tonight," she said. "How about...let's see, oh, make me a Negroni, why not?"

"My darling!" said Lawrence, spinning around on his stool. "Whatever has caused you to see the light?" He lifted his own Negroni to toast her.

"Oh, I don't know. Not feeling like the usual tonight, if you know what I mean."

"I do not. But it doesn't matter. I'm glad to see you! And please allow me to introduce my friend Stephan," he said, smiling hesitantly and nodding at a handsome young man on the stool next to him.

"Stephan!" exclaimed Molly. "I'm so happy to meet you. And to see that you are in fact a living human."

"Thanks?" said Stephan.

Molly smiled at him and then glanced over at Nico, who was his usual imperturbable self as patrons called out drink orders and jostled to find a place at the crowded bar. "Frances here?" she called to him.

"Nah. Got a job with a quick turnaround. She'll be coming over to use your piano in the morning probably."

"Ah," said Molly, thankful that at least she didn't have to face Frances yet. Of course, she would have to tell her about Nico's photograph at Château Marainte. Or by tomorrow would she have figured out an excuse not to?

"So, tell us everything," said Lawrence, putting a hand on Molly's shoulder and giving it a squeeze. "I've told Stephan all about your sublime powers of detection. What's going on with the baron?"

Molly thought she saw Nico flinch.

"Oh, I—Antoinette did hire me, I guess word of that has gotten out. But nothing to do with the murder. I'm sure you know about the emerald?"

"Darling, *everyone* knows about the emerald," said Lawrence.

"Well, that's the job. It's lost, and she wants me to find it. Sort of a needle in a haystack, to be honest. Apparently the baron usually carried it with him in his pocket, but no one knows where it is now."

"Most assuredly *someone* knows where it is," said Lawrence. "At least, if stealing it was the reason for the murder, which seems reasonable. Do you think it was?"

"I have no idea," said Molly. "Maybe. I guess it's suspicious that it wasn't found on him. Did you know it's supposed to be unlucky, that emerald?"

"With a name like *La Sfortuna*, no surprise," he said drily. "And what about Esmé Ridding hurling herself on the casket after crashing the funeral? Castillac has never *seen* such drama!"

"I know," said Molly. "But...it's weird. That's the kind of story that normally I would think was funny, or deliciously horrifying or something. But instead, I don't know, the whole thing just makes me sad."

"Investigators are not supposed to get emotionally involved with their cases," Lawrence said, and then he and Molly laughed, both knowing that such a rule was never going to apply to Molly, who always got more involved than she should with anyone who crossed her path.

"I guess anyone who tried to sell the emerald would get caught immediately?" said Stephan.

"Well," said Lawrence, "you couldn't sell it through any legit organization, for sure—Sotheby's won't be putting it in their catalog. But for someone with contacts in the black market, it's likely easy enough. I'm sure there would be no end of takers, curse or no curse."

"Antoinette just wants to sell it," said Molly.

"Who can blame her? It probably got her husband killed."

Stephan had a polite expression on his face but Molly could see that he'd heard enough speculation on Castillac's crime of the moment. She asked him the usual list of questions—where was he from, how did he like to spend his time, what in the world did he see in Lawrence—but the conversation never picked up steam. Molly blamed herself. She was distracted and kept stealing glances at Nico as though she could catch him doing or saying something that would explain his photograph at Château Marainte.

Nico had always been vague about his history, at least since Molly had known him. He was one of the first people in Castillac she had gotten to know, having frequented Chez Papa often in those early days just after her arrival, fending off a potentially lethal combination of loneliness and homesickness. He had been curious to her because he was obviously university educated and well traveled, clever and drop-dead handsome...yet content to tend bar in a shabby bistro in a small village far from any of the intellectual and social action people his age usually gravitated toward. Molly had wondered why, and even with Frances living with him, she was no closer to finding out.

"Another Negroni?" Nico asked.

"You devil. No, I'll pass. Say, this is an out-of-the-blue question, I know—but what's your last name again?"

She saw a shadow pass over Nico's face, just an instant of concern before he looked into her eyes and smiled. "Bartolucci. You getting me something monogrammed?"

Molly laughed. "A smoking jacket in blue silk, how's that?"

"Smashing," said Nico, and then he drifted down to the other end of the bar. Molly said her goodbyes to Lawrence and Stephan, knowing she was not being the best company, and went home to snuggle with Bobo in bed and carefully go over the events of the day in her mind before falling asleep.

She missed Ben. That was the last thought of that Tuesday in October. Not only because she wanted his thoughts on the case, which of course she did. But she missed him reading in bed beside her, missed the skeptical look he got when she told him a new plan she was hatching, missed the scratchy tone of his voice and the way Bobo leapt for joy when he showed up.

She put an arm around her dog, closed her eyes, and fell into a restless sleep.

❧

ESMÉ RODE the elevator up to her penthouse, having spent a night in a hotel in Bergerac after her meeting with Maron, and returning to Paris by train the following day. The weather was wet and blowy in the city; people hurried down the sidewalk, umbrellas up, and by the time she was home, she was damp and irritable. Her agent had said there were a million offers on the horizon but she had no work at the moment, and for Esmé, having no work was an unstable place to be. When she did not have a character to inhabit when she got up in the morning, she was not entirely sure who she was, though she did not think of it that way.

Once inside her penthouse, she let her coat drop to the floor and walked to the window and looked out, but the gray sky depressed her and she went to the wet bar and poured herself a glass of whiskey.

I'm well out of it, she thought, and then said the sentence out loud, just to see how it sounded. Then she said it again, in a lower register, allowing her voice to crack just at the end.

The whiskey was harsh on her throat, which was one thing about it she liked.

She had no close friends to call, no one to talk to about any of it.

Tossing back the rest of the drink, she slammed the glass on the counter of the bar and strode to her desk with a sense of purpose. The desk stood in front of a window but the view was dulled by low clouds and rain. Esmé opened the slim drawer and took out a letter, addressed to her in a masculine hand, jagged letters in black ink. She opened the letter and read it once. Then methodically she tore it up, into smaller and smaller bits, until the bits were the size of her little fingernail, and then she threw them into the air so that they fluttered to the floor like confetti.

❧

"YES, MAMAN," said Paul-Henri, who had called early in the morning hoping to catch his mother before she went out. She was a very busy woman and so far had resisted getting a cell phone, preferring to do her visiting and shopping without having to worry about receiving calls that might throw off her rhythm. "I'm only asking because it's an active case and we're running into a wall," he added. "It's not like you're going to be dragged into court to testify. I just thought you might know something useful, you know, for background."

"I'm not in the habit of gossiping that way, as you know perfectly well," said Madame Monsour, sipping on the single cup of coffee she allowed herself each morning. "And just because you decided to be rebellious and join that odious gendarmerie doesn't mean I'm going to change into another person just to suit you."

"Of course not, Maman," he said, rolling his eyes. One thing about Maman, once she sank her teeth into something, she never, ever let go. She did not approve of his choice of career, as she made clear every time they spoke, and she was not going to give him any help on the Fleuray case. But the prospect of having some useful bit of information to pass on to Maron was too gratifying to pass up. "Come on, Marcel de Fleuray was living in Paris almost full-time for at least three or four years. He was once minister of the interior, for heaven's sake! Surely you must have run into him. Or know someone who knows him."

"I might. But as I'm trying to explain to you, that does not mean I'm ready and willing to blab to the police."

"I'm—oh for heaven's sake, Maman! I may be a gendarme, but I am also your son. And I would hope you could find it in yourself to give me something that will cost you nothing."

"You could have been a creditable lawyer, you know."

"I believe you have mentioned that."

"It's not too late."

"That's not going to happen, Maman. So, maybe you met him at a dinner party? I know your friend Agathe Beauchamp always goes in for the government types, and Fleuray was apparently a good-looking man, which is the other quality she cares about."

Madame Monsour said nothing.

"I'm right, you did meet him at the Beauchamps'!" Paul-Henri stood up from the table, spilling coffee on his trousers.

"I might have."

"And? Was he with anyone? Esmé Ridding? His wife? What was he like?"

"Do not pepper me with questions as if I am some kind of suspect," said his mother.

"I beg your pardon. Please continue at your leisure." He mopped at his lap with a napkin and gritted his teeth.

"All right then. I did not go into this earlier because I honestly don't see how it matters. I did have dinner with the baron, I believe it was in January. At the Beauchamps'. There were ten or twelve people there, so it isn't as though he and I sat down for an in-depth conversation. I can't remember what we talked about—though as you say, Agathe does go in for politics and so doubtless, as usual, half the table was aghast at the latest move by the president and the other half defended it."

"And Marcel? Do you remember anything he said?"

"I do not. I am not sure he said much of anything. That actress was all over him the entire night, I do remember that. Agathe and I spoke about it the next day. Constantly rubbing his back, kissing him, holding his hand. Like a pair of teenagers. I even thought—"

Madame Monsour let the pause lengthen until Paul-Henri was about to explode. "What, Maman?"

"Well, I was merely going to say that during dinner they did not keep their hands on the table, in view. You can infer from that anything you like."

Paul-Henri rolled his eyes so hard his head ached. "Thank you. If you remember any other detail, please give me a call. How is Father?"

"He is well. His hip has shooting pains if he walks too much in one day, so he has begun playing bridge."

"Wonderful," said Paul-Henri, and he managed to continue

the conversation for another fifteen minutes, saying all the right things at the appropriate moments, while at the same time thinking about Esmé and Marcel, and how easily infatuation could turn to rage. He had felt it himself, when he was younger—and who hadn't?

22

Just before dawn Antoinette woke with a start. She was used to sleeping alone, used to the noises of the château and Grizou's stirrings, and was unsure what had disturbed her. But it hardly mattered, she thought, swinging her thin legs over the side of the bed and sitting up. She rested there a moment, not feeling quite ready to face another day. A soft light, just a faint glow, came in through the leaded windows of her bedroom. She heard a whistling wind, a sound she loved.

In the bathroom she stood before the mirror and gazed at herself. She saw that her nose was too long and bulbous at the end, her lips too thin. She sighed and reached for her toothbrush.

"Grizou," she murmured, feeling the dog's nose at the back of her knee. "Dear, sweet friend." She turned to him and got down on the wooden floor, putting her arms around the dog and weeping into his fur. Grizou licked her face and put a paw on her leg. "All right then, enough of this," she said after a few moments, and struggled to her feet.

Georgina was at her cottage at this hour, doubtless still in bed. It occurred to Antoinette, not for the first time, that if something went wrong—if she choked on a hunk of baguette or slipped in the bathtub—there would be no one to call, no one to help her. The thought did not scare her, especially, because she understood that death was inevitable for everyone, and there was no controlling when it would come. Besides, it was statistically unlikely that a dry baguette would be the agent of her demise. For whatever that was worth.

She made coffee and ate several pieces of toast with jam made from strawberries she had grown. Grizou got a small piece of liver and a raw chicken wing, which he took outside and gnawed happily under a leafless birch. Fortified and dressed for the cool weather, Antoinette walked out and breathed in the morning air, taking a moment to look around the courtyard before continuing on through the narrow passageway and out to the barn, where the goats and donkey were standing by the fence waiting for her.

She let herself into the enclosure and the goats butted their heads against her legs, causing her to hold on to a fencepost. For close to fifteen minutes she just stood in the paddock and petted the goats, watching them gambol about, the donkey ambling over for her share of attention as well. Then Antoinette went back out through the gate, picking up a rubber bucket for the animals' grain, falling into the rhythm of the morning chores. For the next hour, with tremendous resolve and working as slowly as she needed to, she shoveled manure, filled the water buckets, hauled in plenty of hay, and stood among the animals, running her hand on their backs and murmuring to them and breathing in their comforting animal smell.

It was Thursday, two days after seeing Nico's photograph at Château Marainte, and Molly was no closer to figuring out what to do about it. She texted Lawrence and asked to see him—alone—for a consultation about something important she didn't want to talk about over the phone. He suggested getting breakfast at

Pâtisserie Bujold and then taking it to eat on a bench somewhere, teasing her about the need to talk where their conversation could not be bugged.

Molly, of course, had never said no to Pâtisserie Bujold in her life. Twenty minutes later she parked the dented scooter right outside and went in, as blissed out by that first inhalation of coffee mixed with vanilla as she'd been the first time she'd entered the shop.

"Bonjour, Molly!" said Edmond Nugent, the round-bellied proprietor and Molly's great admirer.

"Bonjour, Edmond," Molly answered, leaning over the counter so they could kiss cheeks. "What's the latest in the world of pastry?"

"Oh, you don't want to know. I attended a competition in Poitiers last weekend and it was *rigged*. I myself was not a contestant, but I was able, by means unimportant to my story, to taste some of the various entries. And the chosen winner was absolutely subpar. The judges had to have been bribed. The entire thing was a travesty from start to finish!"

Molly nodded along with Edmond's tale while feasting her eyes on the day's offerings in the glass case as he feasted his eyes on her. When he mentioned a contest she looked up sharply. "Interesting," she said slowly. "I've had an idea. Might be useless. But you know, the gîte business in the off-season is a real struggle. I've got someone coming this Saturday for a week, but then three weeks with nobody."

"I could always use a pair of talented hands in the bakery," he said, licking his lips.

"You're very kind. But so—I don't know if you heard, but I tried a sort of theme dinner, thinking I could do one a week or every couple of weeks—not to make a lot of money but just enough to pay my electricity bill, you know? Anyway, utter flop. For various reasons. So I was—"

"—are you sure you wouldn't consider joining my staff? The

hours are awkward, I don't deny that, but you would be welcome to take home unsold pastries at the end of the day."

"You're kind, Edmond, really—wait, what? I'd be able to take home pastries?" Molly paused, allowing herself to wallow in the gluttonous glory of that thought for just a moment. "You're too generous. But I'm afraid I can't tie myself down like that."

"I do know you have other irons in the fire," said Edmond. "Detective work can be time-consuming, no doubt?"

To her relief, the bell on the door tinkled and Lawrence came in, shivering and stamping his feet. "Bonjour Edmond, Bonjour Molly," he said, kissing Molly on both cheeks. "The temperature is dropping fast out there. It feels more like January than the end of October."

"Have some hot coffee," said Molly.

"I'll do that. Did you get our pastries yet? Edmond, do you have that apricot thing I love?"

"Wrong season, Monsieur Weebly," Edmond said stiffly. He did not approve of other men hanging around his Molly.

"So Edmond—I've got to have a meeting with Lawrence about something, but I want to come back and talk about my idea with you later. Just broadly: what do you think about having a cooking competition at La Baraque? We could have a few contestants, judges—thinking of you in that role—and we could make it free to attend but charge for snacks?"

"This American obsession with snacks...you know that we in France are not cramming our faces all day long the way Americans do."

"Okay, we'll talk more later. Just think about it."

Molly and Lawrence got their orders, paid up, and said goodbye to an increasingly irritable Nugent.

"Is he always so crabby?" said Lawrence, grinning as they headed down the sidewalk.

"Not always. Half the time. Listen, it's way too cold to eat outside. And you laugh, but I do want some privacy. Where can we go?"

After considering and discarding several options, they ended up walking to Lawrence's house on the edge of the village. It was small and very well kept, and every time Molly went, she remembered the night she had spent there during the Amy Bennett case, when she had been too frightened to stay at La Baraque by herself.

And now she was investigating another murder, if not officially. This time she had assumed—along with everyone else—that the murder had happened as a result of the theft, or attempted theft, of *La Sfortuna*. But now that she had seen Nico's photo, she wondered.

Why had he told no one of his connection to the Fleurays? And what *was* the connection?

"Hello? What planet are you on?"

"Oh, whoops. Got a little carried away with my train of thought."

"Well, have a seat while I get us some plates and put on some more coffee. I can't believe how chilly it is, honestly, it's been so warm I feel betrayed by the turn in the weather! And while I'm doing that, why don't you get started. Tell me what's on your mind, darling. I can hear perfectly well from the kitchen."

Molly was suddenly starving and could barely wait for Lawrence to come back with the pastries. She took a deep breath and tried to settle herself down. It felt as though her thoughts were zinging all over the place, and she wanted to be able to speak rationally about the case.

"I'm glad I can talk frankly to you... I agreed to search for *La Sfortuna* just so I could hang around Château Marainte and figure out who killed the baron and why."

"Tell me something I don't know, sweetheart. Though I heard you'll get ten percent, which won't be a bag of nothing."

"Yeah, well, I can't go pinning my hopes on that. But listen. I went over to the château on Tuesday. I have carte blanche to snoop all over the entire place trying to find that damn emerald. I wandered into a salon that looked like it was where Marcel spent time when he was home—all manly, you know, with a gun rack and stuffed heads—and it felt as though it had been used recently. Not like a lot of the rooms, which are shut up and no one goes in them for months or I imagine even years at a time." Molly stopped, remembering Nico's expression in the photograph, so young and full of confidence.

"Go on," said Lawrence, coming over with two plates laden with pastry. "The coffee will take a minute. So what did you find? Is that where he was shot?"

"Yes. Big nasty bloodstain on the rug. You'd think they'd throw the rug out, wouldn't you?"

"Maybe Maron, or Nagrand, told them to wait for some reason."

Molly shrugged. "So...here's what I want to hear your take on." She bit into an almond croissant, the buttery soft layers inside contrasting with the crackly exterior, a sensation she never tired of. "There were framed photographs in the salon. You know, you can tell a lot from photographs, sometimes. They show things people don't include when they talk about stuff."

Lawrence nodded, becoming frustrated with Molly's dragging out what she wanted to say.

"It's Nico. There's a photograph there of *Nico*. It's faded, he's maybe ten years old. Looks like it was taken on a vacation or something—he's standing on a rock with water behind him."

"You're sure—"

"It's him. No question."

Lawrence jumped up to get coffee and Molly ate more of her croissant. "Thing is, he's never once mentioned having any sort of association with the Fleurays. Which might be no big deal, something understandable, him simply not bragging about his fancy connections. Except, once Marcel was murdered? How does he continue to keep that secret when the whole village is talking about the family and wondering what happened?"

"And what *is* the connection? Maybe his parents and the Fleurays were friends, they were on vacation together, it was years ago, nothing he even thinks about anymore."

"But if that were so, Marcel would not be featuring his photograph. It was not a group shot—Nico was alone in the picture. Very clearly he meant something to the baron. Something powerful."

"But what?"

"You know Nico is notoriously guarded about his history."

"I don't especially like giving people my own resumé, so I have no problem with that."

"We're not talking casual acquaintances, Lawrence. You've told me things about your past."

"But that's you, my dear."

"Exactly. Nico is not talking to Frances about any of this. Yet he wants her to marry him."

"Excuse me for being slow-witted here, Molly. Do you think you know what the connection is?"

"I don't. But I have...suspicions. Start with the photograph. There are only three, all in silver frames. These are not random photos but obviously have deep meaning for Marcel."

"I love how you're on a first-name basis with him."

"We're tight. And we'll be even tighter once I figure out who killed him. So listen. One photo was, I'm pretty sure, his sister, who from all accounts he loved quite dearly. *La Sfortuna* belonged to her. The next photo was after a hunt, with a dead boar and maybe Hubert, the gamekeeper—whom his wife says he's very close to, plus hunting was like the main thing in his life, the thing he cared about over everything. Then there's Nico."

"What about Antoinette? No photos of her or his sons?"

"I wondered about that. But they were still around, he could see them whenever he liked. I don't know about you but I'm not that interested in keeping photos out of people I can see any old time, even including people who mean a great deal to me."

"Have you got a picture of Ben anywhere?"

"Stop changing the subject! Look, I have no idea what Nico is doing in a silver frame in the baron's salon. But I intend to find out. And I'm hoping you will enlist your super-secret information network to find out what they know as well."

"This network is a figment of your fantasy, my dear."

"How do you always know the instant anyone dies in Castillac?"

"If I drink any more coffee I may have a heart attack," said Lawrence. "But let's finish up these pastries, shall we? They won't be any good tomorrow."

Molly sighed and picked up a mini-éclair with mocha frosting. She was going to have to tell Frances about the photo. But she winced at the explosion she expected as a reaction.

23

Maron was home in bed asleep when he got the call. Someone breaking into the Baskerville's house, newly renovated, out on route de Canard. He threw on some clothes, jumped on his scooter, and got to the house in a matter of minutes. Shining his flashlight around the yard, he saw no sign of anyone.

"Officer Maron!" a man called out, after opening the door a crack.

Maron trotted up the steps and pushed his way inside. Mr. Henry Baskerville, formerly of London, was standing in the foyer in his pajamas, holding the arm of a teenaged boy twisted behind his back. The boy had an innocent face, young and open—and frightened.

"What's this about?" said Maron gruffly.

"Found him trying to jimmy open a window. Car was parked around back, guess he figured no one was home. That it, kid?" asked Baskerville, giving the boy's arm a wrench.

"Ow!" cried the boy.

"All right," said Maron, "let him go. You're not going to run off, are you? I didn't think so. Thinking you'd get into Monsieur

Baskerville's house and see if any valuables were lying about? Shouldn't you be home in bed on a school night?"

The boy looked down at the floor and did not answer.

"What's your name?" asked Maron.

"Malcolm."

"Malcolm what?"

"Barstow."

"You part of that Barstow family out on route de Fallon? Your father been in jail recently?"

Malcolm nodded.

Maron sighed. "All right, Mr. Baskerville, I'll take him in. Look around and make sure nothing's been taken, and give me a call in the morning if so."

"I appreciate your coming so quickly," said Baskerville, suddenly feeling embarrassed to be standing there in his pajamas.

Maron gripped Malcolm's upper arm and walked him outside, regretting that he'd brought the scooter. "You're going to have to ride behind me," he said. "No funny business, hear me?"

Malcolm nodded glumly and got on behind Maron but did not deign to put his hands on Maron's hips, holding on to the edge of the seat instead. Maron sped down route de Canard to the station. It was 3:30 a.m.

Just before stopping, Maron reached around to hold Malcolm's wrist tightly. Maron was strong and fit, and Malcolm undernourished and young—both of them knew escape was not really an option.

"All right then," Maron said with a sigh, as once they were inside, Malcolm dropped into a chair. "Why don't you tell me what you were thinking, breaking into that house? You're too young for that foolishness, Malcolm."

"We don't have enough to eat," Malcolm said quietly. He flicked his eyes up to Maron to see if he bit.

"Who do you live with?"

"My parents and my little sister. But my father's been...away... and my mother...."

Maron waited for the kid to finish. Castillac wasn't tiny, so it was possible he didn't know if a family was enduring particular hardship. Nevertheless, so far he wasn't buying Malcolm's story. "You're saying you broke into the Baskervilles' because you and your little sister are starving? That's your story?"

Malcolm could see it wasn't going well, so he nimbly changed tactics. "That's all true, sir. But I'll admit, I've gone into some people's homes just because it gives me a thrill." He shrugged and smiled, and Maron felt himself almost smile in response.

"Is going to jail worth it for a thrill?"

"Naw, I don't want to go to jail, you're right about that, Chief Maron. Maybe we could make a trade? I'll promise not to break into any more houses if you'll let me go. And I have something I think you might be interested in, that I'll give you absolutely free of charge."

Maron laughed. "What, you're trying to horse trade?"

"You've got a murdered baron on your hands, am I right?"

Maron narrowed his eyes at the boy.

"Well, I happen to have a pretty good idea who plugged him. And not only that, I have evidence. Rock solid evidence you can hold in your hand."

"Pfft," said Maron, looking away. "You're nothing but talk."

"No sir! Drive me home and I'll show you exactly what I'm talking about. As long as you let me go," he added.

"It's the middle of the night, Malcolm, and I'm not in the mood for a wild goose chase. Why don't you tell me what it is you think you've got that's so important, and then I'll decide whether to take you downstairs to a cell or not."

"It would have more of an impact if you saw it in person. But okay, it was like this. I was...I found myself inside Château Marainte one day, by chance—"

Maron couldn't help snickering.

"—and I happened to be in the salon where I believe the baron got shot. If the bloodstain on the rug is any sort of clue. And in that salon, in between the pages of a book, I found a letter..."

"People don't write letters anymore."

"Well then what do you think, a ghost wrote this one? An alien? Come on, Officer Maron! I'm telling you I found a letter, written by Esmé Ridding to the baron. Her handwriting is nothing so great, I'll tell you that much. Or maybe it's just that she was so angry when she wrote the letter that it made her hand jump all over the place. Anyway—she goes on and on about how mad she is at him, how betrayed she feels, blah blah blah, and at the end, she promises to kill him. Her actual words were 'I'm going to shoot your blankety-blank head off!' She wrote out the curse words but I know cursing in front of an adult is rude so I'm not saying what those words were." Malcolm looked at Maron, his freckled face the picture of virtue.

"You are some piece of work," said Maron, shaking his head.

But of course he would not be doing his job if he did not follow up on a potential piece of evidence as explosive as Malcolm claimed, though he decided a night in the rarely used jail might have an overall positive effect on Malcolm, and that they would fetch the supposed letter once the sun came up.

24

Friday was a more typical late October day, with a light rain off and on, and sweater rather than coat weather. Constance sped down rue des Chênes on her bicycle, feeling a little proud that Molly had given her the job of welcoming the first guest at La Baraque in weeks.

"Molls!" she said, her cheeks flushed, when Molly opened the door. "Have you written down all my instructions? I don't want to mess this up!"

"You won't, don't worry," said Molly, suddenly filled with anxiety at all the things that could go wrong. It *was* Constance, after all. "There's really not much to do. It's a couple coming in from New York. They're renting a car so they'll be getting here that way and won't need picking up at the station or anything. They've got directions and probably a GPS in the car. All you have to do is wait for their text that they're almost here, come over and greet them when they arrive, show them around a little, give them the key, and that's it."

"But what if they don't speak any French?"

"I'm trying to remember...I don't know if they do or not. Probably best to assume no. But really, Constance, it doesn't make any difference! Just smile a lot and make sure they see the bottle of wine I put on their dining room table. I left a note explaining that I had to make an urgent trip to Paris and would be back in a few days."

"Urgent, huh?" Constance looked skeptical.

"Actually, it *is* urgent. In a way. As you know, Antoinette hired me to find the jewel, and a logical place for me to look is the baron's apartment in Paris."

"You just want to get in there and look for clues to his murder."

"Is it that obvious?"

"Uh, yeah, Molls. But only to anyone who knows you."

"Well, too bad. I'm going. I haven't been to Paris in forever so I'll probably do a little sight-seeing while I'm there. Check out the Louvre and the Luxembourg Gardens."

"No you won't."

"Huh?"

"When you're sniffing around a case, that's pretty much all you do. Can't really picture you strolling through museums soaking up culture when there's a murderer on the loose."

"I can do two things at the same time, you know."

Constance shrugged, grinning, clearly not agreeing. "Do you want me to do any cleaning before the guests come? What are their names, anyway?"

"If you'd look around and spot clean, that'd be excellent. The place is in pretty good shape, but I might have missed something. They'll be staying in the cottage. Ervin and Sissy Chubb."

"What?"

"I'll write it down for you." Molly tore a sheet off a pad of paper sitting on the kitchen counter and wrote out the guests' names. "I know you can handle this, Constance. And if there's any trouble at all, just text me. If you have to tell me a long story call me. I'm expecting to be by myself for the whole trip so there's no bad time to call."

"No secret lover waiting for you in a glamorous bar?"

"Hardly."

It was not until she was enjoying the comfortable seat on the TGV that it occurred to Molly that she might not be the only person thinking that *La Sfortuna* might be in Marcel's apartment. But she reassured herself with the fact that she was the only one to whom Antoinette had given a key.

Right?

❧

AT LONG LAST, after endless procrastination and only about twenty minutes of actual work, the jingle was written. All Frances had to do was sit down at Molly's piano and play it through a few times to make sure. Sometimes the things just sprouted up whole, and didn't need a lot of tweaking. She very much hoped this was one of those times. Because...Nico.

She slid out of bed, giving a long look to her beloved, fast asleep on his side with his sensuous mouth slightly open, his olive skin still dark even months after summer had ended. "So beautiful," she murmured to herself, and then quickly put on a pair of emerald green leggings and a tunic that had a large Egyptian eye over her chest. She brushed her hair until it shone, falling stick-straight and black, with bangs and the rest grown to her shoulders.

Since Chez Papa was only a few blocks away and Nico could get to work on foot, Frances borrowed Nico's car for the drive to Molly's. Molly had been acting a little weird lately, and Frances wanted to ask her what was going on. Did she miss Ben but not want to talk about it, or was it just that the Fleuray case was taking up all her attention?

As she started the car and turned around, insidious little thoughts about Nico tried to rise up to consciousness, but she swept them away, forcing herself to run through her jingle a few more times, singing out loud.

Frances had always like singing in the car. Of course, cars didn't have the acoustics of showers, but still, something about being alone in a car always made her start belting out songs. She sang along with Aretha Franklin belting out R-E-S-P-E-C-T as she drove out of the village on the way to Molly's, and that felt so good that she drove right past Molly's driveway and into the country, going from Aretha to hymns she had learned when her grandmother took her to church, and then snatches of a Rossini aria she halfway knew.

Way, way deep down, Frances knew she was singing and driving because there was something going on she did not want to face. She didn't know exactly what it was, and did not want to know. It was an amorphous fear that she could keep away for an indefinite time, and hopefully, eventually, whatever it was would simply fade away without harm. Her plan for the rest of the day was beginning to solidify: keep singing, keep driving, and at some point stop for some wine and maybe some chocolate. And then repeat.

❧

THE TGV GOT MOLLY to Paris in only a few hours. She had brought only a light shoulder bag, easy enough to carry, and thought she would walk around the city and then eat a leisurely dinner, in no hurry to get to Marcel's apartment. If the emerald was there, it would wait.

Ah, Paris.

Molly had only visited there in warm weather, and she found Paris in October to be even more wonderful—more intimate, without floods of tourists around every corner. More neighborly somehow, which was surprising for one of the major cities of the world. She was proud that she was able to chat with shopkeepers easily now, comfortably and without nervousness, instead of dealing with the constant misunderstandings and confusions that come with having a fragile purchase on another language.

Instead of looking for recommendations on the internet, she felt like choosing a restaurant the old fashioned way, by reading the menu out front and deciding whether she liked the feel of the place. In the 6th arrondissement, she found a small bistro tucked in between two big apartment buildings. It had no name but an elaborate sculpture of a blue pig over the door.

Inside, the restaurant was old-fashioned in the best sort of way. The tablecloths were a dazzling white, and places were set with more flatware than Molly was used to. The place seemed full, but with a wink the aged maitre d' found a tiny table for Molly next to the kitchen. She didn't mind. The flow of waiters in and out of the swinging kitchen door gave her something to pay attention to, and she did her best to eavesdrop on their gossiping, though she could only catch a few words when the door was open.

But even the hubbub of a Paris restaurant was not enough to keep Molly from thinking about the latest developments in the baron's case. She kept going over and over that photograph. Surely Nico was merely a friend of the family, not anyone currently significant in the Fleuray's lives, and the photograph nothing more than an artifact from an earlier time, which the baron hadn't bothered to remove. It's not as though a hunting man like Marcel was likely very involved in room decoration, she thought. It's probably nothing.

Molly was not known for moderation when it came to French food, and she certainly wasn't going to stint now that she was in Paris. When the waiter came around with a basket of rolls, she took two, breaking off hunks and slathering them with sweet butter, reveling in the yeasty soft interior and the crackly hard exterior. For a starter she ordered escargots Bourguignon, because she was helpless to get anything else when they were on the menu, and followed that with *lapin au cidre* and a *pichet* of table wine. The meal was so stupendous—and she was so tipsy—that she seriously wondered whether she had made a grievous error not moving to Burgundy instead of the Dordogne, the Burgundian food was that good.

She over-tipped (which was her habit even when not half-drunk) and staggered to her hotel, happily flopping face down on the bed. The window was cracked open and even though it made the room too cool, she liked listening to the sounds coming up from the street: a group walking by laughing, a young girl calling out *Maman*, a low murmur of conversation.

By eleven o'clock, Molly decided it was time to do what she had come to Paris to do, no matter the lateness of the hour. Still a bit unsteady on her feet, she took the elevator down to the lobby, waved at the concierge who did not notice her, and headed out to the street. She had chosen the hotel because of its proximity to Marcel's apartment. She could have spent the night in the apartment itself, and Antoinette had even suggested doing so, but the idea gave Molly the creeps, though she didn't know exactly why. It's not as though the murder—or anything untoward at all—had taken place there, as far as she knew.

Though the building was old, the interior was modern, which surprised her at first. But then she supposed if you had grown up in a 15th century château, you might perhaps yearn for something completely different if you had the chance. There was no concierge, but three keys to get in: the door to the building, the door to the elevator or stairs, and the apartment itself. Molly navigated all that without trouble, for the first time feeling a tingle of excitement at the prospect of actually finding the jewel, and allowing herself to indulge in some fantasy of how quickly and easily the windfall would solve a lot of problems at La Baraque.

She understood that her faculties were not sharp, thanks to the wine, but told herself a little story about how perhaps the wine would allow her to see the apartment in a different light, and anyway, she would come back in the morning for a sober look.

Molly fitted the key in the door to 7C. She turned it and pushed open the metal door.

In the foyer, lying on the rug—old and Turkish, she noticed—was a bra.

Molly stood staring at it, trying to form some kind of narrative for why a silky, lacy bra would be in the foyer, on the floor of a dead man's apartment. Her mind was dull and she felt an incipient headache crowding into the base of her skull. A sound no louder than an exhalation came from somewhere close by. Molly took a few steps, listening. She almost called out hello but stopped herself.

And then a woman burst out of a room with a sheet wound around her body, shrieking with delight. Molly gaped. Words jumbled around in her throat but she was unable to get any of them out, until finally—the woman looking at Molly with horror—she managed to say, "Esmé?"

25

Percival looked out at the street and then at his Cartier watch. His brother was late, as usual, and he allowed himself to glower and feel annoyed, knowing that once Luc showed up he would have to keep those feelings under wraps. They didn't see each other often in Paris. Luc kept odd hours, and their friends belonged to such different social groups—one conformist and conservative, the other dabbling in radical politics or at least a lot of marijuana consumption—that on the rare times they did get together, it was always just the two of them.

Percival went to the bar and ordered an Armagnac. He was lost in his own thoughts, not noticing the other patrons. Eventually, when he was on his second drink, Luc sauntered in. His boyish good looks attracted the attention of a group of young women sitting in a booth, and although Luc noticed, he paid them no mind.

"What the hell," said Percival, giving his brother a rap on his bicep that was a little too hard.

"Sorry, got stuck somewhere. Sort of a stakeout, but that makes it sound more exciting that it was. I spent the last three hours hanging around a street corner waiting for a guy to leave a building so I could try to ask him some questions."

"That's lovely."

"Oh, don't be like that, Perce."

"So how does it feel to be a semi-orphan?"

"Can't say I've looked at Father's death that way."

"Can't say I miss him."

Luc shrugged. "What's to miss? It's not as though we ever spent any time together, really. Even when we were all home at the same time, he was out in the woods with Hubert more than anything."

Percival nodded. He knew it would be smart to soften Luc up a little, but he couldn't calm down enough to think of how to accomplish that.

"So what's on your mind?" Luc asked.

Percival paused for a second, wishing there were another way. "Believe me, I did not want to call you. I suppose you can guess what I...I am forced to ask."

"Some thoughts have crossed my mind, yes," said Luc, leaning back against the bar and looking at Percival with a languid smile.

"Look, starting a new business, it's quite tricky in the early stages but can be marvelously remunerative in the end. Everything is going just as it should be. The product is of very high quality, the market is in place, details are being meticulously taken care of both administratively and in marketing. The team could honestly not be any better at what they do."

"So what's the problem?"

"Time. As is so often the case. Unfortunately, creative people are not good at estimating how long a job will take them. And even though I know that perfectly well—anyone in management knows it—that still leaves me with a hole when I'm trying to block out the tasks of the rest of the company with respect to that product. All of which to say—there's a...a shortfall. I was forced to put my own money into it. And that's left me..." Percival swallowed hard and visibly steeled himself. "That's left me needing to ask for a loan. Not a big one," he hastened to add. "And not for a long time. The turnaround should be short, even allowing for some extra padding in case of another deadline missed."

Luc smiled. He had not ordered his drink yet and was in no hurry. "And...excuse me for asking, it must be embarrassing for you...would this need for money have anything at all to do with your gambling problem?"

He caught the eye of the bartender, who was at the other end of the bar flirting with the young women in the banquette, and held up his finger to show he was ready to give his order.

"That's in the past," said Percival. His face looked deflated, as though Luc had, with that one remark, opened a valve and all the air—and hope—had suddenly whooshed right out of him.

"Ah, the past. Let's talk about the past, shall we? About how you borrowed every last *centime* I had to pay off those thugs who were threatening to break your legs? About how you've only paid some of it back, though apparently judging by your watch, you don't mind lavishing yourself with some expensive presents. Or do you owe other people this time?"

"You don't understand, you have never understood—in my business, one must look the part. Without that, no one takes you seriously. You can't get anywhere at all."

"So buying yourself the Cartier, that's just a burden put on you by your profession that you were forced to bear?" Luc laughed. "I think I'll have a shot of tequila," he said to the bartender. "Do you have any lime?"

"What an unpleasant drink," Percival said, unable to help himself.

Luc just laughed. When the bartender set a dish with some lime slices on it, and then the shot glass, he sucked on a chunk of lime and then tossed the tequila back. Setting the glass on the bar, he looked over at the young women and gave them a half-smile.

"Why don't you ask Maman for the money?" he asked. "I don't think she's doing too badly. Do you figure your share of Father's inheritance isn't coming quite fast enough?"

Percival did not answer. Nervously he scraped his teeth over his bottom lip, trying to think of some way to change his brother's mind.

"There's nothing you can say," Luc told him. "So really—don't bother. You got me to fall for your bull once, but twice? That's getting close to insulting." Luc stood up, threw a couple of bills on the counter, and left the bar.

❧

ONCE HOME, Malcolm Barstow gave Maron a thin sheaf of papers, which he tucked under his arm while giving the boy a stern lecture about the trouble he would get into if caught breaking into any more houses. Malcolm had a talent for looking remorseful and he laid it on thick, knowing Maron would feel competent and good about himself, which he did.

Outside, on the stoop of the Barstow house, Maron stopped to quickly riffle through the papers to see if they contained "something juicy," as the teenager had claimed. A scrap that simply said "Zimbabwe? Canada?". More interesting, a handwritten note saying that *La Sfortuna* should go to the baron's nephew in the event of his death. Maron snickered at that, amused at how often people tried to do their children out of inheritances. Next, a letter. He quickly read through it, then again. He was suddenly alert, his heart pounding. If authentic, the letter stolen by Malcolm Barstow appeared on the surface to hand Maron the solution to the Fleuray case on a silver platter.

Maron sped to the station and settled at his to reread the letter. After pulling it from the envelope, he closed his eyes for a moment, almost afraid that when he read it again, it would not be as incriminating as he first thought.

Dearest Marcel,

I am undone. Shattered. To find out that you are not the man I believed you to be...it is beyond devastating. And understand, these are just words I am spilling upon the page, they do not begin to express what I am feeling in my heart.

Was it only a few days ago that you held the emerald in your hand, and moved it up and down my body, caressing me with it? What sweet things you murmured to me then! How you devoured the sight of the emerald on my skin, how your eyes were on fire!

And barely a few days later...not so much as a note, or a call, only silence. I sat at the Ritz bar for nearly an hour with tears gathering in my eyes, the whole world there to witness my humiliation at your hands.

I tell you Marcel, I want to wrench that stupid gun out of your hands and shoot you with it! And then alas, I would have to turn it on myself and pull the trigger, for how on earth can I continue to live in this world without you in it—

Adoringly,
Your Esmé

MARON NOTICED that Esmé had not cursed the way Malcolm had said, and admired the boy's glibness while shaking his head. Then he smiled as the contents of the letter sunk in.

Motive, check. Means, check. Opportunity, check.

But...he knew that once he arrested Esmé Ridding for the murder of the baron, Castillac would turn into a circus beyond what any of its inhabitants could imagine. Maron could see it unfolding, too fast to control: the tabloids would be camped outside the station every day, and clamoring at the gates of Château Marainte. Powerful people in the film industry would be exerting any and all pressure to prevent their valuable actress from being arrested and convicted. Villagers would be accosted by journalists looking for anyone who had seen the couple together or even set foot in Château Marainte for any reason whatsoever.

And he himself would quickly become more despised than anyone else involved. Maron did not fear that. To his mind, the question he needed to answer first was simply whether someone like Esmé Ridding was too famous for jail. Whether she was too important to too many powerful people, and he would not be allowed to push forward no matter what evidence he had in hand. Would a swarm of defense attorneys descend on the gendarmerie, disallowing evidence and muddying his case? Would they malign his integrity, even have him transferred?

Maron knew that for him this was brand new territory, and he did not have the experience to navigate it. Again he wished Dufort were still in town and he could consult with him. Sure, Dufort was a small-town fellow and did not have the requisite experience either, but he was level-headed and would at least know whom to ask for advice and counsel. And more important, villagers trusted him implicitly.

He could see it now:

ESMÉ MURDERS BARON BOYFRIEND

The Daily Mail couldn't write a more explosive headline.

Paul-Henri was constantly bragging about his big-city connections, and with distaste, Maron realized that he might actually be of some help on a case like this. Maybe the mother he droned on about endlessly might know someone who would be willing to advise them about the publicity angles. Maron was confident about the police work, finding the evidence and building the case against her. The actress had been seen at the château the night of the murder, she had lied about the state of her relationship with the baron, and she had threatened him with the murder weapon not a week before he was killed.

Yes, he was confident about the case all right. It was all the rest of it—an out-of-control press, public opinion, her rich backers—that was making him worry, and wish for the millionth time that he was not acting chief. Maron was not going to go off half-cocked and make an arrest—not yet. Given her celebrity, he understood that a confession was his best chance for bringing her to justice, so while he would pressure the forensics team to see if they could come up with anything else, he tried to think of how in the world to make that happen.

❧

HE HAD no idea where Frances had gone off to, which Nico did not like. For the second day in a row, he had woken up alone, the apartment empty, no note. He put on water for coffee, then threw on a pair of gym shorts and went outside to the small porch where he kept his weight-lifting equipment. He lay down, closing his eyes as though to shut everything out—including his anxiety over Frances—and bench-pressed, exhaling as he lifted the bar, then breathing noisily in through his nose, six repetitions, his muscles nearly failing on the final lift.

Nico ducked into the kitchen to pour water into the coffee press, then back to the porch for squats and then rows, until the coffee was made and his exercise finished.

Alphonse wasn't expecting him at Chez Papa until eleven. He ate a prune yogurt and neatened up, washing a few dishes Frances had left in the sink. He showered and got dressed, then sat on the sofa flipping through a magazine, which, like almost every magazine in the country, had photographs of Esmé Ridding all through it. Esmé in a slinky, glittering gown at a movie première; Esmé in a bikini, glamorously stretched out on a beach, in a perfume ad; Esmé showing a sad face to the paparazzi as she left the hottest restaurant in Paris with one of her girlfriends.

She is stunning, no question about that. What did she see in Marcel, he wondered.

The apartment felt like a tomb without Frances there to liven things up. Nico had had a steady stream of girlfriends ever since he was a teenager, but he had never really fallen in love before. It was news to him that this thing people talked about so reverently was so painful and difficult. Even so, he would do anything for her. Anything.

He managed to fritter away the rest of the time before he had to leave for work, but before leaving, he checked under the bed to make sure his overnight bag was there. He knew it almost certainly was; it wasn't as though Frances spent any time vacuuming up dust bunnies under there or anything like that. Pulling it out, he unzipped it and looked inside to reassure himself: his passport, change of clothes, a thick sheaf of euros that were his bar tips for many months.

All set, if it came to that.

26

Molly had no trouble recognizing Esmé even though she was wearing a headscarf and sunglasses, and by the size of the group of paparazzi waiting outside the restaurant, she wasn't the only one. The maitre d' showed her to Esmé's table, but before she could sit down Esmé jumped up to kiss cheeks.

"Thanks a million for meeting me. I'm just so, so sorry about last night," she whispered in Molly's ear.

I bet, thought Molly.

"And it's, well, you know...*so* awkward, now that we've met under those...circumstances. I've heard about your work and had tried to get in touch with you, but now I'm afraid...you won't be interested in anything I have to say."

"Heard of my work?"

"Of course. After Marcel...once he...after the murder, I spoke to the local gendarme. Jérome? Gilles? I forget his name. Between you and me, he did not inspire confidence. It's extremely important to me, you must understand, that justice is served in this case. I wondered if there was anyone else in Castillac who might be able to do something, to find the person who...and right off, once I started asking around, your name came up."

Molly was both thrilled and utterly uncomfortable. She knew she was being flattered, yet the delicious sensation of it was hard to reject.

"I only came to Paris looking for some property of the baron's," Molly said.

"Right," said Esmé with a twinkle in her eye.

Any advertising firm would pay a couple million for that twinkle, thought Molly, trying to hold on to a semblance of objectivity and not get sucked in by the actress's charm.

She spoke, trying not to sound judgmental. "Look, let's just get it out in the open, all right? I understand I don't have any standing in this situation—Marcel wasn't my husband, obviously. But I have to ask—what were you doing in his apartment last night?"

"I imagine that was rather plain."

"I mean—why *there?*"

Esmé picked an olive out of a small dish and chewed it, looking straight at Molly. "I don't know, Molly. It seemed like a good idea at the time. Haven't you ever done anything, um, inexplicable? I am in deep mourning for Marcel and I'm afraid sometimes I find myself doing things, saying things...that perhaps I should not. I can't even express to you how difficult this whole thing has been for me. It's terrible enough when a relationship ends and you have to move on and there's this hole in your life now that this person you cared so much about is gone. But to have to go through that because the man you love was murdered? It's beyond horrible. And to be clear," she added, her dark brown eyes looking deep into Molly's, "I understand perfectly that it is a thousand, a million times worse for poor Marcel, and horrible as well for his wife and children. I am not trying to corner the market on emotional pain."

"So you're saying...the man last night...."

"Oh, he's nothing to me. Nothing! As for him, believe me, I am nothing more than a notch on his belt, something for him to brag about to his friends." She cast her eyes away from Molly for the first time, and ran her fingers along the edge of her napkin, which still sat on the table in the shape of a peacock. "Perhaps I sound ungrateful or whiny about my good fortune, but when you get to be as famous as I am, it is almost impossible to have a normal interaction with a man. I am no longer just a woman, no longer even human—I am a character from one of my movies, or some kind of untouchable icon, something inert to put on a shelf and prove your own worth through owning it, do you see what I mean?

"Like *La Sfortuna*," said Molly.

"Rather," agreed Esmé. "Though that is not why Marcel loved it. He only cared about it because it reminded him of his beloved sister."

"That's what I've heard. But I wonder. Marcel had all those trophy heads in his salon—animals he shot and stuffed for his wall. So maybe he was more of a collector in that way than you think he was."

"Oh no," laughed Esmé. "Of course I have never been to his salon at Château Marainte, but he described it to me. I heard about those beastly heads, if you will excuse the pun!" Her eyes twinkled again, and Molly tried and failed to figure out whether the effect was makeup, or personality, or acting. "Marcel had nothing to do with them, Molly. Not my dear *Petit Ours*. You have to understand, Château Marainte has been in his family for hundreds of years. Most of it—the furniture and the decoration—has been exactly the same ever since he was born, and for untold years before that. Some ancestor shot those animals and put them on the wall, not my Marcel. What he hunted, he brought to the table for dinner."

As interesting as it was to watch Esmé do everything she could to defend herself and Marcel from any criticism, Molly did not forget that she was in Paris, at a very good restaurant, and her stomach was growling. She looked over at a pair of waiters standing by who were trying and failing not to stare at Esmé.

"So...you and Marcel were happy together?" asked Molly.

"Rapturously so," said Esmé, a pink glow coming into her cheeks. She had a way of looking so sophisticated and sensuous, but then a gesture or a tone in her voice would sound so girlish, as though she were still around ten years old.

"And the age difference wasn't a problem?"

"No," said Esmé forcefully. "I was trying to explain that to Gilles, the gendarme...that Marcel had a way of looking at me, of seeing right down through me in a way no one else ever has. Or ever will," she finished, her voice breaking.

Oh that's just going over the top, thought Molly.

"You ever fired a shotgun?" she asked, nonchalantly.

Esmé laughed, and the waiters all turned to gaze upon her. "My grandfather taught me how to shoot when I was a girl. I never actually shot anything except a few tin cans off a fence. But yes, Molly, I can handle a gun if I need to. Can you?"

"What do you say we go ahead and order? It's been a long day already and it's barely the afternoon."

"I'm terribly hungover myself. I think I'll just have some soup."

"But—here? In a three-star restaurant, only soup?"

Esmé shrugged, leaving Molly to figure out that coming to good restaurants was simply where she had meals, and nothing to mark down on her calendar as notable.

❧

ACROSS TOWN, in a less distinguished arrondissement than the one where Molly and Esmé were having lunch, Alexandre Roulier lay back on a hotel bed looking up at the ceiling, which was not marred by cobwebs or a sloppy paint job, though it was too plain for his tastes. He much preferred a coffered ceiling or elaborate moulding of the kind that takes a fleet of cleaners to keep dust-free, but alas, that is not the sort of room one gets for the amount of money he currently had to spend. He was far from broke, but at the moment his liquidity was not what he might have wished.

Though as ever, he expected that to change very, very soon.

He had spent two full days at the hunting lodge in the baron's forest, turning the place inside-out looking for *La Sfortuna*, with no luck. It had taken half a day to find his way out of the forest, and only by the kindness of a farmer on a tractor giving him a ride had he gotten back to what passed for civilization in that part of the country.

The desire for the jewel burned just as bright, despite his failing to find it. Sticking to his idea that the hiding place of the stone was in some way connected to hunting, Alexandre closed his eyes and concentrated, remembering the one time Marcel had held the emerald out to him, allowing him to cup it in his palm, its green light sparkling even in a dimly lit room.

Come to me.

Maybe Marcel had sewn it up in one of those stuffed heads, he thought. But there was no way to take them down and cut them to pieces to find out, not without getting tossed out of the château for good.

Then, much as he would like to think about *La Sfortuna* all day, he got up and sat at the small desk, opening his laptop. His other business didn't stand still just because he was on the trail of a fortune, and he ran through various spreadsheets, caught up on email, and made some trades on the *Bourse* with money he had successfully laundered.

After a few hours, Alexandre got up to stretch his legs and shoulders. He unwrapped a piece of butterscotch candy and sucked on it. Nodding to himself, he picked up a throwaway cell and tapped in a number he had committed to memory.

"Yes. It's me. What we discussed? I want it done as soon as possible...yes, that's right. Just do it." He hung up, called room service, and ordered a gigantic lunch.

There was nothing quite like ordering a hit to stir his appetite.

27

Another careful sweep of Marcel's apartment had garnered Molly exactly nothing: no emerald, and not so much as a hint of a whisper of a clue about who might have killed him. She had gone through his desk and bedside table looking for letters or notes. She had riffled through all the books on his bookshelf, though there were not very many. She had looked in trash cans, but the cleaning service was efficient and there was nothing in them. As far as Molly could tell from spending time in his apartment, Baron Marcel de Fleuray had been a man whose complications were hidden; his outward life was one of simplicity, despite his title. The apartment was roomy but not conspicuously so. He did not have many belongings. The view was unremarkable, the furnishings of good quality but not luxurious.

Marcel read Wendell Berry and the essays of Montaigne. A handful of pheasant feathers lay on the mantel. The kitchen was tiny, but looked well used, so Marcel—or someone—cooked, and he did not appear to spend all his evenings out. There was no television or computer. The closet had a few good suits, but far more clothes for the outdoors—waders for fly-fishing, waxed jackets for crashing through underbrush, sturdy boots, various garments in camouflage. She looked for more photographs, feeling trepidation about seeing more photographs of Nico, but none were displayed and none hidden as far as she could find.

Molly considered staying another night in Paris, not because there was anything left to do at Marcel's, but just because...*Paris*. But she knew she couldn't afford any more meals out, and besides, she was feeling pangs of homesickness. On the train back to Castillac, Molly went over the details in her mind, trying to picture Marcel in his apartment, going about his business unobserved. Given the lack of entertainment options, she concluded that he must have spent most of his time traveling out of the city, perhaps to the hunting and fishing preserves of his friends, or in company, romantic or otherwise. Was he really as uncomplicated as that? Just a good-looking man of aristocratic blood who preferred to be in nature, with the odd dalliance on the side?

As for Esmé, Molly did not know what to think. She was false, certainly, a great pretender. Always taking the moment by the hand and working to make it more dramatic. Molly had found having lunch with her to be exhausting. But had the actress's flair for drama led her to shoot her lover?

Well, maybe.

Though Esmé had just told her she hadn't ever been in Marcel's salon, and there was no question that was where the murder took place; Molly had seen the bloodstain on the rug.

Of course—the actress could easily be lying.

It would be such a relief if Esmé were the killer, Molly thought. Anything to get Nico out from under suspicion. But, she reminded herself, as far as she knew, she was the only person who had any questions about Nico at all. She wondered what evidence Maron might have uncovered, and how he would react if she paid him a visit—just to say hello, of course.

The train ride was uneventful and Molly was in Castillac before she knew it. Her scooter was locked up outside the station, only a little damp from a recent rain. She rode toward La Baraque, very happy to be home even though she'd only been gone one night. She looked forward to meeting the new guests and hoped Constance hadn't found a way to irritate them. When she pulled into the driveway, Bobo leapt up in a crazy dance of welcome, and Molly saw Constance's bike leaning against the side of the house.

"Coo-coo!" she called, coming inside.

"Molls!" called Constance, who was lying on the sofa with her feet up, reading a magazine. "Hey! How was Paris? The Chubbs are super cool, no worries! Bobo and I have been having a high old time, eating liver for breakfast and chasing balls in the backyard."

Molly laughed. "So the Chubbs settled in okay? Did they get here on time?"

"More or less. Ervin owns a nightclub in New York City. He says anytime I come to New York, he'll comp me the whole time I'm there. Molly, I *live* for nightclubs!"

"Then why on earth do you live in Castillac?"

"Good point. Maybe I'll try to convince Thomas to move to New York. At least then he might be out of the clutches of *her,*" she said, pointing at the cover of her magazine, which featured none other than Esmé Ridding.

Molly laughed again, not sure why. Because everywhere she looked, there was Esmé? Because she realized that, having been away for the first time since moving to Castillac, La Baraque was truly home now, in a way that no other place had been?

"So listen, if you think I've spent the whole time lying around reading magazines, you're all wrong. You said something about your plan for a cooking contest, and I've been giving it a lot of thought. Wanna sit down and do some strategizing, or do you have other stuff to take care of first?"

Molly thought a moment. If only she had found that damn emerald. She let out a long sigh.

"Okay, Constance, lay it on me. Amaze me with your brilliance."

"No need to get sassy," said Constance, looking a little hurt.

Molly went to a drawer and got out a pad of paper and a pen. "I don't mean to sound sarcastic," she said. "I'm just crabby because...well, never mind, let's get to work."

"Awesome! So I was thinking, look, those successful TV shows, why not just copy what they do? People will get a kick out of it even though obviously they won't be getting on TV. I was thinking we could have three cooks, all making the same dish. A panel of judges, natch."

"Is my kitchen big enough to handle three cooks at once?"

"No way. You're going to have to use the *cantine* at the school."

"Hmm. Well, I do know Caroline Dubois, who works in the school office. Not sure she likes me very much though."

"Oh, that's just Caroline! She's always been a big grouch. I'll ask her if you want?"

"Thank you! I'll talk to Edmond at Pâtisserie Bujold about being a judge. Maybe Nathalie from La Métairie. And...Lapin? Just for laughs?"

Constance nodded and let out a cackle. "He'll love it. So...just figure out what the dish is they're going to make, do some publicity, and you're on the road to riches." Constance gave Bobo one last pat and jumped up to go. "But Molls? Explain to me how you're making any money on the deal?"

"I'm going to sell snacks during the show."

"Snacks?"

"Every time I say the word 'snacks', some French people give me the side-eye. Okay, they're not snacks, they're hors d'oeuvres, and we'll do the show at *apéro* time and serve drinks too, how about that?"

"Nailed it," said Constance happily. "Do I get a cut of the profits?"

"Want to serve?"

"I'm...I'm gonna be absolutely honest, because you know I love you like a sister...I've been fired from a...a few waitressing jobs. It's not my best thing. But I'm game to give it another try!"

Molly smiled weakly. If only she had found that emerald, she wouldn't need to go through all this bother just to scrape together a living. The dream of sudden and complete relief from her financial bind was so tantalizing...but she squared her shoulders, said goodbye to Constance, and prepared to push thoughts of murder and jewels aside, and buckle down to the business of making the contest a success.

❧

THE NEXT MORNING Molly spent a solid couple of hours writing out a to-do list for the contest, making some calls, and choosing which *hors d'oeuvres* to make. She knocked on the door of the cottage but the Chubbs's car was gone and so were they. As for *La Sfortuna*, she reminded herself that she might as well depend on playing the lottery to improve her financial situation. Not only that, it was seeming more and more likely that the murderer had made off with the emerald anyway, simply removing it from the baron's trouser pocket where everyone said he kept it most of the time. Molly told herself these things, yet after her chores were done and she found herself more or less at loose ends, she drove out to Château Marainte, dropping by Pâtisserie Bujold on her way to make sure Edmond was on board to be a judge at the contest. As she expected, he readily agreed.

After crossing the drawbridge and entering the courtyard, Molly was surprised to see Antoinette sitting on a bench next to one of the parterres, hands in her lap, Grizou by her side.

"Bonjour, Antoinette!" she said, leaning down to kiss cheeks. "I don't remember a bench being here, but it's in a very nice spot."

"Hubert arranged it for me," said Antoinette. "It's nice to sit here and feel the warmth of the sun, even this late in October." She leaned her head back slightly and closed her eyes, just as a cloud passed over the sun. She was dressed in a long tweed skirt and leather boots that looked so soft Molly wanted to touch them. "At any rate, I am glad you've returned. I expect you had no luck in Paris, or you'd have called me?"

"I'm sad to say you're right. Marcel's apartment was in good order, not crowded with a lot of stuff, so there weren't that many places to look. I didn't find *La Sfortuna*."

I did find Esmé Ridding without any clothes on, but you don't need to know that.

"Ah, well. In that case, I'm glad you've come back to the château for another look around. And," she said, lowering her voice even further, "that odious Alexandre Roulier has come back, and...I don't like to say so, but I don't like him, Molly. Heaven knows why Marcel had anything to do with that sort of person. He must have come back to sniff around after the emerald, and I don't know how to get rid of him."

"Can't you tell him you're sorry, but you're not up to having visitors right now?"

"I've said as much. He responds by going on and on about how he's going to be so helpful to me now that there's not a man in my house. It's as though he wants to point out to me that I'm...more or less alone here, at least a night. Defenseless."

"Oh my. And he and Marcel were friends?"

"Yes. I know at least that Alexandre isn't making that up. Marcel brought him here once, for a hunting party. I never had much to do with any of that, but I do remember meeting him then. I'm probably making more of this than it deserves; at my age, you do feel more vulnerable and I'm doubtless seeing menace where there is none. But—as you go around the château on your search—do keep an eye out for him, just in case. I don't want you to find yourself alone with him in some remote corner of the château."

"I'll do that." Molly reached over to pet Grizou, but the dog kept his eyes on Antoinette, and Molly got the feeling that he was tolerating her attention rather than enjoying it, so she stopped. "Well, on a different subject—I've decided I'm going to hold a cooking contest in the village, possibly as early as next week if I can get it organized. Perhaps you would like to come?"

"A cooking contest?"

"Yes, like the ones you see on TV? We'll give the cooks the same ingredients and see which one makes the best dish. I'll be serving hors d'oeuvres and drinks to the audience."

"I see. And what dish will the cooks make?"

"I haven't quite decided. I was thinking maybe I would give them something that wasn't French, to make it a harder challenge."

"Georgina's gnocchi, perhaps? They're quite famous, at least among our family. She's our housekeeper, not a cook, but occasionally she makes this one dish and all of us go mad for it."

"Mmm, gnocchi. Actually, that's a brilliant suggestion—maybe the challenge is that they all make the same gnocchi but each chef gets to devise his own sauce. How do you like them best?"

"Hard to say," said Antoinette, and her eyes looked lively for the first time in weeks as she considered. "You can't go wrong with simple butter and Parmesan. But the right tomato sauce can be excellent as well, perhaps with a bit of porcini."

"I'm suddenly starving," said Molly, forgetting all about the almond croissant she had eaten a half hour ago while chatting to Edmond Nugent. "All right then. I'll go search for the jewel, and then ask Georgina for that recipe if she'll part with it. Any ideas pop into your head while I was away? Sometimes clues can seem like nothing, and it's only later that you notice them."

The baroness just shook her head and smiled.

"Enjoy the sunshine," Molly added, petting Grizou on the top of his head before heading inside the château.

28

Deciding to talk to Georgina first, Molly found her in a hallway on the second floor by following the sound of the vacuum cleaner.

"Excuse me!" she said, loud enough that Georgina could hear over the machine.

Georgina glared at her and flicked the vacuum off with her foot. Her French was quite good, although she had not moved to France until she was in her twenties, and still spoke Italian at home with her husband. Molly's accent was pretty good—at least it was not burdened with any Bostonian flair—but it was foreign enough to throw Georgina off.

"Sorry to bother you, but I was just talking with Antoinette about a cooking contest I'm hoping to hold soon, for chefs in the village. She was telling me about an amazing recipe you have for gnocchi? That's one of my all-time favorite foods, and I think it would be perfect for the contest if you'd allow it. Of course you would get all the credit for the recipe."

Georgina stepped back. "My grandmother's gnocchi?" She laughed harshly. "Do you think there are many in France who could make gnocchi, even with my recipe? Oh no, Madame Sutton, excuse me for saying it, but you are out of your mind. First of all, making gnocchi takes more than just following a recipe. There is heart and soul that goes into that dish, you understand?"

"Yes! I do understand! And that's why it would be so perfect for a contest. If a chef just follows the directions and that's all...it won't be any good, right?"

Georgina looked up at the ceiling and chewed on her lip. "What kind of credit are you talking about?"

"Well, at the beginning I'll introduce the chefs and explain what the challenge is. I'll say that they're all to make Georgina Locatelli's famous gnocchi, and that they may invent their own sauce to put on it."

"Dio mio!" shrieked Georgina, laughing with a bit more amusement. "You know they will be putting lumps of foie gras in the sauce or some such nonsense!"

Molly laughed. "Well, it'll be interesting to see what they come up with. Please do it, you can stand up and take a bow!"

Georgina crossed her arms and pretended to be annoyed. "Maybe." She did like the idea of being the center of attention. "I suppose it would be a tribute to my grandmother."

"Exactly!"

"Do you want this recipe now? I have it down in the kitchen, written out on an old piece of stationery of my grandmother's. God rest her soul."

"Right now would be terrific. One less thing for me to worry about later." The two women walked down the long hallway on the way to the kitchen, Molly glancing in rooms along the way. "I hear Monsieur Roulier is back," she said, offhandedly.

"Horrible beast," said Georgina simply. "If Doriane could see the type of person her brother started to hang out with—"

Molly realized that Georgina was a far better informant than

Antoinette about what went on in the château, and kicked herself for not seeing it sooner. "So I was wondering, because he's a friend of mine," she said slowly, "I saw Nico in the salon, and was curious about what he was doing there?"

Georgina snapped her head in Molly's direction, her eyes wide. "What?"

"Nico. The bartender at Chez Papa. In the baron's salon?"

Georgina stopped walking and put her hands over her face. "I did not wish this!" she cried out.

Molly had that tingly feeling she got when the landscape of a case was about to change dramatically. She waited for the housekeeper to continue.

"But how did you find out he was here?" Georgina asked. "I thought I was the only one who knew. I would never, ever have said a word about it. Did Nico himself tell you what happened?"

Molly looked confused.

"I would have taken that secret to my grave, Madame Sutton. I would do anything for the boy, you must understand—"

Molly stared. "Wait, are you saying he was here, in person? Not just his photograph?"

Georgina looked stricken. "The photograph!"

The housekeeper kept talking. She rattled on about gnocchi, her grandmother, and then back to what a pig Alexandre Roulier was, but Molly was barely listening. Through the jumble of their miscommunication—with each speaking in a second language, it was no surprise—she had gotten the point that Georgina was trying so hard to cover up, which was that Nico had been at Château Marainte, in the flesh, the night of the murder.

He had been there. And hadn't told anyone.

ALEXANDRE WAS UP LATE. The château was hardly a place of

hustle and bustle; nevertheless, he felt less constrained moving about the place late at night, when he was fairly sure the baroness was in bed, the ill-tempered housekeeper had gone home, and he could search for the emerald at leisure. He had gone through all the rooms on every floor of the wing where his bedroom was, and the rooms the family regularly used as well. That left the north wing, which apparently the housekeeper ignored. It was quite dusty, and many rooms were empty of furniture. In some were stacks of cardboard boxes, while a few others were piled with furniture that was woefully in need of repair or reupholstering.

By this point, Alexandre had a system: he used the flashlight on his phone to get around without bumping into things, because the darkness was complete in the château. He felt underneath tables and looked behind curtains and books on bookshelves. He checked armoires and drawers and any container that was closed. As he went along, he snapped a few pictures on his phone of things he found interesting, such as a lamp that was a life-sized bronze sculpture of a naked goddess holding a wreath of light-bulbs over her head, and a round stained-glass window depicting what looked like marijuana leaves.

But he was not there to sight-see, and as his interests did not especially lie in the direction of architectural novelties and antiques, he advanced more quickly through the rooms, not bothering to put anything back after moving it, not caring about his footprints in the dust.

He reached the last room on the top floor, pausing briefly in the corridor to look out a window to the courtyard. The moon had come out, bathing the view in a ghostly light, and it occurred to him that what he was seeing at that moment was no different from what Fleurays would have seen from that window three or even four hundred years earlier. The slate of the turrets gleamed in the moonshine. All below was still. He imagined that the circular towers facing the road were crammed with archers, ready to let fly with arrows if anyone were stupid enough to approach in the middle of the night when the moon was shining.

Perhaps Marcel should have been taken out with an arrow, he mused. *Mon Dieu*, he could go on for hours about how much he loved bow hunting—an arrow would have been delicious in a way. But not so reliable, not to mention the awkwardness of carrying and using a bow.

It was very late and Alexandre was getting fatigued. He lifted the latch on the last room and went in. It was smallish, with a pair of made-up single beds and a table between them. An armchair stood in a corner with a blanket folded over its back. Alexandre felt a small surge of optimism because the room was not dusty; someone had been there quite recently.

He stood in the center of the room, closed his eyes, and imagined the jeweled box containing the emerald slowly and inexorably traveling toward him.

"Come closer," he murmured out loud.

A built-in bookshelf ran along part of the wall across from the beds. It was jammed full of children's books and novels for young readers. Alexandre guessed correctly that the room had been a sort of playroom for Doriane and Marcel when they were young. He took out four and five books at a time, looking behind them, and in the process of putting them back, he heard a click, then the sound of wood scraping on wood...and the bookshelf slowly began to move, to rotate.

Alexandre stepped back and watched as a secret compartment —no, a whole room—was revealed behind the bookshelf.

He laughed aloud and ducked his head into the small space, and then squeezed in his whole body, sure that he had found the location of the famous stone. The room was closet-sized, with a tiny round window letting in faint light. He directed his flashlight quickly over the space, to see any particular places where the jeweled box might be tucked, but nothing presented itself. He saw a stuffed pig on the floor, and a dusty puzzle box in a corner.

There was a lumpy chair with a loose pillow, and Alexandre pounced on the pillow, smashing it between his hands, but there was nothing in it but feathers.

On the floor was an empty mug with vestiges of chocolate around the edge, and a book. Alexandre picked up the book and threw it at the wall because there was no place else to search. Then he felt something. A tiny prickle on the back of his neck. His hands were resting on the back of the chair and he picked it up and looked underneath, and to his almost complete surprise, there was the jeweled box, taped to the bottom with a piece of gray duct tape.

Carefully he set the chair down on its side, as gently as though the box were an egg. He pulled at the tape and the box fell straight into his hand. "I knew you would come to me," he breathed, forcing his eyes closed for a split second before unhooking the clasp on the box and opening it.

It was empty.

Alexandre felt a sickening sensation of disappointment flood his belly and he actually thought for a moment he was going to throw up. Still, however—he recovered quickly—the box itself was worth quite a lot. He ran his fingers over the much smaller diamonds and emeralds that covered the top. It looked just as he remembered, exquisitely made with no expense spared.

After stuffing the box in his trousers, he pushed himself back out of the secret room and shoved the bookcase sloppily back in place, then walked to the part of the château where Antoinette lived. She must have the jewel, he reasoned, because otherwise, he would have found it by now. It would have come to him.

When he got to the corridor where her bedroom was, he checked his phone for the time. It was nearly three in the morning. He took a step onto the stone floor, off the Turkish runner, so that his footstep would be as noisy as possible. Then he waited. Two seconds, three. Another loud step. This time, he waited six seconds, then two steps in quick succession.

The irregularity would wake her up, he felt confident, and he was not wrong.

Antoinette lay in bed, eyes wide open, listening. She knew it was Alexandre, knew he was trying to frighten her.

It was working.

29

He wished that coming home was something other than a chore, but since he had never known any different, Percival rode in the taxi up the hill to the château without any expectations of gladness at the sight of the place or its inhabitants. The main childhood memory he had was of trudging around the forest in the freezing cold, trying and failing to defend himself from his father's disappointment. His mother had been kinder, certainly, but far more interested in her dogs and various farm animals than in him. At least, that was how Percival saw it.

The young man grabbed his bag, under-tipped the taxi driver, and crossed the drawbridge. It was early in the morning, and the air was clear and the weather pleasantly chilly, though he did not notice it. He wrenched open the heavy door, calling out, "Maman! Georgina!" but was met with silence.

He wondered idly how much Château Marainte would bring if it were put up for sale, though he knew his mother would never allow it. Enough to solve his current financial trouble, that was for sure. It was humiliating, having to come home to beg, but Percival did not feel it especially; when any inkling of a negative emotion began to bubble up, he stomped it down hard, down and out of sight, where it did not trouble him.

Wandering into the kitchen, he found Georgina sitting at the table eating a piece of toast with apricot jam.

"Bonjour, Percival," she said politely, while grimacing at him.

"Not glad to see me? Make me breakfast," he said, dropping his bag and putting his hands on his hips.

"Make it yourself," said Georgina, taking another bite of toast.

"Do you want me to tell Maman about that night? About what we did before the fête that summer?"

Georgina did not change her expression but inside she was cursing Percival up, down, and sideways. The Fleuray parents weren't half bad, but this child? A complete jerk. *Stronzo*. "There's coffee in the pot. Here's toast," she said, pushing the package toward him.

"I like my toast freshly made," he said, enjoying himself.

"I like to see pigs fly," said Georgina.

"I'll just go find Maman then."

"Oh all right. What do you have in mind, then? Fresh toast and what else? I'm not the cook, you know."

"Toast with strawberry jam and butter. And a cheese omelette. *S'il vous plaît,"* he said, sarcastically.

Both turned as they heard footsteps in the corridor.

"Maman!" shouted Percival, his voice brimming with false joy. "So good to see you. I thought I'd just pop down to give you some company. Paris can be so dreary at this time of year."

"Oh, I doubt that. But it's good to see you again so soon, and very thoughtful of you to come."

"Madame, may I pour you some coffee?"

"That would be lovely, Georgina, thank you. Shall we sit in the lounge, Percival? You can tell me stories about what you do at work that I won't understood a word of."

Percival laughed and took his mother's arm but she pulled away.

"But you must wait a bit, my dear—I'm afraid I slept badly and I'm behind in my chores this morning. The animals still need tending. I'm going to go out to the barn but I'll be right back. Don't harry Georgina while I'm gone," she said with a smile.

"Never," said Percival. He went into the lounge and waited for Georgina to bring his breakfast. Before long, she came in with a tray. She was wearing her usual work outfit: a short dress with an apron and low heels, which might not have been every housekeeper's choice for work clothes but helped Georgina feel a little less resentful about her job than she otherwise would have been.

"Come here," said Percival, as she set the tray on the coffee table. "Sit on my lap," he said, taking hold of the hem of her dress.

But Georgina slapped his hand. "Never in this life," she spat at him, moving quickly through the door and down the corridor.

"I'll have you fired!"

"Be my guest!"

Percival's heart rate had not had time to settle back down after this rejection when Antoinette came back inside and sat on the sofa.

"Eat your eggs before they get cold!" she said, pouring coffee. "Oh, I'm sorry, I'm talking to you as though you're still a child. Sometimes it is hard to stay in the present."

"Dear Maman," said Percival lovingly. "Tell me, what kind of job are the gendarmes doing? Do you think they've figured out who killed Father?"

Antoinette slowly shook her head. "I don't know. I should give Officer Maron a call and ask what progress he's made in the case. I'm afraid it looks like someone came to the château for the emerald, and killed your father in the process."

Percival shook his head. "He should have listened to us and put that thing in the bank where it belonged."

"Yes. Of course. I'm sure all of our lives are filled with moments we wish we could go back and change."

"Very true," said Percival, and his voice got suddenly much

younger. "Speaking of regret, I...there's a situation in my own life..."

Wearily, Antoinette turned to her son. "What is it this time, Percy?"

❧

ONE BIG DIFFERENCE between the States and France was that in France, if money got tight, you couldn't just say oops, overdraw your bank account, and pay a fee. In France, the bank can dump you for that kind of thing.

And Molly did not want to get dumped.

She sat at her desk early that Tuesday morning, glancing from the computer screen to the gray October skies, the ball of anxiety in her belly growing worse by the minute. She needed some cash, and she needed it yesterday. Daydreaming about getting a cut from *La Sfortuna* was not solving the problem. Of course, the sensible thing would be to spend a good month or six weeks organizing the cooking contest. She still needed to find contestants, secure the venue, get the word out, and buy the ingredients and supplies—in other words, everything. But her electricity bill allowed no such luxury of time. She had to make this thing happen, and fast.

So, running down the daunting checklist, she called Nathalie Marchand at La Métairie, who graciously agreed to join Nugent on the panel of judges. Molly was ninety-nine percent sure Lapin would want to do it as well. She wrote out two shopping lists—one for the hors d'oeuvres and drinks she planned to make herself, and another for the ingredients in Georgina's recipe, plus a wide variety of things for the contestants to use in making sauce for the gnocchi.

Oh right, *Georgina*. One thing about money troubles—they have the ability to block out everything else, including anxiety about Nico which was frankly terrifying. All right, she told herself, he didn't actually lie about not being at the château the night of the murder, or about having some relationship with the Fleurays. He just somehow made sure it never came up.

A lie of omission, if it's big enough, is still a lie.

"Come on, Bobo," she said. "Let's go for a walk in the woods before it rains." Bobo perked up and ran in circles, very clear on the meaning of the word 'walk.'

Molly shoved an apple in her pocket and did not bother brushing her tangled hair, but put a cap on instead.

Nico.

The questions were obvious enough: what was his connection to the Fleurays? And why was it secret? And then, the big enchilada: what on earth was he doing at the château on that night of all nights?

Molly's family life growing up had been relatively uncomplicated. Her parents had been decent people who went faithfully to their jobs and took care of their children without much drama. Once Molly was older, she felt distant from them only because her parents' interests were so narrow that they struggled for anything to talk about. Same with her brother. They had not been a close, happy, exuberant family, the kind practically anyone would love to part of—but neither was it ugly or mean.

There had been no skeletons in any closets, no secrets at all, as far as she knew.

And that was the most troubling thing about Nico, as Molly saw it. She could understand not wanting the whole world to know your private thoughts or personal business, but she and Nico were good friends. Not strangers, and not mere acquaintances, but friends. And of course—Frances? How could he keep whatever happened at the château that night from Frances? Even if it was something terrible?

The woods looked almost wintry. The ferns had all died back and the trees were down to their very last leaves. Everywhere she looked were different shades of brown, yellow spotted with brown, faded green, and gray. She understood the cycles of nature and knew that the dying off was necessary to the bursting forth of life in spring, but that didn't make her like it when it was happening.

She heard a church bell tolling, and it made her remember a scene she had witnessed in Castillac earlier in the month: men walking down the sidewalk toward the church with a casket on their shoulders, with women in black following along behind. Autumn is the season of death, and it felt implacable, inescapable, relentless.

Abruptly she called Bobo and turned back toward home. The woods in fall had their particular beauty, but at the moment, she was not in the mood for it. A man had been shot in the face on the same night Nico had been to visit, and she had better find out why before Maron did.

30

To-do list tucked in her bag, Molly sped into the village toward the *primaire*. Constance might have remembered to ask Caroline about using the cantine for the contest, but Molly figured she would confirm in person, wanting to know if that first step was in place before spending any money on ingredients. The school was in the center of town. The offices were in a modern building that had large windows, as Molly remembered from visiting with Ben on an earlier case.

Ben. She didn't even have an address for him, and he had been offline for weeks. Open to anything, Molly tried sending telepathic messages that she needed to speak with him urgently, but apparently those hadn't hit the mark either.

She saw Caroline through the window and waved, hoping she was in a good mood.

"Bonjour, Caroline!" she exclaimed, going a little overboard with friendliness. Caroline kissed cheeks with her and then stepped back, looking suspicious.

"Has Constance come to see you recently?"

Caroline shook her head.

"Well, never mind. I'm sorry to bother you, I'm sure you are overloaded with work this time of year, but I have an idea—something fun for the whole village—and wanted to run it by you and see what you think."

"Yes?" said Caroline doubtfully.

Molly made her pitch. With a flash of inspiration, she suggested that students could act as servers, passing hors d'oeuvres and drinks to the audience while the cooking went on.

"While I appreciate your ingenuity in finding free help, I don't see why our students need to be involved," said Caroline.

"Oh, I didn't mean they need to be. Just if any of them wanted to! And using the cantine is only one of the things I want to ask you about. Obviously I'm going to need contestants as well. Do you have any suggestions for talented cooks who might be interested? How about you?"

Caroline snickered. "I am happy eating potato chips and yogurt," she said. "Believe me, I am not who you are looking for. Besides...."

Molly waited.

"Besides, as long as you're here...I've been wondering...if you've found *La Sfortuna* yet?"

"I thought its existence was a big secret."

"Ha! Haven't you figured out that in Castillac, there are no secrets? Not for long anyway," she added bitterly.

"I do know what you mean. But no, I haven't found it. Do you know the family at all?"

"Hardly. The sons would have been at school before my time, but of course they did not attend the local school in any case. Shipped off somewhere much fancier than here," she said, gesturing across the courtyard to the small *primaire*. Molly smiled at the children tearing around the playground, coats off, though inevitably the sight gave her a pang of yearning.

"Well," said Caroline, "I don't see any reason why you can't use the cantine, as long as we don't have anything scheduled there at the same time. When are you thinking this contest will take place?"

"Friday?"

"My heavens! How will you ever manage to pull it together that quickly?"

"I have no idea. But I'm going to try!"

Her words were brave, but the only thing really driving her was the inbox of unpaid bills that she could no longer push out of her mind. Leaving the school, she pulled her list out of her bag, figuring to knock off another couple of items before swinging by Chez Papa. If she had any luck at all, in the middle of the afternoon Nico would be there alone, and Molly would have a chance to see if he would come clean about the Fleurays and his activities the night of the murder.

She had the unsettling feeling that she was making her way through fog, barely able to see where she was going, and with the ominous sense that unseen danger was all around. Maybe her friend Nico would, finally, provide some clarity.

THE FIRST PART of the afternoon went better than expected. She bought enough glasses for a crowd and had them delivered to La Baraque, same thing for bottles of crème de cassis, since surely kirs would make most of the audience happy. The salesgirl at the kitchen supply shop suggested her neighbor might want to be a contestant. She called while Molly was there. The neighbor was enthusiastic and agreed to do it, although she asked what the prize for winning was and Molly had to tell her it was a secret, something "very good" while feeling aghast that she hadn't even considered prizes yet.

She ended up spending quite a bit at the kitchen supply store, since if you have three chefs working at once, you obviously need three of everything. The plan was happening too quickly, and she knew there would be mistakes and doubtless wasted money along the way, but by then she was like a pony with a bit in its teeth and a view of the barn, with nearly zero chance of changing course.

By three o'clock there was nothing else on the list that she could do just then. It was time to swing by Chez Papa and see Nico. There was a light drizzle, off and on, not too cold. Villagers were mostly inside and the streets were quiet. Chez Papa, Molly was relieved to see, looked empty.

She parked her scooter and came inside. "Hey Nico!" she called. "Bonjour!"

No answer.

Molly plopped onto a stool, trying to quiet the imps of anxiety that were dancing in her head. Then she heard footsteps—heavy footsteps. She jumped off the stool. "Nico?"

Alphonse, the owner of the bistro, swung around the corner, having come from the cooler or the office. He shook his big shaggy head and smiled. "Bonjour, *ma petite chou!* It is magnificent to see you on this gray Tuesday."

They kissed cheeks. "Very nice to see you, too, Alphonse. I guess a drizzly day keeps people home, huh?"

"Eh, it is all right. If this place was filled to the brim every minute, it would run me ragged. Nothing wrong with a slow day every now and then. The space has to breathe too, yes?"

Molly had always thought Alphonse had a mystical side, and she felt pleased at having it confirmed. "Any idea where Nico is?"

"Oh, he'll be back soon enough. The bar is out of lemons, and he ran down to the épicerie to get a bag. Even on dreary days like this, we get children in who want their *citron pressé!* And I, like their mamans, would much rather they drink that than some American soda drink, if you won't be insulted."

"Not at all," said Molly smiling.

"Here he comes now," said Alphonse, gesturing out the big window at the front of the bistro. "I'll be heading back to the office then. A wee bit of paperwork left before I knock off for the day." He gave Molly a wink and lumbered out of sight.

"Bonjour, Molly!" said Nico.

Was she imagining it, or did his face fall just a bit when he saw her?

"Bonjour, Nico. I was hoping you'd be here."

"Looking for a kir and a plate of frites?"

"Well, sure. Can't ever go wrong with those." She paused, unsure how to jump in. "Look, Nico, I've got something a little awkward to ask you about."

He looked up quickly, tilting his head to the side. "Is Frances upset about something?"

"No, no, it's not about Frances. It's about...okay, I'll just start at the beginning. You know that Antoinette de Fleuray has asked me to find *La Sfortuna*?"

"Uh, sure. Any luck with that?"

"No. The point is that of course the château was where I started my search. I went all over, but gave a careful look where the baron spent time, namely his salon." She stopped, watching his face, but Nico's expression did not change. He waited with a look of bland curiosity on his handsome face, but no unease that Molly could discern.

"In the baron's salon, sitting on a bookshelf, is a photograph of you."

Nico jerked his head back, his eyes wide open.

"This is a surprise? I wonder that you didn't know about it, since I was told—and believe me, Nico, I know how awkward this is and I just hope that whatever is going on, whatever happened, you'll just be open with me about it, I'm on your side for God's sake—I was told that you were at the château the night the baron was murdered."

Nico shook his head, smiling. "Oh, is that all? You had me nervous there for a second. It's true, I was there that night. Percival, one of the Fleuray sons, is an old friend of mine. I'd heard he was in town and so I went over to see him. I got there, the housekeeper told me I was mistaken and Percy was in Paris, and I went home. Of course, later, when I heard what had happened, I was stunned. But the murderer must have gotten there after I left, because there were no other cars in the lot at that point, probably around nine o'clock."

"But why keep all that a secret? We were talking right here in Chez Papa about the murder. Wouldn't it be natural, if you had nothing to hide, to say, 'Yeah, whew, I must have nearly crossed paths with a killer!'"

Nico shrugged and began making Molly a kir. "I guess I could have. But you know, the Fleurays have never mixed with the village much. People don't know them, they're this family of aristocrats living in the huge château on the hill, looking down at everyone in Castillac. I figured it would make people uncomfortable, like I was trying to show off my connection with the upper class."

Molly thought this over. "Okay, I sort of get that. But why wouldn't you at least tell Frances? You're all 'love of my life' and marriage and everything...well, wouldn't that mean sharing who your friends are?"

"I guess you're right. I don't...it's just been a sort of habit, you understand. But of course I could have told Frances, I only didn't because I honestly didn't think of it at the time."

"You men and the way you shove different parts of your lives into boxes!"

"Are making a sexist remark in my bar?" Nico deadpanned.

Molly laughed. "Hurry up with those frites, will you? I could eat a horse."

"Well, you *are* in France. You probably have."

Molly looked at Nico in pretend shock, but underneath she was feeling tremendously relieved. She had hoped so hard for a reasonable explanation and felt she had gotten it. She crossed Nico off her mental list of suspects for the baron's murder.

Problem was, now there was no one on it at all.

31

It was after dinner in the middle of the week. Although Esmé had been invited to several parties, they weren't personal invitations made by anyone who actually wanted her company. They were either from people she'd barely met who wanted to be able to brag about a connection with Esmé Ridding, or by companies who wanted publicity for some product or another. And she had far too much of that already in her work for Chanel.

She was hungry, but used to it. Dinner had been salad with only a small scrap of fish on the side, and an even smaller spoonful of sauce on it. Esmé put on a raincoat and a hat she could pull down so as not to be recognized, and went out for a pint of ice cream.

Double brownie chocolate chip, to be exact, from the only place she knew of to get American ice cream, the glorious Ben & Jerry's brand, at a hole in the wall down the block.

And so she was sitting on the sofa with a dishtowel spread across her lap eating the ice cream out of the container with a big spoon and watching music videos when her agent called.

"A thousand apologies, darling, you can't imagine how difficult everyone has been. I swear, *The Kruger Protocol* that flopped last month? It's got everyone so on edge. Anyway. I've got some very good news. They want you for the lead in something Bishop is doing next year, I've already sent the script over tonight."

Esmé sighed, long and loudly.

"What? You said you were dying to get back to work! This part is perfect for you, absolutely perfect!"

"I'll read it when it gets here," Esmé said dully.

"It will be there in two minutes. It might already be there! Buck up, darling, you're going to love it, I'm telling you. Although, a few minor things—there always are, aren't there? You will have to ride; that's not a problem, is it?"

"Of course not. You've seen me on horseback before, you ninny."

"And—this is awkward—but they want to know if you have any experience...if you can handle a gun."

Esmé rolled her eyes. "Really, that's what they're asking? Is this even a legit offer?"

"Of course it is, darling, you know I don't wast my time otherwise."

"Well tell 'em I can shoot all right. Pistol, rifle, *shotgun*. If they give me a bad guy, I'll blow him right off the screen."

❧

MOLLY HAD BEEN PLANTED on her stool at Chez Papa for hours. Once Nico had reassured her about his involvement with the Fleurays, she almost relaxed and enjoyed bantering with him like old times. Then friends starting to drift in—first Lawrence, then Lapin, followed by Frances. Each arrival caused a flurry of greetings and cheek-kissing, and then inevitably, the newcomer asked Molly about progress on the baron's case.

"I swear, people, you aren't listening to me! I'm not *on* the case. With Ben being away, I have no way to get inside information. No idea what the forensic evidence is, or how Maron is doing with his interviews. I know he's spoken to the baroness and Georgina, I can tell you that much, though that's pretty obvious."

"Do you think any of us believe that for one second?" said Lawrence affectionately. "Especially since you've been given a pass to roam all over Château Marainte looking for *La Sfortuna*? And by the way, how's that going? I assume you haven't found it?"

"Are you kidding? If I had, my screams would have been heard all over the Dordogne."

"Well, at least you have a guest now, right?"

"One guest does not a positive cash flow make," said Molly. "But you're right, I should look at the bright side. And the cooking contest is coming along nicely—I hope you're all planning to be there? This Friday night at the cantine. I do need one more contestant...."

"Nico!" shouted Frances. "Come on, you'd be perfect!" she said, as he shook his head.

"I'm not...really don't...."

But Frances got a chant started and everyone in the bar was saying, "Ni-co! Ni-co!" until he shrugged and said yes.

"So what's involved, exactly?" he asked.

"The three contestants will be making the same dish, which is a surprise. One hint: it's not French. Well, two hints: it's something that requires a sauce. So all three of you will make the same dish, but decide on your own sauce once you see the variety of ingredients I have on hand. The panel of judges will taste what everyone makes and decide on a winner."

"What does the winner get?" asked Frances.

"Um, good question," said Molly. "Any ideas for a good prize? Satisfaction in winning has got to count for something."

"Maybe something from my shop?" said Lapin.

"Great, I slave all night and come out with a broken chair!" said Nico, making the others laugh.

Lawrence looked down at his phone. "Not to change the subject," he said, "but apparently Maron is headed to Paris on police business. Are you thinking what I'm thinking?"

The bar was silent.

"He's going after Esmé Ridding," said Lapin. "I knew she was a real firecracker!"

Molly looked at Nico and grinned. His explanation had soothed her anxiety, but the news that Maron was interested in Esmé calmed her even more. An arrest of the most famous face in all of France might even bring more business to Castillac, mightn't it, if that wasn't an entirely selfish thought?

"Hey Nico," she said, "make me a Negroni, will you? I feel like celebrating."

Lawrence smiled and put his arm around her. "Only one, my dear, or I'll have to bring you home with me to keep you out of trouble."

Molly laughed. "Hey, where's Stephan?"

Lawrence raised his eyebrows. "Must people be joined at the hip if they're seeing each other? Stephan and I are fine. But he does not understand the Negroni. Or Chez Papa, for that matter."

Molly nodded, but inwardly she thought, okay, that's the kiss of death. But before getting sidetracked by the subject of Lawrence's love life, she wanted to hear more about Maron and Esmé.

"So do you have more information than that? I haven't seen Maron in ages, no idea what he's been doing. Do you think he's headed to Paris for an arrest, or just further questioning?"

"Can't say," said Lawrence. "But I don't see how either way is any good for Miss Ridding. Much as I admire her."

"Yeah," said Nico dreamily, and Frances threw an olive at him and hit him square on the forehead.

It was a wonderful evening, that Tuesday. The contest was coming together beautifully, suspicion was off her friend, and the Negroni further lifted Molly's spirits. That's the thing about betrayal, isn't it—you don't see it coming until it smacks you right in the back of the head.

32

The news that Maron was headed to Paris to see Esmé Ridding alone did not shock Paul-Henri, since from the beginning of the case Maron had shut him out at every turn. He had hoped his mother's bit of gossip about the baron and Esmé would be useful enough to make Maron less selfish and allow him into the process even if only for consultation. But no, Paul-Henri was sent out to find lost dogs and lost husbands with dementia until he thought he would die of boredom.

At least Maron was away and Paul-Henri was captain of the ship for two whole days. He performed a thorough cleaning of the station and checked his uniform, making sure buttons were polished and creases pressed perfectly. And then, because he didn't know what else to do, he went out and walked the streets like Maron usually did, keeping an eye on the village, and making an effort to listen when anyone had something to tell him.

Meanwhile, as his train sped toward Paris, Maron methodically went over the facts of his case. The baron had been shot with his own shotgun at close range. According to Nagrand the coroner, the Holland & Holland shotgun—the murder weapon—

was designed to kill nothing larger than a pheasant, so it was possible that the shot had been impulsive and not meant to kill him. The baron usually kept an extremely valuable jewel on his person that was still unaccounted for. His mistress, Esmé Ridding, was the only person apart from the family and staff who visited the château that night, as far as they knew; her sports car was seen tearing down the drive at a high speed around midnight.

And the pièce de résistance, Esmé had written an angry letter to the baron specifically mentioning shooting him. But it was that letter, oddly enough, that made Maron distrust his conclusion. Or —not distrust entirely—but the letter gave him pause, because it simply seemed too neat, too obvious, and in his limited experience with murder cases, they had been neither.

He had leaned on Nagrand and the forensics team for something more, anything at all, but they had not been forthcoming. There was some DNA in Marcel's salon that could not be assigned to any of the people they knew had been there that night, but that wasn't unusual. Tradespeople and visitors, out-of-town relatives, guests to the baron's hunting parties—any of them might have left behind a hair or a thread that Georgina had missed in her cleaning.

The gun had been wiped clean, which was evidence of knowledge of guilt, but no help in pointing out whose.

So forensics was a bust, and there was no eyewitness. The only way the case was going to be solved was through a confession.

Maron was a solid detective, more skilled than he gave himself credit for. And he was not a complete pushover when it came to beautiful women. But Esmé Ridding...she was not just any beautiful woman. She was the glamorous, seductive women in movies he'd seen for the last fifteen years. She was, no exaggeration, a goddess, her image and voice everywhere.

The train pulled into the station at Montparnasse, and Maron impatiently waited for the doors to open. Now that he was close, he wanted nothing more than to face his suspect, get her talking, and wrap the whole thing up. He hustled through the crowd and out onto the street, hailing a taxi and giving the address in the 6th arrondissement. The sights and sounds of Paris were lost on him as he focused on his opening gambit and the few questions he had thought of to prompt Esmé to open up to him.

❧

A LOT CAN GET DONE in a few days if you're motivated enough, and Molly absolutely was. She tacked posters up all over the village and in Bergerac as well, advertising the contest as *Chef du Monde*—perhaps overstating it a little bit, but hey, that's what puts fannies in seats, right?

The three contestants were briefed on the rules and busy making what few advance preparations they could, given that they were not told what they would be making. The panel of judges was enthusiastic and ready. Since she wasn't selling tickets but putting on the contest for free, Molly had no way of knowing what kind of crowd to expect, but word on the street was positive. She had lucked out and chosen a weekend when the weather was supposed to be mild, and nothing else was going on.

Thursday and much of Friday she spent preparing hors d'oeuvres. Devils on horseback (bacon-wrapped prunes), a fluted little paper with a mouthful of tuna tartare, ham-butter cornichons on slices of baguette, mushroom pâté with toasted baguette to smear it on, deviled eggs, and savory *sablés* made with rosemary and thyme. Her kitchen smelled amazing as she baked, chopped, and cleaned, then did it all again for the next group of appetizers. By lunchtime on Friday, the day of, Molly was about to drop from exhaustion, but took a break and went over to the cottage to see how the Chubbs were doing on their last full day at La Baraque.

"Molly!" said the jovial Ervin. "I was just going to come have a word with you. Sissy and I have had such a fantastic time here, we were wondering if it might be possible for us to stay on another week?"

Molly beamed, hoping the dollar signs weren't popping up in her eyes like in a cartoon. (Or euro signs, she reminded herself.) "Of course you can stay longer! This is something of a slow time for tourists, though that just makes everything better for you. No lines, no crowds...."

"We've spent the last week doing some high-octane sightseeing—went to Rocamadour, saw the cave paintings at Lascaux, which were incredible, the chateaux at Beynac and Castelnaud. Our life in New York is so hectic—up half the night at the club, tearing around all day with so much to do and people to see, you understand—so what we'd really like to do this week is hang around La Baraque, read, and take long naps. Sissy's taking one now, actually."

Molly nodded. "La Baraque is excellent for reading and napping, I can vouch for that. You're welcome to stay as long as you like. I know you just told me you want to stay in and recharge, but just to let you know—I'm putting on a cooking contest in the village this evening. It's nothing sophisticated like you'd find in Paris or New York, but you might find seeing a slice of the village entertaining. Now, I wish I could stay and chat but I've got a ton of stuff to do to get ready."

"Go go go!" said Ervin, gesturing to the door. "Tonight sounds fun. You may see us there."

"The cantine, center of town—"

"Wonderful!"

Molly hurried back to her house and leaned on the kitchen counter, staring at the master list. Lapin had come over with his truck earlier and taken a load of stuff to the cantine, so that was done. The food was prepped and ready to go. All she had to do was shower and get dressed, and then head over to the cantine to set out chairs and get the equipment organized.

"What do you think, Bobo? Am I out of my mind?"

The speckled dog nuzzled Molly's hand, giving her some comfort as the specter of unpaid bills loomed up in her thoughts again. Tonight's just got to work, she thought. Or I'll be trying to convince the Chubbs that candles really are better than having electric lights.

33

To Molly's delight, the cantine was packed a full half hour before showtime. Sensibly, everything was meant to be served at room temperature, so there was no worry about keeping food hot. To make things even easier, she decided to charge one rate for an hors d'oeuvres plate consisting of a variety of nibbles, rather than having people pick and choose. At that point, Molly had sampled so many *sablés* and devils on horseback during the cooking that they no longer looked all that appealing, but the audience was gobbling them up with gusto. Constance was helping serve the plates and running back and forth to peek through the window in the kitchen door as the cantine filled up.

"My God, Molls, I think you may really have hit on something! Everyone and his night nurse is out there!"

"Huh?"

"Do you think I should put two deviled eggs per plate or just one? And listen, I heard Esmé Ridding is going *down* for the baron's murder!" she chirped happily.

"I heard the same," said Molly. "I think one deviled egg per plate is fine. Make sure to add a little parsley on the side, yep, that's it. Whew," she said, peering out at the crowd. "I can't believe this is actually happening."

"Look, when I hand over the plate and take their money, where do I put it?"

"Didn't think of that. Just shove it in your pocket for now. If your pockets get too full—and I hope they will—just put the money in my bag, over there in the corner. It'll be safe there, don't you think?"

Constance shrugged. "The way Castillac is these days? All bets are off." But she winked as she backed up to the swinging door and pushed her way to the other side.

Twenty minutes until showtime.

Thomas was pouring kirs and two of his teenage cousins were boisterously handing them out. Two of the three contestants milled in the crowd, talking to friends and supporters. The shop-girl's neighbor, Anne-Marie Poulin, a grandmother famous in the village for her soufflés, wore a snowy white apron and toque. Molly had found the second contestant thanks to a suggestion from Madame Tessier, who knew more about the villagers than they knew about themselves, and was always happy to lend her advice and opinion on any subject at all. He was a teenager named Hugo Sargent, who had another year before finishing at the *lycée*. He had ambitions of becoming a famous chef and the minute he heard from Molly, he had texted back that he was thrilled to participate; she found out later that his parents wanted him to be a doctor and were thoroughly against their son doing anything related to cooking.

Well, when you're putting on a show, it's always good to have a little tension, right?

Nico was the third contestant, but so far he was nowhere in evidence.

Lapin had banged together a small raised platform where the judges sat, near enough that they could watch the chefs closely. And he had talked the cooking supply company into bringing three used stoves and setting them up so that the audience could observe every step as well. Nathalie Marchand sat looking amused, chic as ever, while Nugent prattled on in her ear, so besotted that he seemed on the verge of producing a knife and fork so that he could eat her up. Lapin was everywhere at once, making sure the stoves all worked, setting up more chairs, welcoming people at the door, and generally being a stand-up guy.

Molly had a quick flash, remembering her terrible opinion of Lapin when she had first met him. Just goes to show that first impressions can be wildly wrong, she thought. Sometimes what you see when you first meet someone is entirely misleading.

She went back in the kitchen to set up more plates for Constance to take out, and once she was caught up there, to the front door to greet people as they came in. And they kept coming and coming, *Chef du Monde* proving itself to be the social event of the season, outdoing even the gala if number of attendees were the only measure.

Ten minutes until showtime. *Where is Nico?*

Molly grinned, seeing Antoinette, Percival, and Georgina walking across the playground on their way to the cantine. "So happy you could come!" she said, in a flurry of cheek-kissing. Antoinette was dressed elegantly in a long gray skirt with a black velvet blazer, while Georgina looked ready to go clubbing in a super-short dress with makeup troweled on.

"Of course, we are tremendous fans of Georgina's gnocchi," said Antoinette. "And maybe...it is past time for us to be more involved in village life."

Molly nodded, smiling. "I hope you enjoy the show. Well, Percival, your old pal Nico is one of the contestants! Tell me, can he really cook? All I've ever had is plates of frites at Chez Papa!"

Percival shook his head slightly. "Nico?" he said, looking baffled.

"Um—Nico Bartolucci? Your old friend?"

"I've no idea where you got that idea. I hardly know him at

all," said Percival. "Come, Maman, let's get seats before they're all taken."

Molly stood with a fake smile, nodding at the Fleurays like one of those bobblehead dolls people put on their car dashboards. Hardly know him at all?

What?

❧

ACROSS THE ROOM from the Fleurays, Madame Tessier sat next to Molly's next-door neighbor, Madame Sabourin. "You know," said Madame Tessier, jabbing the other woman in the ribs perhaps more firmly than was necessary, "Percival de Fleuray is not someone the village can be proud of, not if what I've heard is true."

"And what is that?" asked Madame Sabourin.

"Gambler," said Madame Tessier simply. Both women craned their necks to get a good look at him.

"Is it bad?"

"Oh, I think very," said Madame Tessier, "though you'd never know it to look at his clothing. That is not a cheap shirt, I can tell you. Custom, unless my eyes deceive me."

The two women nodded their heads slowly.

Six rows down, Lawrence and Stephan were balancing plates of hors d'oeuvres on their knees and munching away happily. "Your friend can cook," said Stephan, looking around for Constance so he could get a second plate. "This tuna tartare is to die for."

Lawrence nodded, his mouth full.

"So where's Nico? I thought he was going to be one of the chefs in the competition?"

Lawrence turned in his seat and looked around the room. He saw Frances standing in the back near the door, looking unhappy. Then he pulled out his phone to check the time, and saw a text.

"Uh oh," he said. He leaned over and said in Stephan's ear, "Looks like the case against Esmé has fallen apart."

Stephan ate his last devil on horseback. "Then Molly had best get cracking," he said.

Lawrence felt himself bristle. "I'm sure she's doing all anyone could do. It's not as though she's part of the gendarmerie, after all."

Meanwhile, Frances paced the back of the room. The contest was supposed to start in five minutes. All three judges were seated on the platform with pads of paper and pens. The other two contestants stood nervously in the makeshift kitchen. Molly was all over the place, checking that all the necessary ingredients were on each chef's worktable, making sure she had three copies of the famous gnocchi recipe ready to hand out, consulting with Thomas over whether someone needed to make an emergency run for more glasses.

All the hubbub made Frances feel sick to her stomach and she stopped pacing and stared out of the window, praying for Nico to appear.

❧

SHOWTIME. Fifteen minutes past showtime, to be precise.

Molly took a deep breath and stepped onto the platform where the judges sat. She only had two out of three contestants but the audience was understandably restive and she had no choice but to start without Nico.

"Welcome everyone!" she began, with forced cheer. "I'm so glad you came out to the first ever Castillac *Chef du Monde*!" She went over the rules, making no mention of the missing Nico. "In this head-to-head battle, Anne-Marie and Hugo will be making the glorious recipe for gnocchi that belonged to Georgina Locatelli's grandmother. Thank you so much for letting our talented chefs have a go at it, Georgina. All right, I'm going to hand over the recipe, and our chefs will get to work. They'll have forty-five minutes to prepare their dishes. In the meantime, if you'd like something else to eat or drink, just give Constance or the boys a wave. And now, Anne-Marie and Hugo: *Bonne chance!*"

The two chefs took a long moment to read the recipe and then flew into furious action, throwing potatoes into pots and then running into the actual kitchen of the cantine where they could fill the pots with water.

Molly saw Frances still standing at the back of the room, facing away from the show, watching for Nico. Her posture was slumped and the sight of her broke Molly's heart. "Bastard," she said under her breath.

She swept her eyes around the room, checking to see if there was anything that needed doing, while telling herself that Maron was in Paris probably arresting Esmé Ridding right that second, that Nico probably had the time wrong, or overslept, or...or... something. Her thoughts went around and around and around, until the chefs were already draining the potatoes and beginning to mash them up with egg and flour. Nugent leaned forward to watch Anne-Marie's technique, Hugo dropped a measuring cup on the floor, and with satisfaction Molly saw that the crowd seemed to be mesmerized by the whole thing.

But no matter how hard she tried to keep her attention on the show, the same thoughts kept swirling through her mind:

Nico was at Château Marainte the night of the murder. *Didn't tell anyone.*

Said he was great pals with Percival. *Lie.*

Said he would be in the contest. *No show.*

What's that saying again? When someone shows you who they are, believe them.

34

For Molly, the rest of the contest sailed by in a blur. Anne-Marie and Hugo entertained the crowd by making a few messy mistakes, with Anne-Marie muttering an audible *merde* when she dropped a whisk on the floor. Both of the chefs made creditable gnocchi; Anne-Marie chose a simple but perfect sage butter sauce while Hugo sauced his with a walnut pesto. At the end, Anne-Marie won by a vote of 2-1, though both judges had substantial compliments for Hugo as well. His parents, who Molly had feared would be accusing her of leading their son down the wrong path, instead came up to her afterward to argue that the contest had been rigged and Hugo should have won.

All during the event, Molly's face was fixed with an unnaturally bright smile and eyes too wide open, as though she could defend herself against dread by pretending with her facial expression that nothing terrible had happened. Because, sickeningly, all the wisps and threads of thoughts had converged into one: Nico.

It's Nico.

Continually she stole glances at Frances, who stood near the door, her head bowed. Molly had never, ever seen her friend look so defeated. She managed to go to the front of the room and congratulate Anne-Marie while the audience clapped, and present her with an antique mixing bowl she had found at Lapin's shop, sturdy porcelain with a deep blue glaze, a gorgeous treasure. She thanked the judges profusely, and for a brief moment, was able to appreciate how extremely well the evening had gone and how satisfied the audience looked as they rose and put on their coats to leave. Piles of dirty plates and empty glasses waited in the kitchen, but Molly hurried outside to catch up to Antoinette, Percival, and Georgina as they made their way down the sidewalk to Georgina's car.

"Pardon!" she called out, and Antoinette turned and smiled at the sound of her voice.

"That was quite entertaining," she said to Molly. "Thank you for putting it together, and especially for inviting us. Castillac is lucky to have you."

"I'm glad you enjoyed it," said Molly, trying to smile at the compliment, and breathless. "I wonder if I could have...a private word with you?"

Georgina looked alarmed and Percival concerned, but Antoinette told them to go on to the car, she would meet them there in a minute. Antoinette was not easily disobeyed. "What is it, my dear?" she said, turning back to Molly.

"Well, I just...I found something out that's confusing me and I wanted to ask you about it. My friend Nico...Nico Bartolucci? He was at the château the night of the murder. Did you know this?"

Antoinette's mouth opened slightly but she betrayed no real alarm. "Who told you that? No, actually, I did not know he was at the château—that night or any recent night, for that matter."

The two women looked searchingly into each other's eyes.

"But clearly..." the baroness said, "You do not know the entire story, and maybe it is time you do."

Molly held her breath.

"I SUPPOSE every family has its share of dirty laundry, yes? A few secrets, that don't matter to anyone else? The fact is, Nico is my nephew. I've told you about Doriane and Gianni Conti, my sister- and brother-in-law? He is their son. Poor child, of course it was horrible to lose his parents as he did, at such a young age. He's never wanted anything to do with us, sad to say. I've heard he's a bartender in the village, if you can imagine such a thing. I don't mean to sound like such a snob, Molly! But the son of the noble Gianni Conti, and nephew of the Baron de Fleuray—you'll admit, it's something of a come-down." She sighed and looked at Molly sadly. "Of course, I don't believe for one instant that he had anything to do with Marcel's murder, no matter what night he was at the château. Certainly not. I rather imagine he was sniffing around after that emerald, if I had to guess. Surely his wages as a bartender might not cover everything that a young man might wish?"

"Nico is your *nephew?*"

"Yes, Molly. Estranged nephew, I guess you'd have to say. We did our very best for him, you understand, but he went to boarding schools after his parents died and has spent very little time at Château Marainte over the years, by his choice. Marcel, especially, reached out to him—wanted to take over as a father, you know—he loved the boy very much indeed. But Nico rejected all of the Fleurays completely. I don't know if he somehow blamed us for his parents' death, or the trauma just turned everything upside-down and sideways. I can't explain it. But he's not been to the château more than three or four times over the last, oh, twenty years."

"I see," said Molly, though she did not. "Why is his last name Bartolucci then? Shouldn't it be Conti?"

Antoinette made an exaggerated shrug. "I cannot answer your question. Of course, when we heard he was going by that other name, we wondered as well. But I do not think we ever had an answer. I would suppose that taking a different name was one more way to put distance between himself and his past?"

Molly nodded slowly.

Antoinette said, "Do you see what I was saying about the poisonous effect of that damn emerald? Now it's casting suspicion on our dear Nico, where it does not belong. Please, come over one last time to look for it, won't you Molly? I know you're busy and getting tired of what must seem like a fool's errand. Of course I do understand that *La Sfortuna* might be in the hands of a thief and far from Castillac by now. But I don't think so. I can feel its effects still, and believe it is somewhere in my house. Marcel did sometimes hide it away somewhere, when he was traveling a lot and worried about having it in his pocket. Please. I beg you."

Molly took Antoinette's hand and squeezed it. Their eyes got moist and they broke apart, giving a last wave, unable to find the right words to say.

❧

MOLLY SLEPT until nearly ten o'clock the following morning, after staying very late to clean up at the cantine. After seeing how much money Constance had stuffed in her bag, she figured she would be having more contests in the future, and wanted to make sure that she left everything shipshape so the school wouldn't mind allowing her to use the space again.

Every minute that she washed dishes, she thought about what the baroness had said. Nico—an aristocrat! She had always thought there was something hidden about about him, and now she knew. But Frances was entirely in the dark about the fact that her almost-fiancé was at the château the night the baron was shot, and that he was the baron's nephew. Molly considered going over to their apartment right then to talk to her, but decided to wait until she had more complete information. Was Nico's no-show at the contest related to any of this? Frances was suffering enough without having to panic over Nico's possibly being guilty of murder.

Nico had mentioned to Molly recently that he was worried about money, feeling that he didn't have enough of it to suit Frances. Molly had done her best to tell him he was really barking up the wrong tree, that for one thing, Frances made plenty of money on her own, thank you very much, and she was most definitely not looking for a man to give her all sorts of expensive stuff. Just not what Frances was interested in. Molly had thought she had gotten through to him.

So why *had* he gone to the château that night? Clearly not to see Percival as he claimed.

It felt awful being lied to, thought Molly. And it would be much worse for Frances. Lies on top of omissions on top of lies, by the man she loved, the man who was asking to marry her.

Well, Antoinette had been kind enough to attend *Chef du Monde*, so Molly figured she would do as asked and give the search for *La Sfortuna* one last crack. A thick sheaf of euros was tucked into her handbag thanks to the night before, but that wasn't enough to pay all her bills, or even close. Expenses had been high and would eat up over half of the gross. Sighing, Molly thought that maybe Antoinette would give her a token payment for having put in so much time looking for that damn stone.

It was the brink of November and the sky was gray. Riding the scooter was a little cold, and she stopped at one point to reach under her helmet and pull her wool hat down over her ears and button her coat. As she parked in the lot and made her way across the drawbridge of the château, she was hit with another pang of missing Ben. Of wanting, just in that moment, to feel his strong arms around her and let her head drop onto his shoulder. What would he think of this business with Nico? Would he be able to help Maron prove that Esmé was guilty?

Antoinette was waiting for Molly on the bench, with a camel-colored mohair blanket over her lap. "Bonjour, *ma chérie*," she said as they kissed cheeks. "I knew you would come. I've been sitting here for over an hour, lost in memories."

"Some parts of grief are bittersweet, aren't they?" said Molly.

"Indeed. The impact of death lasts far longer than one would imagine. So. Would you like coffee before beginning?"

"No, thank you. If it's all right with you, I'm going to dive in and make this last search the most thorough of all. I do have a bit of an idea, so we'll see where that leads me."

"An idea! I like the sound of that very much. I think I will continue my reveries in the barn. Often the goats are the best company one could wish for."

Molly nodded and watched the baroness as she walked across the courtyard with Grizou at her side, and then went inside and up to the second floor in the east wing where the family lived.

The baron had been a sentimental man, she had been thinking. He carried his sister's jewel around in his pocket, as a way to feel connected to her. He hired her maid for the same reason. So, she speculated, what does a sentimental man value above everything? His childhood. This grand château, where his ancestors had lived for hundreds of years, where the decoration barely changed from generation to generation, where he continually returned even though he had a distinguished life in Paris with a place in national politics—Château Marainte was the baron's emotional center, the place all his memories of learning to hunt in the forest and growing up with Doriane sprang from.

Molly had been in the nursery before, on her first run-through of that floor back when her search began. She had looked in the armoire and opened the drawers of the child-sized bureaux, and found them empty, then moved on. Truthfully, it made her uncomfortable spending time in rooms designed for small children. Her desire for her own little ones bubbled up painfully, and she had found no relief for that pain except distraction. But this morning, feeling as though she understood Marcel better than she had when she began, she did not give in to the desire to leave the nursery and think about anything else besides little children.

The light blue paint on the plastered walls had faded to the color of a pair of old jeans. The window faced east and morning light spilled into the room, though the light was not enough to make it feel anything but long abandoned. It was clean enough, and uncluttered, but the feeling of the room was of a place shut away and unused.

An elaborate antique crib stood pushed into a corner. Molly ran her hands along the carved endposts and lifted the wool mattress to look under it. She imagined baby Marcel standing up in the crib, reaching his chubby arms to be picked up. But then she realized no, it would be beautiful little Doriane in the crib, and Marcel in the small bed in the opposite corner. She could see them whispering together, laughing. She could see Marcel, four years older, coming over to the crib to console his baby sister when she cried, pushing his hands through the slats to pat her and making silly faces.

Molly went through the drawers again and found nothing. Then she opened a wooden toy chest that stood at the foot of the small bed. She had rummaged through it on her first search, feeling disappointed when she did not see the jeweled box, but this time she didn't rush. In the chest were three stuffed animals: a rabbit with a chewed-up ear, a lamb whose wool had been rubbed smooth, and a little bear. A *petit ours.*

Molly picked up the bear. *Petit Ours.* Her breath was suddenly fast and her fingers shook as she felt it all over, pressing into the stuffing, trying to see if...and then, in the bear's right foot, she felt something hard, about the size of an apricot.

With both hands she palpated the hard object. She could move it around in the stuffing, but there was no opening that she could see. Inspecting the bear's leg closely, she saw thread freshly sewn, as though a seam had split and been repaired. Swallowing hard, she grasped the fabric on either side of the seam and pulled mightily, but the thread held. Frantically she dug in her bag for the tiny Swiss pocketknife she had been carrying with her since she was twelve, and sliced the bear's foot open.

She lifted the little bear and gave it a shake. Out tumbled a green stone, so big that it looked like costume jewelry, so beautifully cut that its facets glittered even though it was partly covered with stuffing.

35

Her eyes cartoonishly wide, Molly picked up the emerald and blew off the stuffing. Her first thought was *I'm rich!* She jumped to her feet, letting out a whoop of joy and pumping her fist in the air. Then she felt like an idiot, and a selfish one at that...though it was true that ten percent of whatever that whopping stone sold for was going to be more money than she had ever had in her life.

She jammed the emerald in her jeans pocket and ran down the hallway, looking for Antoinette. She sensed danger all of a sudden, as though someone was going to jump out of one of the empty rooms and tackle her to the floor and go through her pockets. She laughed weakly, thinking of Frodo carrying the Ring with half the world on his tail.

Molly made it downstairs and into the courtyard without seeing anyone. Before going on to the barn, she turned to look back at the east wing, and saw a man standing at a window, looking at her.

Totally creeped out, she waved and kept going, wanting very much to put the emerald in Antoinette's hand, as though its storied bad luck might cling to her if she had possession of it for too long.

"Antoinette!" she cried, seeing the baroness inside the paddock, sitting on a bale of hay surrounded by goats.

Antoinette could tell by the excitement in Molly's voice that she had news. She got up and walked quickly to the gate, bits of hay stuck to her skirt. Grizou began barking.

Molly said nothing but dug into her pocket and held out the stone in her palm. "Can you believe it?" she murmured.

Antoinette put her hands over her mouth. "At last," she said. "At last.

Though grave shall sever

Lover from loved

And all they share..."

Molly cocked her head, listening. "Um, I don't want to spoil the moment or anything, but I gotta tell you, I'm nervous holding something this valuable in my hand. I think you should get it someplace safe right away."

Antoinette took the stone and held it up. They admired its glinting in the sunlight. Then she closed her hand over the gem, opening her fingers almost immediately as though worried it might have disappeared. "*La Sfortuna*. At last."

"Not to be a nag—but what are you going to do with it? And was that Alexandre Roulier I just saw? Is he *still* here?"

"Unfortunately it's Saturday, I'm not sure what can be done. I can take it to the bank first thing Monday morning." She kept opening and closing her hand over the jewel, pressing it hard into the skin of her palm. "Yes, Alexandre is still here. I fear I do not rule Château Marainte with the firmness that is sometimes called for. However, once the stone is safely at the bank, we can let people know it has been found. I suspect his desire to comfort me will end abruptly once that happens.

"You know, I should never complain. Heaven knows I have been very lucky in this world. But I feel you and I...we have gotten close, Molly. I will tell you that the financial picture of the Fleuray family...it is not what you might think to look at the château. I am not claiming poverty, but at the same time...well, simply understand that the proceeds from selling this awful emerald will allow me to breathe much easier at night. Georgina and Hubert depend on me, you know, and it is a tremendous relief to be able to continue on as we have. I owe you so much, *ma chérie!*"

Molly thought for a split second that the baroness was going to hug her—an altogether un-French impulse, though Molly would have welcomed it. But Antoinette instead reached out and shook her hand, smiling. "And I believe your portion of the sale might make a difference in your life as well?"

"Oh Antoinette, you have no idea," said Molly, the reality starting to sink in a bit. "Do you...not to sound greedy...but do you have any idea how much it is worth?"

The baroness opened her fingers again and both women looked at the jewel. She tilted her palm and cupped it, and the stone threw out dots of glittering green light. "We must admit, it is rather dazzling, is it not? I believe I remember Marcel telling me...in the neighborhood of eight million euros. Gianni Conti, he loved Doriane very much, and he was a not a shy man when it came to spending."

Molly gasped. She tried to take ten percent of eight million, but was so agitated that zeroes flew around in her head like confetti.

"Not a word to anyone," Antoinette said, giving the goat one last scratch behind the ears. "Grizou!" she called, and the dog streaked to her side. "You're right—the last thing we want is for anyone to get the idea that *La Sfortuna* has been found, not until it is safe. So please—say nothing, even to your closest friends."

"Of course not," answered Molly.

They kissed cheeks, and Molly took off on her scooter, swinging by Pâtisserie Bujold on the way home.

She was rich.

And as she struggled to wrap her mind around that delicious new development, she was also, in the back of her mind, still wondering about the baron's murder. Had Maron made an arrest? Was Castillac about to become ground zero for tabloid reporters and paparazzi?

Molly ordered a big bag of almond croissants, a couple of *religieuses* for good measure, and breathed not a word to Nugent about anything.

36

Molly spent the afternoon on a cloud. She didn't dare call anyone or go to Chez Papa—the secret of finding *La Sfortuna* would be too hard to hold back. So instead, she turned off her phone, ate a prodigious number of croissants, and gave Bobo an extravagant amount of petting and liver treats. The orange cat even got a saucer of cream. Molly was feeling generous to the universe and ecstatic that the ugly pressure of those bills had been lifted from her shoulders all at once. It was hard to believe it was really happening.

Of course, it is the way of the world that no happiness is a hundred percent pure, and even while she gorged on pastry and wandered around La Baraque seeing a million new things to spend money on, she was still wondering whether Maron had arrested Esmé. Worrying about where Nico was and how he was going to explain himself. And anxious about brokenhearted Frances.

Molly's bedroom was very plain. Since funds had been limited from the beginning, she had wisely decided that any money spent on décor should go to rooms where guests would stay or visit. Her comforter was lumpy and not quite warm enough, the windows had no curtains, and Bobo had chewed up one end of the throw rug. Now, with as much as 800,000 euros coming her way—eight hundred thousand!—she imagined toile curtains and a sumptuous duvet cover. A thick, soft rug on which to put her feet when she got out of bed in the morning.

It was a staggering amount of money. Yes, she had made a very good salary back in Boston when she was a fundraiser, but her expenses had been ridiculously high and somehow she had always felt she was on the verge of being broke. Here in Castillac, she walked and worked in the garden instead of going to a gym. She did her own nails, when she thought of it, which wasn't often. Prices at Chez Papa were absurdly low. But more than that, she realized, opening another bag of liver treats for Bobo, she no longer spent money as a way to cheer herself up. In retrospect, it was no wonder she had felt half-broke a lot of the time, because she used to go on shoe-shopping sprees and kitchen-gadget sprees because, well, bottom line? She had been in a bad marriage and living in the wrong place.

The irony of realizing this as she was considering blowing a big chunk of cash on a bedroom makeover was not lost on her.

Bobo jumped up and ran barking to the door, and Molly went to see who it was, glad for company and warning herself to keep quiet.

"My dear!" said Lawrence, kissing her on both cheeks and giving her a quick hug. "Have you turned off your phone? It's not like you."

"Ha! No, I guess not. I don't know, I just...needed to chill out a little. You know how it is."

Lawrence looked skeptical. "Well, I tried texting you but got no answer, and this seemed important enough news to deliver in person. I just heard that Maron is back from Paris. No arrest of Esmé, and from what my mole told me, there's not going to be any arrest either."

Molly was quiet. "Damn," she said finally.

"You have something against that glorious creature? Do all women just hate her, is that it?"

"No, Lawrence, it's not that. It's...there are other considerations...what do you mean, 'mole'? Who the hell gives you your information?"

But Lawrence just smiled serenely as he always did when questioned about his sources. "You know I can't say, dearest. Castillac is a den of gossips, as you surely know by now. Madame Tessier is not the only one who can't bear to keep a juicy tidbit to herself. Or himself, make no assumptions as you often remind me."

"They can be so sneaky, assumptions," Molly said, thinking about Nico. "Sometimes I even try to write out everything I think I know, and go through them one by one to see if maybe some items I considered facts were actually just wishes or hopes. Assumptions come in all flavors. Eh, sorry, I'm rambling. This time I'm not even properly on the case. Tell me what *you* think. If you had to guess right now, who do you think killed the baron?"

Lawrence looked up at the ceiling and tilted his head. "Hmm. Well, I'm really in no position to make any guesses. I haven't met any of the family and don't know any of the details. The idea that it was Esmé certainly made sense, and was gloriously thrilling, in a way. A bad movie sort of way, admittedly. I'm a bit sorry to see her crossed off the list, if that is what's happened. Can't you go see Maron and weasel some information out of him? You two get on fairly well, don't you?"

"More or less. I give him credit for never acting put out when I've helped on cases before."

"'Helped on'? Molly darling, you solved those cases while the gendarmes of the village ran in circles chasing their tails."

Molly laughed but her eyes were distant. She was thinking that she had a duty to go to Maron, and right away, because if Esmé was out, he had to be told about Nico...but how could she rat out her friend, and her best friend's almost-fiancé?

What in the world was she going to do?

❧

Alexandre stayed at the window waiting for the baroness to come back from the barn. He had seen the hurry Molly was in when she ran through the courtyard, and watched her leave after speaking to Antoinette. With the finely tuned senses of an expert con man, he knew without a doubt that something was up.

That morning, he had made some calls, several to Paris and one to Geneva. *La Sfortuna* was going to be tricky to move, and some of the details needed to be arranged in advance so that the transfer could take place without a moment's delay. He looked forward to going to Switzerland. The air was so fresh, and he did appreciate fondue.

He thought about the expression on Molly's face as she had left the château. In his mind, he zoomed in on her eyes and the way her mouth was set, and he had not a single doubt that something had occurred to make that woman very, very pleased. They had *La Sfortuna*, he was sure of it. Impatiently he muttered to himself, so tired of the endless waiting and the long hours that Antoinette seemed to be able to waste at the barn. It wasn't as though she had a herd of cows to look after! Nothing but a couple of mangy goats and an old donkey. How in the world did looking after them take so many hours a day?

Alexandre pondered some more about the safest ways to get himself and the jewel to Switzerland, about the deep pleasure he was going to feel when he finally held the gem in his hand, and a bit more about fondue. He did not once remember his friend the baron.

At long last, Antoinette emerged into the sunshine of the courtyard. He could see straw clinging to her skirt.

This is going to be extremely enjoyable, he thought, and went to meet her.

37

Molly arrived at the door of the station the next morning at nine. She had fortified herself with two cups of strong coffee and a fresh croissant from Pâtisserie Bujold, but she was far from content. Half of her wanted to dance in the street with joy of being rich, and the other half was in agony over Nico and Frances, and at having to be the one to tell Maron her suspicions. She held out hope that perhaps Maron had missed something, that the case against Esmé could be strengthened again somehow. There was nothing to do but try to ask as many questions as Maron would allow.

"Bonjour Gilles," she said when he opened the door. They kissed cheeks and Molly was relieved to see that Paul-Henri was absent, thinking that his presence might have made it more difficult for Maron to speak with her freely. It was obviously not at all according to protocol for anyone in the gendarmerie to share the details of a case with a civilian.

"I hope you don't mind my coming over. Things pretty slow this Sunday morning?"

"You know how it is in the village. Half of them are still asleep. The others are thinking about lunch."

Molly smiled, uncertain of how to start.

"Is there something I can do for you? Has there been some trouble?"

"Well, I...I have some information...but first, and I understand that it's really none of my business but it would help immensely to know...I heard you had gone to see Esmé Ridding in Paris?"

Maron nodded but did not elaborate.

"I take it...that no charges will be filed?"

"I really can't comment, Molly. As you know."

"Of course. I understand. Well. You see, I've gotten to be friends with the baroness, Antoinette de Fleuray. She asked me to...perform a service for her that required my spending time at the château, and so naturally, we got to know each other. And...."

Maron waited. He had the clear sense that Molly was going to tell him something valuable, which if so, would allow him to stop slamming his head against the wall in frustration at this dead end case. "Yes?" he prodded, as she looked away.

"I don't want to say anything about this. I would much rather keep quiet. The guy involved, he's a friend of mine, and I don't like tattletales any more than the next person."

Maron nodded sympathetically, wanting to reach down her throat and pull the words out.

Molly stood up and walked to the window. "Is there any way you could just tell me a little bit about why Esmé was cleared? I know—along with the rest of the world—that she was having an affair with the baron. I know she made a scene at his funeral. And I saw her in Paris too, behaving in a way that, well, did not exactly look like bereavement. Seems to me that's a lot of strikes against her."

But after she spoke, Molly's head drooped. She knew she had no real evidence against Esmé and was only trying to divert Maron's attention in the actress's direction, away from Nico. She was supposed to be all about the truth, not trying to confuse the picture, which could possibly allow a murderer to go free.

"Okay look, I guess there's no putting this off any longer. I was talking to the housekeeper at Château Marainte, who told me that Nico—yes, that Nico, Nico Bartolucci—was at the château the night of the murder. He failed to mention that to me or any of his other friends, which seemed...odd. And then something else came to light. Do you know Nico at all, Gilles?"

"No. I stop in at Chez Papa occasionally, of course. I know him by name, to say bonjour, but nothing beyond that."

"I've known him for over a year. He's one of the first people I met when I moved to Castillac last year. I've spent a lot of time sitting at the bar talking, and not about football and politics all the time either. We got to be real friends. And never once did he mention that in fact, he is the baron's nephew."

Maron sat frozen. "Nephew?"

"Yes. On his mother's side. His mother was Doriane de Fleuray, Marcel's sister. Married to Gianni Conti. I'm sure you've heard of him."

"Yes, of course. And do you have some idea why he kept this a secret?"

"I don't believe it was, not from the Fleuray side, anyway. But Nico, for reasons I don't entirely understand, did not want the connection known. Maybe that's why he changed his last name."

"Why would he do a thing like that? Did he have a falling out with his parents?"

"They were killed in a plane crash twenty years ago."

Now Maron stood up and flexed his shoulders. "Do you have evidence that he killed the baron?" he asked Molly point-blank.

"I don't know," she said, holding back tears. "I don't know."

Maron went back to his desk and pulled open a side drawer. He took off the rubber band holding the Fleuray documents together, the ones he had gotten from petty thief Malcolm Barstow: the letter from Esmé, the short list of countries, and the torn-off piece of paper with a note in the baron's handwriting. "Take a look at this," he said, knowing he had already far overstepped police procedure, but feeling as though he and Molly together were on the verge of pinpointing the killer, and he did not dare shut her out now.

The note was written with pen and ink and though a few blots marred the short paragraph, it was perfectly legible.

This emerald, known as La Sfortuna, belonged to my sister, most beloved Doriane Lisette de Fleuray Conti, and though it has deep sadness associated with it, once I am gone, it rightfully belongs to her heir, my nephew.

Marcel de Fleuray

'There is no sorrow
Time heals never;
No loss, betrayal,
Beyond repair.'

"Do you know that poem?" asked Molly, feeling queasy at the realization that if the emerald did not belong to Antoinette, she was not going to be getting ten percent of anything.

"Nah. I was never much for literature. So you're telling me that this nephew in the note is Nico, bartender at Chez Papa. If he came from such an illustrious family, why on earth would he be filling glasses of beer for Alphonse? The baron was minister of the interior, you realize."

"I can't say. Of course...it's not uncommon for children to want a different path than their family wants for them. Maybe the Fleurays were pushy, wanting him to...I don't know...be a minister too?"

"Molly. Answer truthfully please. In your opinion, is Nico capable of murder?"

"Oh Gilles, who can say? Maybe we all are, if the right circumstances present themselves. I can tell you I've never seen Nico do anything at all violent."

"I can't say the same for Esmé Ridding. She has an arrest record actually, though of course she was let off with nothing more than a sanction. But she assaulted a young man in a nightclub a few years ago. Broke his nose."

Molly's first thought was that the young man probably deserved it. "So, is she cleared or not?"

Maron hesitated. "In my view, no, Esmé is not off the list of suspects completely. She was at its top, at least before this information you have given me about Nico. But see, I've got nothing but the flimsiest circumstantial evidence against her. No forensics, no eyewitness. I needed a confession and I did not get one. She claims that indeed she fought with the baron the night she was killed—she wanted him to leave his wife and marry her. She confronted him at Château Marainte, but drove off furious and spent the night in a hotel in Bergerac, crying on the phone to a girlfriend. As far as I can tell, those check out, though of course we have no idea what she actually said to the girlfriend. She could have been crowing about having done in the baron."

Molly sighed. "What a mess."

"When did you last see Nico?"

Molly went through everything she could think of to help Maron in his search for Nico, and then headed back home, utterly dejected. If the scrawled note held up legally, she had just won and lost 800,000 euros in less than twenty-four hours. And perhaps ruined Frances's life.

❧

ONCE HOME, Molly was no longer thinking about toile curtains and soft rugs. The unbelievable windfall had not even been hers for a day, and its loss was like a stabbing pain between her ribs. But there was not a thing to be done about it. If news of Nico's inheriting a famous jewel had come just a month ago, she would have been ecstatic, but now she had no idea what to think. She sat on the sofa staring into space, idly rubbing Bobo's chest and then belly as the dog flipped onto her back, running over the facts of the case, looking for any soft spots, any weaknesses, anything she believed to be true but did not know was true. She came up empty and went to bed hugging a pillow to her chest, feeling bereft in ten different directions.

It was not until the next morning that she went to the computer and did some searches.

Curious. Once again, my first impression was...incomplete.

She went to check in with Ervin and Sissy but their car was gone. She tried to rake some leaves, unsure about how to proceed with what she was piecing together. Then, impulsively, she jumped on the scooter and took off for Château Marainte, unable to let things sit for a moment longer.

The lot in front of the château was empty, but Molly parked and crossed the drawbridge anyway. She hoped to find Georgina before seeing anyone else. And she had not forgotten the man who watched her from the window.

Molly let herself inside when no one answered her knock. It was overstepping, but surely the situation warranted it. Gratefully, she heard a vacuum running upstairs and she flew up the wide staircase and walked toward the sound, finding Georgina in a sitting room she did not remember seeing during her search—not surprising in such a vast house.

"Bonjour Molly," said Georgina, scowling and turning the machine off with her foot. "Antoinette is not here. She and Percival left yesterday, stopping by my house on their way out to ask if I would take care of the animals for a few days. Figured I'd get ahead on the vacuuming as long as I'm here."

"Actually, it's you I came to see."

"Me?" Georgina laughed suspiciously. "Did you not approve of the gnocchi?"

"Heavens no, it's not about that! The gnocchi were fabulous, and thank you again for letting me use your grandmother's recipe."

"May she rest in peace."

"Yes. So. I was wondering...you've known the Fleurays a long time, yes?"

"Eh, I suppose you could say that."

"How about we make a cup of tea while we talk?"

Georgina nodded and they walked toward the kitchen.

"Well, this situation with Nico...it doesn't look good for him, to be honest."

"It breaks my heart. I was devoted to his mother. Devoted. And to see what this family—"

Molly waited. Georgina had filled a teakettle with water and plugged it in, but she stood looking down at the floor with her mouth pressed closed.

"What about the family?" Molly prodded, trying to be gentle.

Georgina just shook her head. "Not for me to say."

"Who is your loyalty toward? Your mistress, Doriane—don't you think she would want you to help her boy?"

"I do want to help him! I never should have said anything to you, it was a terrible mistake!"

"But Georgina, covering up that he was here—that isn't going to solve anything. What would fix things for Nico is finding the real killer."

The housekeeper still stared at the floor, fidgeting. Silent.

"Just tell me this: why is Nico estranged from the Fleurays? You're right here in the thick of everything, Georgina. And you're clever, too, anyone can see that. I bet you have a pretty good idea what happened. I'm not asking to be nosy, please understand—more than anything, I want Nico cleared of any suspicion. That's what we both want."

Georgina sat down on a stool and then got up and walked around the table. She ran one of her apron strings through her fingers over and over. "It was terrible," she said, her voice guttural.

"What was?"

"You know anything about jealousy? You ever seen it eat somebody alive?"

Molly nodded, thinking she might finally understand who she was talking about.

Georgina poured boiling water into a teapot and dumped in some tea. The pause got longer and longer. Molly heard a clock chiming somewhere far away in the château.

"Save Nico," said Molly quietly.

Georgina looked up at her, biting her lip. "When I get fired, you gonna take me on out at La Baraque?"

"Not sure I can afford to, to be honest, but I'll make every effort to get you another job. I wish I could offer you more."

The housekeeper took a deep breath. "All right, all right. You're pushy, you know that? Look, I was very young when Doriane hired me. Best thing that ever happened, you know? I was just a kid in a family barely scraping along, and all of a sudden I was flying to Paris, Gstaad, the Riviera. And Doriane was super kind to me. Taught me all kinds of things. She really wanted me to have a good life." She wiped a tear away with the back of her hand. "We used to come here to the château too, a couple of times a year. Doriane and Marcel were close. And that's what the problem was, right there. Crazy, isn't it?"

"I don't understand."

"Antoinette *hated* Doriane. I mean hated her with a blinding passion. Who gets jealous of a sister, I ask you? That's nothing but crazy. Marcel and Doriane were close, they loved each other. Nothing in the world wrong with that. But Antoinette, oh, she didn't like it. Couldn't stand how they would laugh together and talk about old times. Couldn't stand how good-looking Doriane was either, if you ask me. And so, when Doriane and Gianni... when the plane went down..."

"...their son wasn't welcome here."

"That's right. Antoinette absolutely refused to take him in."

Georgina got two teacups out and poured the tea. Molly was so intent on getting the story she'd been missing all this time that she drank the tea without thinking about how she detested it.

"So what happened then? Nico was a twelve-year-old orphan. Where did he go?"

"The baron begged to keep him here. The two of them went at it for weeks, let me tell you, screaming, tears, throwing lamps. In the end, little Nico was sent off to boarding school, some fancy place outside of Paris. And he barely ever came here anymore."

"Why in the world did Marcel allow that?"

"What, you think I was running around listening at keyholes? I don't know, I honestly can't say. The baroness can be...I don't think you've seen...."

"Intent?"

"Something like that." Georgina laughed. "I think I'd call her ferocious. Like a man-eating tiger. And anyway, don't forget, there was all that money...."

Molly put her hand to her mouth. How had she not thought of that? The Conti fortune must have been immense, even putting the emerald aside. "Nico must be worth a fortune!"

"Ha. *Should* be. I can't tell you all the ins and outs of all that. All I know is, the Contis were richer than God and Nico tends bar. Doesn't seem like he'd be doing that job just for fun, eh?"

"Are you saying...somehow he was cheated out of his inheritance?"

Suddenly they heard a noise. Georgina looked past Molly at the door and the color drained out of her face. Molly turned to see Antoinette standing in the doorway, her cheeks reddened from being outside, her expression stony.

☙ 38 ❧

"Bonjour, Molly," said Antoinette. "I'm rather surprised to see you again so soon. Georgina, you may leave us."

The housekeeper threw Molly a surreptitious look of solidarity and scurried out of the room.

"So tell me, chérie, why you are hanging about the kitchen with my housekeeper? I believed you had a more subtle sense of social manners."

"Oh," said Molly, with a fake-sounding chuckle, "Georgina and I get on quite well. I'm very interested in Italian cooking, you know. Well, any kind of cooking, really. Food. Food of almost any type—I love it all." Her coat was over the back of a kitchen chair and she removed it and started to put it on. There was much to ask Antoinette, many holes that still needed filling in, but perhaps this wasn't the moment.

"Don't speak such foolishness, it's beneath you." Antoinette closed the door behind her and stood in front of it. She was smiling but there was no warmth, no humor in her expression. Her plain features were lit up with some other emotion, and Molly swallowed hard, fighting off fear.

The baroness stood in front of the door so that there was no way to leave save shoving her out of the way. Molly took a deep breath, glanced quickly around the room, and decided to take a risk. "I did a bit of research," she said, looking hard into Antoinette's eyes. "And without much trouble I found Walter de la Mare."

Antoinette shrugged. "Third-rate poet." She kept her eyes fixed on Molly's.

"Maybe so. But you quoted him the other day. When I brought you the emerald."

"So what? It's nothing more than the mark of an educated person. Would you like to hear more? I have committed endless verses to memory over the years, and without too much thought, I should be able to come up with something appropriate even for this awkward moment, when I came home to find my friend fraternizing with the help behind my back."

"You quoted lines six through eight of 'Away.' The first four lines of the poem was in a note Marcel wrote."

Antoinette's head jerked to one side. "I have no idea what you're talking about," she said, but her voice was not so strong.

"A note in which he writes that the emerald belongs to Nico," Molly said simply.

"No idea where you're getting your information, Molly," Antoinette said, laughing. "Nothing but fantasy and meaningless coincidence."

"I don't think so. I think you knew all along that the emerald was Nico's. You saw that note, didn't you? Maybe you were even there when Marcel wrote it? That's why you blurted out those lines from the poem."

Antoinette leaned back against the door and smiled. "Ah well, it takes the American to pull the covers back from our little family secrets, is that it? But I understand Americans quite well. I know what you all care about most of all is money. I saw how your eyes glittered when you looked at *La Sfortuna*, how you were calculating in your mind how much your take would be. So tell me, chérie, how much more do you require to keep your little thoughts and musings to yourself?"

Molly was aghast. Who *was* this person? "How much?" she repeated, in disbelief.

"I know I told you ten percent before, which was tremendously generous, anyone would agree. But I would be willing to increase your share, if you make certain promises...you must realize that my family's reputation means something. I do not want you to sully it by running about the village spreading rumors."

"Rumors? I'm not interested in rumor," said Molly, pulling herself together.

"I do not misunderstand your motives, chérie. I am many things, but stupid is not among them. I will give you twenty-five percent. That would be plenty to buy that baby you've always wanted, right?"

Though her eyes got very wide and the remark hit like a cold stab in the heart, Molly pushed back. "How did it feel to shoot your husband?" she asked, taking a quick glance around to see if there was knife or anything else she could use to defend herself lying in reach.

"It was delicious," said Antoinette, dragging out the words, her eyes closing for a moment, and then flicking back to Molly. The baroness reached into the roomy pocket of her barn coat.

Molly held her breath as Antoinette drew out a pistol and pointed it at her, smiling.

❧

WELL, the job was a goner and there was nothing to do about that, Georgina thought as she flew to the coatroom where her handbag with her cell phone hung from a peg. Probably should have left years ago and gone back to Italy, but no use thinking about that now. She had heard many troubling things over the years at Château Marainte—not that she had started out as a snoop, but Antoinette tended to forget she was there, and say things over the phone that would have better been unheard.

Georgina knew, for example, that Antoinette had bullied her husband into allowing her to manage Nico's trust. And one way or another—Georgina didn't know whether from outright stealing or just making a hash of it—twenty years later, the trust had dwindled to practically nothing. All that money, Georgina had thought, shaking her head as her mistress had yet another screaming fit on the phone with someone at the bank, all that money down the drain and for what? Out of spite?

But the housekeeper did not stop to ponder the long history of what she had seen and heard, not now. She got to the coatroom, snatched her cell out of her bag, and called Maron at the station.

"Officer Maron, it's Georgina Locatelli at the château. Get up here right away! The baroness—and Molly—I'm afraid she's going to hurt her—"

Maron did not need to be convinced. "On my way," he said. As he ran to his scooter, he asked Georgina a few more questions and then reassured her that he would be there in a matter of minutes.

But she was not confident he would get there in time.

What would Doriane tell her to do now? Probably that she must think for herself, Georgina thought ruefully. She sprinted down the corridor toward the baron's salon, looking for a gun.

39

Alexandre was lying on his bed in the west wing of the château, looking up at the ceiling as he liked to do and trying his best to wait patiently. To amuse himself he remembered holding *La Sfortuna* in his hand, how it had actually been hard to catch his breath. Weeks ago, the baroness had promised him thirty percent if he found it, and once Molly had done the work for him, it had taken very little encouragement on his part for Antoinette to agree to give him twenty percent even though he had not found it—he had reached for her arm and squeezed it a little too hard, given her a look, that was all.

He was a master of implication, and let the baroness's imagination fill in the rest.

Yet in less than an hour she had managed to leave the château with that weasel of a son, and Alexandre was sure they had gone off to put the emerald somewhere out of his reach. Maybe hidden in the hunting lodge this time, or even a safety deposit box. He had been stupid not to take it away from her when he had the chance. If only he had found the thing first! It would be sold by now with none of these idiots any the wiser. He could be lying on a bed at the newly renovated Paris Ritz instead of waiting around this moldy château.

Damn aristocrats, he muttered. He knew full well that the only reason the baron had socialized with him was financial desperation. So often these old families don't realize they're going broke until it's too late—they keep living the way their grandparents did, spending like mad, not understanding that the world has changed and their bank account along with it. Alexandre's shady deals had kept Marcel afloat for a few more years, and no one had been more grateful than the baroness.

Antoinette had even tried to express her gratitude in a physical way, which Alexandre shuddered at the memory of.

Well, she would come back, eventually. And he would not make the same mistake twice.

❧

THE BARONESS SEEMED to relish talking, which was the only thing Molly could be grateful for, since at the moment, stalling was all she had.

"Had you planned to kill Marcel for a long time?"

"Not at all. Of course I hated him for years. Years! He married me for my family's money and then barely glanced at me afterward. You do realize that the Fleurays had the title, and this monstrous château, but otherwise next to nothing? Oh, he was all sweetness before the marriage, believe me. But once he had two sons, I was nothing more than an unwieldy piece of furniture to him, something to trip over and curse. Not love. *Never* love."

"But...was life that bad? I mean, I'm divorced, I know what a bad marriage is like. But you had your sons, you lived in this incredible château..."

"When they were young, my sons were a comfort, true enough. But first boarding school, then Paris—they left home the minute they were able. And the expenses on this place ate up my family money until we were barely able to afford any help.

"The one thing, the only constant—what I have, Molly, is my animals. My goats, my donkey, and of course, dearest Grizou. You do know that no one will ever love you like your dog? They are what have sustained me through the horrors of this life at Château Marainte. And that is what tipped the balance finally, if your small detective mind must know. The night he died, Marcel and I had dinner. He treated me politely, as he always did—but tell me, Molly, what woman wants only politeness?"

Molly shook her head, trying to look sympathetic. She had seen a paring knife next to the sink and edged one step in that direction, trying not to stare at the small barrel of the pistol, still aimed at her chest.

"So that night after dinner, Marcel was getting up from the table and got tangled up with the dog. Grizou likes to stick around in case a tidbit is dropped, you understand, like most dogs will, if they are allowed. And Marcel half fell over, had to put a hand on the floor to right himself. I will say that what he did next was out of character. I can't explain it, he'd never done such a thing before. But he *kicked* Grizou. Kicked my beautiful boy."

The baroness bowed her head for a second before continuing and Molly took a step closer to the sink.

"That night, Nico came to visit Marcel, and for reasons that are not your concern, this was upsetting to me. That tawdry actress showed up as well, but I saw her leave in tears. I stood outside Marcel's salon for some time, considering what I should do. I want to be clear that I did not act impulsively. My husband ignored me for nearly fifteen years, and then he kicked my dog, my Grizou. He deserved to be punished.

"I knocked on his door and went in. When I saw the Holland & Holland lying on the console table, I picked it up and I shot him. And I tell you with something close to pleasure: I am not sorry for it."

"But what about Percival and Luc, Antoinette? Did you not hesitate to kill their father?"

Antoinette made a bitter croak deep in her throat. "They didn't mean half as much to me as my animals. They've taken off, you understand—their lives are elsewhere, I'm nothing but an annoyance to them now. Love, Molly! That's what this is all about! Can you understand what it is like to love and not be loved back, by your husband and then your sons as well? None of them had a care for anyone but themselves." Antoinette drew herself up and straightened her shoulders, looking intently into Molly's eyes. "Rather like you," she said, steadying her hand, an anticipatory smile spreading across her face.

And then, all at once, Molly lunged backward and grabbed the paring knife off the edge of the sink, and Antoinette fell forward as someone shoved hard on the other side of the door.

"Maron!" said Molly, never, ever so glad to see anyone in her life.

40

His skin was so brown he was practically unrecognizable. When he spoke to Christophe, the taxi driver at the railway station, Christophe did a double take.

"Chief?" Christophe said, wonderingly.

"That's right," said Ben Dufort. "Do I look that different?" he laughed lightly.

"Well, yes! Very fit, I'll say that. I heard you were hunting elephants in Malaysia."

"Not hunting, though I did ride some while I was there."

"Was it secret police business?"

"No, as you might remember, I resigned quite a while ago."

"Well, I did hear that," said Christophe. "Was hoping you'd just gone undercover or something."

"Afraid not. Listen, will you take me to Rémy's? I'd like to get cleaned up and then go over to Chez Papa. Will you wait for me?"

"Sure, Chief, whatever you say. Elephants, huh?"

MOLLY SPUN BACK and forth on her stool as she told the story of Antoinette de Fleuray to her friends at Chez Papa. "I'll say one thing for her, Antoinette is a better actress than Esmé Ridding will ever be. I totally thought she was on the level. Not just that—I really *liked* her!"

"One does sort of believe that if someone is a cold-blooded murderer, one would be able to tell somehow," said Lawrence, swigging his Negroni. "Or perhaps we're just flattering ourselves, and we don't really know anything at all about each other."

"I too have hidden depths," Lapin intoned, and everyone cracked up laughing.

But Molly remained serious. "It does make you think. How can sociopaths fake feelings so well? We had some long talks, Antoinette and I, and I'm telling you, I thought she was salt of the earth! I trusted her completely."

"I know that stings," said Lawrence.

"So what tipped you off?" asked Lapin. "I mean, besides the gun pointed at you!"

Molly glanced up at Nico behind the bar, who had been silent. He smiled warmly at her and she started to continue her story but realized she could not blab about Maron showing her the baron's will without getting him in trouble. "Let's just say a poem gave her away, of all things. I'm sorry, but the details of this one are going to have to stay secret, for reasons I'm not allowed to go into, at least for now." Molly knew she had to keep her consultation with Maron strictly private, lest he get in serious trouble.

"Has *La Sfortuna* been recovered?" asked Lapin.

"Apparently it's at a bank in Bergerac. Maron had no trouble tracking that down at least."

Solemnly, Lapin turned to Nico and raised his glass. "To sudden wealth," he said, and the others lifted their glasses and repeated "to sudden wealth!" and cheered, to Nico's discomfort.

"I do have one nagging question, Nico," said Molly, and for

once he waited to hear it without looking like he would do anything to avoid answering.

"If you couldn't stand the Fleurays, why in the world would you choose to live in Castillac?"

Nico nodded. "Good question. And a complicated question. Maybe I can answer simply by saying that...just because I couldn't stand them, I still loved my uncle? Marcel was the only family I had left. Antoinette had been horrible to me, and my cousins not much better, but I did not want to give up on Marcel. Even though he had failed to come through for me when I was a child. We used to meet secretly from time to time, rather often lately. He was a capable, loving man, and utterly terrified of Antoinette."

Frances burst through the door bringing a draft of cold air with her. "Molls!" she cried, seeing her friend. "Oh my God, I just heard—you're okay?" She flung herself at Molly and dragged her off her stool in a full-body hug.

"I'm fine as long as you don't break any bones," said Molly from under Frances's scarf.

Frances let Molly go and raced around the side of the bar and wrapped herself around Nico. "Is it true?" she murmured to him.

Nico nodded. "Look, people, just go on about your business and let me talk to Frances for a minute, all right?"

Lawrence smiled and turned his stool toward the door. Molly and Lapin nodded and looked away but both of them were listening in as hard as they could.

"I'm so sorry," Nico said, kissing Frances on the neck. "I had to leave, I was afraid I was going to be arrested."

"But you could have told me that!"

"No. The last thing I wanted to do was get you involved. You know you'd have insisted on coming with me."

A long pause. Molly glanced over to see Frances kissing Nico so hard that he fell to one side, knocking a glass to the floor.

"Everything's back to normal," said Lapin gleefully.

"No it's not," said Nico, getting his balance back and holding Frances's hand in both of his. "There's still a score left to settle." He let go of Frances and rummaged around behind the bar, coming up with a scrap of paper and a pen. He wrote I.O.U. at the top with flowery letters.

I hereby pledge to give my friend, Molly Sutton, ten percent of the sale price of La Sfortuna, as she had been promised, in gratitude for everything.

Nico Bartolucci Conti

"WHAT?" whispered Molly.

"You deserve every centime," said Nico, grinning broadly and holding out a hand to shake on it. "I should have inherited my father's money, which as everyone seems to know, was quite considerable. But Antoinette managed to lose most of it—quite a job, actually, since if it had simply been invested and left alone, it would be worth...well, it doesn't bear thinking about."

Lawrence agreed, and Lapin stood with a stricken look on his face.

"You are being ridiculously generous," said Molly. "Maybe I'll take something, seeing how I'm almost broke. But ten percent is way too much."

"Not at all. Anyway," continued Nico, "since you found the emerald, I'll have more money than I know what to do with. Certainly enough to buy a house for me and Frances."

Frances beamed and uttered not a single smart remark but slipped her arm around him and pulled him close.

Molly, on the other hand, was thinking about nothing more complicated than toile curtains and a fluffy new comforter. She sipped her kir, so lost in fantasy she did not see the deeply tanned Ben Dufort, former chief of the gendarmes, get out of a taxi and start toward the door of the bistro.

ALSO BY NELL GODDIN

The Third Girl (Molly Sutton Mystery 1)

The Luckiest Woman Ever (Molly Sutton Mystery 2)

The Prisoner of Castillac (Molly Sutton Mystery 3)

Murder for Love (Molly Sutton Mystery 4)

Murder on Vacation (Molly Sutton Mystery 6)

An Official Killing (Molly Sutton Mystery 7)

Death in Darkness (Molly Sutton Mysteries 8)

No Honor Among Thieves (Molly Sutton Mysteries 9)

ACKNOWLEDGMENTS

Once again, Tommy Glass and Nancy Kelley have saved the day. I'm so grateful to know such tremendously talented editors.

GLOSSARY

1:

gendarmerie......police station
traiteur............caterer, takeout purveyor

2:

La Baraque.......house, shack
gîte................holiday rental, usually by the week
allée...............avenue, drive
parterre...........formal section of a garden, often symmetrical
messieurs.........plural of Mr.
3:
arrondissement...section of Paris

4:

département......section of France, sort of like a large county
réligiueses.........custard-filled pastry shaped like a nun
palmiers............flaky, buttery pastry, also known as elephant's ears
la bombe...........attractive, sexy woman
la sfortuna.........misfortune

ma chérie...........my dear
petite chou

5:

pigeonnier........pigeon house

6:

haute cuisine.......fancy food, fine dining
Salut, tout le monde!.....hi everyone!
salade Périgourdine......salad with duck gizzards, a local specialty (and delicious!)
Filet de Bœuf Grillé Sauce Périgueux....beef tenderloin in a Cognac and truffle sauce
pompe aux pommes.......apple turnover

7:

notaire.......government official. Notary public, but performing more functions than an American NP.
bonsoir......good evening

8:

al Diavolo.....hell no

9:

Le Monde....leftish newspaper
épicerie.......small grocery store

11:

potager.......vegetable garden

12:

apéro.......cocktail, apéritif
petit chou.....little cabbage (term of affection)
chérie.........dear

13:

débrouiller.....make do, figure it out

14:

la métairie....farm

15:

petit ours.....little bear

18:

si.........yes

21:

Maman.....mother

22:

carte blanche....free rein, blank check

24:

lapin au cidre.....rabbit in cider
pichet..........small pitcher

26:

Bourse........stock market

28:

Mon Dieu.......my God

29:

stronzo.....jerk (impolite)

30:

citron pressée.....lemonade

32:

sablé.......shortbread
Chef du Monde.....cook of the world

33:

lycée.......high school
bonne chance.....good luck

34:

merde......poop (impolite)

ABOUT THE AUTHOR

Nell Goddin has worked as a radio reporter, SAT tutor, short-order omelet chef, and baker. She tried waitressing but was fired twice.

Nell grew up in Richmond, Virginia and has lived in New England, New York City, and France. Currently she's back in Virginia with teenagers and far too many pets. She has degrees from Dartmouth College and Columbia University.

www.nellgoddin.com
nell@nellgoddin.com

Made in the USA
Coppell, TX
08 August 2024